# "Daddy, over there!" Natalie pointed first this way, then that.

Daniel got a headache trying to follow. Brightly painted wooden marionettes danced across sage green walls. Artificial grapevines festooned the doorway into the dining room. On the ceiling, Japanese kites sailed across an azure sky bordered by fluffy white clouds.

"Isn't it *wonderful*, Daddy?" Natalie pulled herself up on one elbow, her illness momentarily forgotten.

Karina Peterson stepped through the arched doorway, a smile on her face and a swing in her hips. She came to a halt in the middle of the room, talking rapidly.

"I was able to save Petunia's ear, thank goodness. Sorry about the mess. Did you find any vacancies? There's a Sheraton down the road. I could drop you…"

Her words trailed into silence as her huge dark eyes settled on Natalie. "A child," she said in a whisper. "I didn't know you had a child."

Dear Reader,

Twenty-five years ago my mother fought a battle with breast cancer. She lost a breast but won her life. The idea for *A Father's Place* arose from reflecting on how grateful I was she survived and how different my life might have been had she not.

Karina, the heroine of my story, lost her mother to breast cancer at an early age. Her mother's death had a profound effect on her life, particularly when it came to having children of her own. Breaking down her protective barriers takes understanding, humor and a very special man. Daniel is a man of heart and mind with a deep capacity for loving. This is a story about the power of love to transcend fear and to turn abandoned dreams into reality. This is the story of Daniel and Karina.

*A Father's Place* is my first book. Writing it was personal, compelling and fun. Seeing it published is one of the biggest thrills of my life. I hope you enjoy it.

*Joan Kilby*

# A FATHER'S PLACE
# Joan Kilby

## *Harlequin Books*

TORONTO • NEW YORK • LONDON
AMSTERDAM • PARIS • SYDNEY • HAMBURG
STOCKHOLM • ATHENS • TOKYO • MILAN
MADRID • WARSAW • BUDAPEST • AUCKLAND

ISBN 0-373-70777-0

A FATHER'S PLACE

**Printed in U.S.A.**

To my mother, for
being a survivor

# CHAPTER ONE

KARINA PETERSON GAZED into the grinning face of an enormous pig.

It was good, this pig. She liked its pink-and-purple paisley jowls, its corkscrew tail and impossible smile. She liked the squishy feel of the paste and the gradual smoothing of the chicken wire as she built up layers of fabric strips.

Most of all she liked the total absorption she found in its creation. While she worked, her problems didn't exist.

Dishes sat in the sink, magazines and tape cassettes cluttered the kitchen table, high-heeled shoes of various colors and styles peeked from beneath chairs and counters. Karina refused to notice or care. She had her house all to herself, that's what counted. She was through playing den mother to an endless stream of tenants.

On her right breast she bore a tiny scar where an even tinier lump of flesh had been removed. That the lump had turned out to be benign ought to have put her mind at rest, but it hadn't. She was almost thirty-two, the age at which her mother had died of breast cancer. In the coming months she would need her own space in a way she never had before.

She crouched low to work a piece of fabric around the pig's hock, wavy strands of dark hair falling around her face. Tricky getting the angle just right. She pinched and prodded…got it. Time for a coffee.

Her bare feet, dabbed with paste, made little sticking sounds on the blue-and-white linoleum as she crossed from the meals area to the kitchen. Humming to the South American salsa band on the radio, she reached for the thermos jug of coffee, her shoulders and hips moving in time to the music.

Cup, sugar, spoon…cha, cha, cha. She danced over to the fridge for the milk.

Her body stilled as she caught sight of the "Beautiful Victoria" calendar taped to the freezer door. Today's date stared out at her from beneath a color photo of Butchart Gardens.

Saturday, July 8. Exactly one month until her birthday.

Karina shut her eyes and concentrated on reversing the spin of the earth. It was a game she'd played often as a young teenager after Mama had died. In those days, she'd been so desperate to turn back the clock she'd have sold her soul to defy the laws of nature.

She blinked her eyes open, ever hopeful—and sighed. Tulips still tossed their red-and-yellow heads in glossy profusion under July's heading. On the wall above the stove, Felix the Clock's longest arm advanced another minute, his swinging tail blithely indifferent to the passage of time.

Karina laughed at her own foolishness and pulled the milk out of the fridge. But there was a hint of a sob in her laughter. All these years later, she was no less desperate. And the laws of nature were no less immutable. No matter how many times she tried to convince herself that with vigilance she would live to a ripe old age, she couldn't shake the haunting feeling that her mother's fate would be hers.

Turning her back on the calendar, she returned to the counter to add a splash of milk to her coffee. Then she leaned over the kitchen table to crank up the volume of the radio perched on the windowsill. The opening bars of a reggae tune pulsed from the speaker. Karina went back to her pig, gratefully letting the music block her mind to the unthinkable.

No sooner had she plunged her hands into the basin of paste than the front doorbell rang. Karina smiled at the welcome distraction.

"Come on in," she called, though most of her friends just knocked and walked in. The only answer to her summons was another trill of the door bell followed by a brisk knock.

"Darn," she muttered, and gave up the attempt to prod a misshapen lump of fabric into a sow's ear. She looked around for a hand towel and, finding none, hastily wiped her hands on her oversize Hawaiian shirt.

"Coming!" Karina strode down the hall and flung open the door, prepared to give the Fuller Brush man, or whoever it was, short shrift.

But the tall, chestnut-haired man standing on her porch wasn't a salesman. Not unless they went door-to-door these days in faded denim and creased cotton shirts. He had a lean face and clear hazel eyes. And he looked dog-tired.

"Yes?" Karina said. There was more than fatigue in the fine lines around his eyes. Worry? Frustration?

"G'day." His deep voice was tinged with an Australian accent. "I'm Daniel Bowen. I reckon you must be Karina Peterson."

"That's right. What can I do for you?" Karina absently rubbed at her fingers. They were tacky with paste and starting to stick together.

Frowning, he thrust one hand into the hip pocket of his jeans and shoved the other through his rumpled hair. "I'm Betty's cousin."

"Betty? Betty Furness?" The only Betty she knew was married to Kevin in her art department. The thought sounded a vague alarm, but she ignored it and waited for him to come to the point.

"That's right. I've just come in on a flight from Melbourne." He paused, clearly waiting for an appropriate response from her.

"How nice." All Karina could think of was Petunia's ear. It would dry crookedly if this conversation went on much longer.

He smiled, a gritted-teeth kind of smile. "Betty arranged for me to rent rooms in your house. I sent a money order to cover the first month's rent. Didn't you get it? I thought you'd be expecting me."

"Oh, *now* I remember. You're Betty's cousin!" Last spring Kevin had tried to foist some long-lost relative of his wife's on her. But when she'd had to go in for the biopsy Karina had nipped the arrangement in the bud.

"Good," Daniel said. "I'm glad we've got that settled." He glanced over his shoulder at the taxi double-parked on the narrow residential street. "I'll just pay the cabby and get my bags."

Startled, Karina reached out to stop him. "Wait! Don't do that."

His biceps tensed under her fingers and a lock of dark brown hair fell over his forehead. Frowning, he looked down at his sleeve, then back up at her face.

"Sorry." She pulled her hand away, grimacing at the

traces of paste left on his dark blue shirt. "It washes out."

"Never mind that," he said, pushing his hair back into place with lean, tanned fingers. "Is there some problem with our agreement?"

"The room isn't available anymore." She smiled apologetically. "I told Kevin that when I gave him back your money order."

Daniel's frown deepened. "I never received it. Nor was I informed the rooms were unavailable."

He pulled a folded page of airmail paper from his pocket. In the crease was a scrap of neon yellow notepaper that looked disturbingly familiar. Tucking the yellow paper into his palm, he scanned the other page.

"You *are* Karina Peterson?"

"Yes, but—"

"And this is 336 Balaclava Street?" He glanced up at the house number, which undeniably confirmed he was in the right location. "According to Betty's letter, you agreed I could use your garage for a carpentry workshop." He leaned over the porch rail to peer around the side of the house. "Access to the garage is from the alley, I take it?"

Karina almost choked. "Yes, but I'm not renting!"

Then she did what she always did when forced into a confrontation. She laughed. It was an awkward habit that frequently gave people the wrong impression. And judging from the look on Daniel Bowen's face, it had now.

"Is this a joke?" he demanded. "Because I don't think it's very funny. Natalie had a cold when we left Melbourne, and on the flight over she turned really crook. I think she's got the flu."

*Natalie?* Who was Natalie? Kevin hadn't mentioned anything about *two* tenants. She pulled herself together.

"I'm sorry. Of course it's not a joke. It's a misunderstanding. But the fact is, I'm no longer renting."

Daniel held the bit of bright yellow paper in front of her. "I've got your receipt right here. Informal or not, it's still a contract."

She stared in dismay at her distinctive signature—little more than a giant *K* followed by a scrawl. "This is all Kevin's fault," she muttered. "I'll kill him."

"Betty's husband? What's he got to do with it?"

She laughed again. "Kevin's such a space cadet. Great guy, fantastic artist, but he wouldn't think to take out the garbage if it was placed in his hands."

Daniel folded his arms across his chest. Dark brown hair dusted his tanned forearms and peeked from the V of his indigo shirt. "Does this have anything at all to do with me?"

"I remember Kevin asking me about the room," Karina continued. "Right after I approved his design for the RollerDome. Or was it the Frosty Freeze?" She saw Daniel's mouth tighten and hurried on. "At the time I said, 'Sure.' He gave me your money order, I gave him a receipt—well, that piece of paper from my notepad.

"Then...something came up. A personal thing. Even so, I thought about it very hard for two whole weeks. I'm telling you this so you'll know I'm not just..." She cast her eyes upward, searching for the word.

"Scatty? Harebrained?"

Her eyebrows scrunched together in a quick frown. "The word I was looking for is...*capricious*." She wasn't precisely sure what it meant but it sounded a lot better than harebrained.

Daniel Bowen looked as though he might reel right off the porch. "Capricious. Ah. And you're not."

"Of course not. I distinctly told Kevin in March—no,

it was April, because I'd just got the results back from…
Anyway, I told him I couldn't take any new tenants just
now. I probably should have told Betty, but she was in
the hospital with complications. They just had their fifth
baby. But I guess you'd know that. The point is, I didn't
think even Kevin could mess up such a simple message.''

Daniel's eyes pressed shut, the lines of fatigue around
his mouth deepening. ''It never occurred to you to write
directly to me?''

''I suppose I should have got your address from
Kevin, but we had such a rush at work back then. One
of my artists was picked up by a rival firm and I had to
do my own job plus the extra artwork he left behind.
Then my boss got sick and I was doing his job, as well.''

''Look, Ms….Peterson, I don't need to hear all this.
I've sold my house, shut down my business and traveled
halfway around the world on the understanding that I
had a place to live when I got here. Just tell me one
thing—have you rented to someone else?''

''No, you see—'' She broke off. He'd just said he
didn't want to hear about her problems. And she certainly didn't want to discuss her personal life with a total
stranger.

''I'm really sorry about the room. And about your
money order. Knowing Kevin, it's probably still in his
wallet. Why don't you come inside and have a cup of
coffee? You can call a hotel while I see to my pig. If I
don't get back to her soon, her ear is going to dry looking like a cow pie.''

Daniel bowed his head, gripping the bridge of his nose
between thumb and middle finger. Then he glanced up,
his face haggard but resigned. ''I guess a hotel will have
to do for now. I want to get Natalie settled quickly.

We've been thirty-six hours in transit. She needs a hot bath and a good night's sleep.''

"I'm sure your wife will be fine," Karina said reassuringly. "Any of the larger hotels will have a house doctor.''

He gave her an odd look. "Natalie isn't—''

*Honk!* Behind the taxi, a cherry red BMW revved its engine, impatient to get past. Daniel glanced over his shoulder and signaled with a choppy wave of his hand.

"Excuse me," he said, turning back to Karina. "I'll get our things and be right back.''

She watched him stride down the path to the taxi, where the object of all that protective concern waited for her man. For a fraction of a second, Karina felt a twinge of longing. It would be nice to have someone who took care of *her* with such dedication.

Then the gate banged shut and she snapped out of her reverie. Men, especially the nice ones, too often came with expectations of marriage and children. Expectations she could never fulfill. For how could she ever marry knowing she might die young, leaving behind a grieving husband and children? She'd suffered so much when Mama died, she could never inflict such a loss on a child of her own.

Carefully, she unstuck her fingers from the railing and went inside. Besides, she could take care of herself.

Daniel pushed open the wooden gate, not caring that it swung back against the metal latch with a crash. What a bloody, stupid balls-up. How dare she laugh off his problem? Or blame the mix-up on Kevin? What kind of woman was capable of turning a sick child out in the street?

Capricious didn't begin to describe Karina Peterson. Natalie lay across the back seat of the taxi, her favorite blanket tucked up to her chin. Her small oval face was pale and moist and her breath a harsh rattle through chapped lips.

"Nattie," he called softly, worriedly noting the dark circles under her eyes. He'd returned to Victoria to try to heal the ten-year-old rift with his only brother. But in doing so he'd taken an enormous risk with his daughter's happiness, uprooting her from her home and the grandmother who'd been like a mother to her. He prayed she wouldn't pay too dearly for his shot at redemption.

"Natalie," he called again, a little louder. "Come on, sweetheart, we're going inside for a bit."

Her spiky blond lashes fluttered open and a faint spark shone in her dulled eyes. "Are we at our new home?"

His heart ached at having to disappoint her. "Not exactly. We have to find a hotel for the night. We'll go inside and telephone. Come on."

He reached into the cab and pulled his daughter into his arms. Her slender legs dangled to his waist, and it amazed him, as always, how big she'd grown. He could hardly believe his baby would be starting grade one in the fall.

Daniel carried her up the steps and through the open door. To the right, a staircase climbed to the second floor. Directly in front of him ran a short hallway, at the end of which he glimpsed the kitchen.

To the left was a doorway, and he walked through it into the living room. Part of his brain registered a clutter of furniture and overdecorated walls. Intent only on Natalie's comfort, he went directly to the sofa and gently laid her down. He slipped off her shoes and adjusted the cushions under her head, then tucked her blanket around her and went back for their bags.

Leaving the suitcases in the foyer, he picked the Yel-

low Pages up from the hall table and returned to the
sofa, his gaze lowered as he flicked through the phone
book.

Natalie touched his arm and he glanced up. Her
cheeks were flushed and feverish, and she was staring
around the room in wonder. "Daddy, look!"

His gaze followed the direction of her finger, and he
blinked in disbelief. Jet lag must be giving him hallu-
cinations.

Suspended from the ceiling of the adjoining dining
room was a flock, if that was the right word, of life-
size...angels? Not angels. They didn't have wings or
halos, and their entire bodies were clothed in a wild flo-
ral print. There must be half a dozen of the damn things.

Before he'd come to grips with the strange celestial
beings, Natalie pointed somewhere else. "Daddy,
Daddy! Look at the fairy lights! Aren't they pretty!"

He turned his head. In a recess in the wall, a piece of
driftwood the size of a small tree sported tiny, winking
white lights from its twisted, naked branches.

"Daddy, over there!" Natalie's finger pointed first
this way, then that.

Daniel got a headache trying to follow. Brightly
painted wooden marionettes danced across sage green
walls. Artificial grapevines festooned the doorway into
the dining room. Glass baubles and spangled ceramic
masks bedecked the mahogany wall unit. On the ceiling,
Japanese kites sailed across an azure sky bordered by
fluffy white clouds.

"Isn't it *wonderful*, Daddy?" Natalie pulled herself
up on one elbow, her illness momentarily forgotten.

"Fair boggles the mind," he replied, still gazing
around the room. Maybe it was just as well he and Nat-

alie weren't staying. What kind of bizarre imagination had created such chaotic fantasy?

Karina Peterson stepped through the arched doorway, a smile on her face and a swing in her hips. Her hands and face were newly clean, but her glossy black hair spilled from her hair clip in unruly waves. She came to a halt in the middle of the living room, talking rapidly.

"I was able to save the ear, thank goodness. Sorry about the mess. The cleaning lady doesn't come till Monday. Did you find any vacancies? There's a Sheraton just down the road. I could drop you..."

Her words trailed into silence as her huge dark eyes settled on Natalie. "A child," she said in a whisper. "I didn't know you had a child."

Karina pressed a hand to her stomach and forced herself to breathe. What a funny turn the sight of the girl had given her. Almost as though she'd seen herself at that age, home sick from school, waiting for Mama to read her a book or sing her a song in her perfect, clear soprano.

"A *sick* child," Daniel corrected her. "This is my daughter, Natalie," he added, fatherly pride creeping into his voice.

Karina kneeled on the floor beside the couch. "You poor thing," she murmured to Natalie.

Damp tendrils of fair hair stuck to the child's temples, and her pale cheeks held two bright spots of pink. Her round blue eyes glittered unhealthily.

"I've got a kite, too," Natalie confided. "Mrs. Beeton thinks it's the best flyer she's ever seen. Daddy almost didn't let me bring it because he said there are kite-eating trees here. Is that true?"

Karina suppressed a smile. At least part of the glitter in the child's eyes was due to an impish spark that was instantly endearing. "Oh, yes," she replied seriously. "You've got to be very careful. The bigger the tree, the more kites they can eat."

She pressed the back of her hand against the girl's forehead and looked at Daniel in alarm. "She's got a fever."

Daniel nodded silently. His daughter's tiny hand was cradled in his large one, and he gently stroked the backs of her fingers with his thumb. An unexpected lump formed in Karina's throat. Where was the child's mother?

"This changes everything." She reached over to the coffee table and flipped the phone book shut.

Daniel's dark eyebrows pulled together in a puzzled frown. "What do you mean?"

"I can't let you go to a hotel with a sick child. You'll have to stay here, at least for tonight."

His shoulders stiffened and his hand closed protectively around Natalie's. "Thanks, but no. You weren't expecting us."

"You can't possibly move your daughter again today." Karina looked at the girl's pinched face, and her heart ached. "She needs a hot bath and a good night's sleep."

"But—"

"You said so yourself," Karina reminded him.

"We'd be better off at a hotel. At least we could see a doctor."

"I'll call my GP. She makes house calls."

"We can't stay," Daniel said stubbornly.

"I insist." Karina wasn't sure how the tables had turned so quickly, but she did know she couldn't possibly send this poor child away.

He crossed his arms over his chest. "I refuse."

Karina shook her head. "I've heard Australian men are macho."

"Not all. Anyway, I'm from Canada originally. Victoria, actually."

"Then think about your daughter."

"*Please,* Daddy."

Daniel turned to his little girl, and Karina knew by the way his mouth softened the battle was all but over. "It's the height of tourist season," she added. "There probably isn't a vacancy anywhere in city."

He glanced back to her, his hazel eyes narrow. "That didn't seem to worry you before."

Karina smiled at Natalie and smoothed back her damp hair. "Adults can take care of themselves. Children need all the help we can give them."

It was after midnight when Karina clattered up the front steps and called a laughing goodbye to her friends. She kicked her shoes off in the hall and was about to drop her handbag with a thump when she remembered Daniel and Natalie.

She laid her purse quietly on the hall table and went to the foot of the stairs. One hand resting on the banister, she paused and listened. Not a sound came from the second-floor bedrooms. They must have settled in for the night long ago.

She'd had an assortment of tenants before, but never a man and a child. It felt strange, but kind of nice, almost as though a family lived here.

But they weren't family, she reminded herself. They weren't even tenants. Tomorrow they'd be gone.

From the radio in the kitchen, the somber chords of a piano concerto drifted down the darkened hallway. A wave of melancholy swept over her. Suddenly she felt empty. Alone.

Hugging her arms around herself, she wandered into the living room and sank onto the couch. In the low light of the table lamp, she gazed at the framed portrait on the wall directly opposite.

The woman in the photograph looked back at her with dark, soulful eyes and a Mona Lisa smile. Her lustrous black hair, so much like Karina's own, fell in waves around her shoulders.

Karina felt the familiar tightening in her chest and the hollow burning sensation behind her eyes from the river of tears she had never let flow.

*It still hurts so bad, Mama. Why did you have to leave me?*

The silence that filled the room was her only answer. Karina sat on in the semidarkness, as always, hardening herself to the pain. She'd never completely gotten over Mama's death, and her own cancer scare had brought the grief and fear flooding back as though it were yesterday.

She still had her father, but he might as well live on Mars instead of Penticton for all the contact they had. She hadn't even told him about her lumpectomy. He hadn't been able to cope with Mama's disease, or their grief, when she'd died. Stirring up all those awful memories would only increase the distance between them.

SUMMER RAIN PATTERED at the kitchen window. Karina, up to her wrists in paste, hummed along to *Aida*. As the music gave way to the midmorning news, she heard a perfunctory knock and the sound of the door opening.

"Yoohoo, anybody home?"

Karina leaned backward to glance down the hall. "Hi,

Joanne," she called to the tall, gangly woman stepping inside. "Where are the kids?"

Joanne shed her dripping raincoat and gave her shaggy blond head a shake, spraying water like a collie dog. "You mean those changelings that inhabit my children's bodies? Mom's got them for a couple of hours."

"You're so lucky she likes to baby-sit."

Joanne tramped down the hall in her sock feet. "I know. She says she's giving me a break, but I suspect she just likes to spoil them rotten without interference."

She walked slowly around the pig, nodding her approval. "Petunia's coming right along."

"Almost finished," Karina said. "Do me a favor and retie my hair for me? It's driving me crazy."

Joanne gathered up the loose strands that had fallen out of Karina's long, thick braid. "What I wouldn't give to have hair like yours."

Karina tilted her head back so Joanne could wrap a scrunchie around the braid at the base of her neck. "Don't say that. It's such a pain."

"So call me a masochist. Got any coffee?" Joanne's gaze fell on Daniel's brown leather jacket hanging over the back of a chair. Her long, skinny body jerked in an exaggerated double take. "Karina Isabella Peterson. Do you have *company*?" She peered around the corner into the dining room as though whoever it was might be hiding behind the potted palm.

"Don't be an idiot, Jo. You know me better than that."

"I do, indeed. And it's not me who's an idiot."

Joanne took a cup from the cupboard, inspected the interior and gave it a quick rinse under the hot water tap. "Who is he? And if he's not a lover, what's he doing here?"

Karina poked at Petunia's front trotter, trying for a better cleft between the toes. "He's Betty's cousin from Australia. He arrived yesterday under the impression he'd rented rooms in my house."

"Where did he get that idea?" Joanne asked, pouring herself coffee from the jug. "Wait, don't tell me. Kevin?"

Karina nodded, rolling her eyes. She wasn't surprised Joanne had got it in one; she'd been regaling her with stories about Kevin for years. "It's partly my fault. At one point I did agree to rent him the space. Then I changed my mind and trusted Kevin to pass on the message."

"Bad move," Joanne said, spooning sugar into her coffee.

Finished with the trotter, Karina stretched her fingers around the pig's wide neck and began pressing out the bubbles in the fabric. "If Kevin wasn't one of my best artists, I'd strangle him."

"So how come you let this guy stay?" Joanne stopped stirring her coffee and turned to Karina, her blue-grey eyes alight. "Is he gorgeous?"

"Shhh! He might hear you." Karina glanced uneasily at the ceiling.

"Well, is he or isn't he?" Joanne went to the fridge and opened the door. "Hey, you've got real food in here. He *must* be gorgeous."

"Of course he's not gorgeous," Karina said. "He's just a man. Quite ordinary in fact."

It occurred to her that *ordinary* didn't accurately describe Daniel Bowen. He had a sort of quiet certainty about him, a *presence* for lack of a better word. But she couldn't put her finger on anything tangible that made him *un*-ordinary, so she let it go.

"His daughter is ill," she said to explain the bagels, cream cheese and fresh orange juice sitting in her fridge where last night there'd been only half a carton of milk and an assortment of pickles.

Joanne's narrow face reappeared around the fridge door, her eyebrows raised. "Daughter?"

"Natalie. She got sick on the flight over. That's why I let them stay the night. Besides, there are half a dozen conventions in town. Every hotel is probably booked solid."

"True." Joanne took out the milk and poured some into her coffee. "Speaking of which, I'm booking the cabin at Watch Lake for the third week of August. Want to come? Peter will be up north collecting fish samples all summer, and I could use some adult company."

Karina got to her feet and stepped back to take a critical look at her pig. "I'd love to but I can't. The corporate golf tournament is that weekend."

"I thought you didn't like golf." Joanne pushed the Saturday paper to one side and sat down at the table with her coffee.

"I don't. But I've decided I'm going to break into upper management even if I have to spend a whole weekend chasing a little ball around a golf course to do it." She took a sip of cool coffee, made a face and dumped it down the sink.

"For two years," she continued, taking up the coffee jug and giving it an experimental shake, "I've coordinated all of SignCity's art departments across the country, as well as being art director of the Victoria office. I have higher responsibilities than the chief sales executive but am I considered upper management? No. Am I adequately compensated for my efforts? No. Does my title even begin to reflect my responsibilities?"

"No!" Joanne cried and raised her cup. "The time has come. The worm will turn!"

Karina stopped to look at her, jug poised over her cup. *"Worm?"*

"Sorry," Joanne said, grinning. "I was living out my own unfulfilled fantasies for a moment. So tell me, how is playing golf going to get you into upper management?"

"All major decisions are made on the golf course," Karina explained. "I hate playing the corporate game by men's rules—all that striving for success, pretending to be tougher than tough and never, God forbid, admitting you made a mistake. But there's no challenge left where I am. My only choice, if I don't want to be trapped in middle management, is to get out there and schmooze like mad at the annual golf tourney."

*"Schmooze,"* Joanne repeated, picking up a pen to doodle on the front page of the newspaper. "Is that in the corporate rule book?"

"On page one." Karina dropped three spoonfuls of sugar into her coffee quickly before Joanne noticed. "Picture this. I'm on the nineteenth hole—"

"Er, Karina, don't look now but there are only eighteen holes on a golf course. And don't think I didn't notice all that sugar you dumped in your coffee."

"Okay, so I'm on the *eighteenth* hole." She gripped the sugar spoon like a golf club. "I'm playing with three or four members of the board of directors. Just before I tee off—is that the correct terminology?"

"Sounds right." Joanne, busy turning a photo of the mayor into a portrait of Groucho Marx, paused to gaze at her.

"Just before I tee off, I'll say—" She arrested her swing and turned to an imaginary partner. "'By the way,

Bill, or Phil, or Whomever—if SignCity is going to ex-
pand into the Asia-Pacific market, I'll need a title that
will impress. I was thinking of Grand pooh-bah. What
do you say, Philbert, old buddy?'"

Joanne giggled. "He'd be nuts not to go for it."

"Shh, I'm in my stride. And Phil, or Bill, will say,
'Absolutely, Karina, old thing. Of course you'll need a
raise in pay. And a decent expense account.' Then..."
she raised her arms and swung "...I'll whack the ball a
mile down the fairway. And they'll slap me on the back
and say, 'This woman is going places.'"

"Into the bushes to look for your ball?" Joanne suggested with a grin.

"Scoff away," Karina said, waving the sugar spoon.
"I'll have that rack of suits falling all over each other
in a race to upgrade my position."

Joanne's smile faded. "I've no doubt you will." She
put down the pen and sipped her coffee.

Karina dropped her arms to her side with a wondering
glance at her friend. Joanne was usually her biggest
cheerleader. "Don't be so enthusiastic."

Joanne smiled halfheartedly. "You'll be great. You'll
come across as a dingbat. Then when they least expect
it, you'll dazzle 'em with your competence and know-
how. Just like you always do."

Karina stepped around Petunia and sat down at the
table. "So, isn't that good?"

"Yeees..." Joanne picked up the pen again and
clicked the button in and out. "But if you get an even
more high-powered job, when are you going to have
time to get married and have a family?"

Karina fiddled with the radio dial, eliciting a succes-
sion of blaring sound bites until she came to the station
she wanted. "You know how I feel about...mother-

hood,'' she said at last. "Anyway, I wonder if it's all it's cracked up to be. Look at you—your kids drive you crazy.''

"I'm also crazy about them. They're noisy, messy, completely vile little creatures but they're mine. Flesh of my flesh and all that.''

"But when we were teenagers you were always going on about the career you were going to have. You weren't even interested in children.''

"People change. What's wrong with that? Being a mother doesn't mean I've given up sentient life. Or that I'll never go back to teaching. At least with your job you're in an ideal position to freelance. You could have a home office and easily combine the two.''

"I'd get bored working by myself. Say, do you think I should wear shorts on the golf course or one of those kicky little skirt things tennis players wear?''

Joanne rolled her eyes. "You're supposed to dazzle them with your competence, not your legs. Seriously, Karina, I just can't see you being alone all your life.''

Karina jumped up and paced across to the kitchen counter. "I've got plenty of friends. Not all of them are married. I'm sure I'll find someone to sit by the fire with in my dotage.''

"Friends are great, but they're not the same as having your own family,'' Joanne insisted. "Besides, you love kids. You practically drooled over every one of my babies. Why not have your own?''

*And leave them to weep for me when I'm gone? Never.*

Karina busied herself at the counter, rearranging the clutter. "Aunt Maria called the other day.''

"Your mom's sister?''

"Yes. She was crying so much I could hardly make

out what she was saying. Pamela, her eldest daughter, found another lump in her breast last month.''

"Oh, dear." Joanne's mouth twisted sympathetically. "Was it malignant?"

Karina nodded, sorting used twist-ties into piles by color. "Poor Pam. She must be terrified. Aunt Maria went on and on about how every generation since my great-great-grandmother's time has been affected by breast cancer. She made it sound like every female in the family is doomed.''

"Yet *she* never got it," Joanne argued. "And how good could the medical treatment have been in an Italian village in the old days?"

"Not great, probably. But the best treatment in modern-day Canada didn't save my mother. And sure Maria never got it, but she's only one out of how many?" Karina wound a twist-tie around her finger. "I'll be thirty-two next month, Jo.''

"Oh, Karina. You're *not* going to get breast cancer and die.''

"It happened to my mother."

"But it won't happen to you. Not with all the information and screening techniques around these days." Joanne frowned at her. "You do practise self-examination, don't you?"

"I'd be crazy not to, wouldn't I?" She didn't mention the major effort required to work up the courage to do it every month, or the cold sweat that had broken out when she'd actually found something.

"But I very nearly didn't see my doctor about that lump last April," she confessed. "I tried to convince myself it was just normal bumpy tissue. I know it's not rational, but I'm terrified I'll be the next family casualty."

"But you *did* see your doctor. You *did* get it treated. Have you told your dad about it yet, by the way?"

Karina hung her head. "I don't want to worry him. He never got over Mama. If I even try to talk about her, he gets this frozen look on his face and changes the subject. He loved her so much when she was alive, it's as if he hates her for dying. I wouldn't ever want to put anyone I loved through that. He's still suffering."

"Still, he should be told. *You* don't talk about your mother, either," Joanne added, her husky contralto sounding even lower than usual. "I've never seen you cry over her, not even right after she died."

Karina pushed the piles of twist-ties into a drawer, where they scattered among the cutlery. Some things were too painful, too frightening to talk about, even with Joanne. Anyway, what was the point of dwelling on them? She wanted to forget. She wanted to be happy.

"I..." She swallowed. "There's nothing to say, Jo."

Joanne looked skeptical but she crossed the room and pulled Karina into a hug. "If you ever do want to talk, I'm here, okay?"

"I'm fine, really." Karina gave her a shaky smile. "But thanks. I appreciate it."

"That's okay." Joanne released her and stood back. "You know, Karina, maybe you should rent to this Aussie guy. You two might hit it off."

Karina let out an exasperated sigh tempered with a tiny smile. "You never give up, do you?"

"I'm just worried about you. You push away any man who gets too close. Look at Joel. The minute he started getting serious, you told him to take a hike."

Karina's gaze slid away from Joanne's. "I was in the middle of restructuring the art department. It was a bad time."

"That was two years ago! Who've you been out with since?"

"No one special, you know that. For me to fall in love and marry—which I can tell you right now will never happen—I'd have to find one extraordinary man."

The sound of footsteps on the landing overhead made her pause abruptly. "Shhh. He's coming."

## CHAPTER TWO

DANIEL QUIETLY SHUT the door to Natalie's room and paused on the landing. Voices drifted up the stairs from the kitchen. Karina and another woman. Great. How was he going to convince Karina to let them stay until they found another place to live in the middle of a gabfest?

He descended the stairs and walked down the carpeted hallway, drawn by the aroma of freshly brewed coffee. At the entrance to the meals area he paused, his way blocked by a sea of newspapers surrounding the biggest pig he'd ever seen.

The two women fell abruptly silent.

"Mornin'." His brief nod encompassed them both.

"Good morning," Karina said cheerily. "How did you sleep?"

"Well, thanks. Natalie's still sawing logs." Karina wore a sunny smile, he noted, but her eyes were unnaturally bright, as though she'd been crying. Or come close to it. "I hope I'm not interrupting."

"Not at all. Coffee's hot." Karina nodded at the thermal jug. "This is Joanne. Joanne, Daniel."

"Pleased to meet you." He walked into the kitchen under the spotlight of Joanne's avid gaze. Karina, wearing another oversize, paste-streaked shirt over black leggings, was totally rapt in pouring sugar into a royal-blue-and-white sugar bowl. Her feet were bare, her toenails painted the same fuchsia color as her shirt.

Daniel gave the sticky-looking pig a wide berth. It was oddly appealing, he had to admit, with a smile as big as its maker's. He poured himself a cup of coffee and pulled out a chair at the far side of the table. As he sat down he glimpsed Joanne throwing Karina a *look,* her big eyes widening till white surrounded the blue.

Strange woman. He rooted through the newspaper for the "Want Ad" section.

"How's Natalie?" Karina asked, glancing over her shoulder at him. Her dark brown eyes were warm and full of concern.

Daniel paused, cup to his lips. For a moment he found himself wanting to pour out all his worries over his daughter. About how she still cried for her mother. How she spent too much time playing with her imaginary friend, Mrs. Beeton. How she'd clung to her grandma when they'd left Melbourne and had to be carried, sobbing, onto the plane.

He took a sip of coffee and swallowed the hot, bitter liquid. "She's developed a rattling cough."

Karina made a *tsking* sound. "And her fever?"

"Worse."

Her mouth moved outward in a moue of sympathy. Daniel's gaze fixed on the soft curve of her lower lip, noting the gradation from pale pink at the edges to cranberry at its fullest part. Then he shook open the newspaper to the "For Rent" section and focused on the tiny print.

"Sounds like bronchitis," Joanne said cheerfully. She sat down and planted her elbows on the table. "Or maybe pneumonia."

Daniel lowered the paper in alarm. "Pneumonia?"

"Don't mind her," Karina said with a quick smile. "She's a card-carrying pessimist."

Joanne made a face at Karina. "I'm a mother." To Daniel, she explained, "I've got three kids—eight, six and two. They've been through everything, twice."

"Natalie's six, too," he said.

Karina split a bagel and popped it into the toaster. "I called my doctor. She's coming around this afternoon."

Surprised, he glanced up at her, gratitude warming his gaze. "Thank you."

With a flustered laugh she bustled off, chattering about bagels and cream cheese as though she were offering him a full-course gourmet dinner.

Joanne drained her coffee and rose from the table to carry her cup to the sink. "Well, folks, I'll leave you to it."

The toaster popped. Karina whipped out the hot bagels and juggled them to the bread board, her alarmed gaze fixed on Joanne. "Aren't you staying for breakfast?"

Daniel watched Karina over his coffee cup. She seemed surprised at Joanne's departure, and just the teeniest bit annoyed. What was going on?

"Nope," Joanne replied. "I've got to stop at the store before I pick up the kids from Mom." She turned to Daniel. "Why don't you bring Natalie over to play with my girls when she's feeling better? She'll need some company to help keep her mind off her friends back home."

Daniel set down his cup. The offer was appealing, but he hadn't missed the lightning-quick glare and counterglare that flashed between Karina and Joanne. Joanne was probably just being friendly. But Karina obviously wanted him out of the house. Well, she had no worries on that score. He wanted to get Natalie settled as soon as possible.

"Thanks. I'll have to see where we are by then."

Joanne tossed her shaggy blond hair and laughed. "Oh, you'll still be here. I heard on the news the other day the vacancy rate's at a ten-year low."

"Thank you, Joanne." Karina all but pushed her out the door, muttering something inaudible under her breath.

Daniel watched the pair with amusement, but his smile faded as he contemplated Joanne's parting words. He had less than two months to find a place to rent before Natalie started school. Buying a house would have to wait until he'd familiarized himself with prices, schools and locations. Ten years was a long time to be away, and the city had undoubtedly changed.

He could hear Karina and Joanne talking on the front porch, their lowered voices punctuated by the occasional burst of laughter. Munching on a bagel, Daniel took a pen from the pewter beer mug on the windowsill and began to mark the ads that appeared suitable. They were discouragingly few.

Karina came back into the room. "Anything good?"

He threw down the pen. "A couple. Not much."

"Try them." She plucked the cordless phone from its holder on the wall and passed it to him.

Fifteen minutes later Daniel had been through the lot. "Gone, every last one of them." He folded the phone shut. "I'll have to wait till next week."

"Next month, you mean," Karina said, spreading cream cheese over another toasted bagel.

Daniel looked at her blankly. "Beg your pardon?"

"Most apartments are rented by the month, with possession from the first. You missed it by a week." She eyed him curiously. "Didn't you know that?"

"Obviously not." Daniel pushed himself to his feet. He would have strode across the room but the damn pig was in the way. Frustrated, he braced his hands inside the doorless frame that separated the kitchen from the meals area. "In Melbourne, you can move into a rental anytime if the place is vacant. And there are always vacancies."

Karina's eyebrows lifted. "Not here. On the first of every month, there's a mad scramble among renters to grab the few available apartments and houses. People hang out at the back of the newspaper building at 5:00 a.m. to get the paper fresh off the press."

"That's insane."

She shrugged. "That's life in Lotus Land. What made you move to Australia in the first place? If you don't mind me asking."

"My wife was Australian. We can't spend a month or more in a hotel," he muttered, his mind still on the housing situation. "I promised Natalie we'd have a real home. I'll have to contact a rental agency."

"Good idea. I'll ask around at work, too. I guess Betty and Kevin are already overcrowded," she added between bites of her bagel.

Daniel nodded. "Even if they had room, they wouldn't want a sick child coming in contact with their new baby."

"No, I guess not." Karina took a sip of coffee. "I take it your parents don't live in Victoria?"

"They used to. But when Dad retired a few years ago they moved up-island. As soon as we get settled and I get transport, I'll take Natalie for a visit. They haven't seen her since she was a baby."

"I'll bet they can't wait to get reacquainted. Any other friends or relatives you could mooch off?"

"I have a brother...." Daniel's hands stiffened around

the door frame. No way could he contact Brian after a decade of silence and immediately ask a favor.

"Well?"

"I don't know what his situation is. Whether he has room or not."

Karina frowned, looking puzzled. "Give him a call and find out."

Daniel hesitated, reluctant to admit the extent of his estrangement with his brother. "He doesn't know I'm back," he said finally. "We haven't spoken to each other for ten years."

"Ten years!" Karina looked astounded. "Why not?"

"We…had a fight." Daniel straightened, flexing his hands. He turned away from her and crossed the kitchen to look out the window into the backyard. Why on earth was he telling her this? He had a problem and he would solve it, without any sympathy from a woman he scarcely knew.

He and Brian used to be best mates. They'd been through everything together—Little League, Scouts, fishing, girls. *Girls.* That's where everything had gone wrong. But Francine was dead and Natalie was growing up. Surely Brian would forgive and forget. They were brothers, after all.

Behind him, he heard Karina leave the table and set her dishes in the sink. "What did you fight about?" she asked above the clatter of china on porcelain.

The clock over the stove ticked loudly in the ensuing silence. Daniel watched the swinging tail, the eyes flicking back and forth with each passing second.

"A woman," he said finally. "No big deal." *Damn,* that hadn't come out right.

When his inadvertent chauvinism didn't draw a blast from Karina, he turned to see her staring at a miniature

silver frame on the shelf above the sink. Crammed between a vase of dried flowers and a collection of scallop
shells was a photo of a good-looking man with wavy
dark hair.

"My brother, Tom, and I used to fight all the time,"
she said. "About all sorts of trivial things. We were very
jealous of each other."

Were all families the same? "Do you still fight?"

She smiled. "No, we grew out of that. We hardly see
each other since he moved to Toronto, but we talk fairly
often on the phone."

"This is a big house for one person," Daniel said.
"Why did you stop renting?"

To his surprise, the rosy bloom drained from her
cheeks and she stared at him with wide, troubled eyes.
Then, just as he was about to ask what was wrong, she
laughed, though her laughter sounded forced.

"I've had a string of bad tenants," she said, turning
away from her brother's photo. "Everything from a lech
to a loser who couldn't pay the rent. I'm fed up."

"I see." What he saw was that behind her bright and
beautiful facade she was afraid. Of what, he couldn't
imagine, but her problems were none of his business. He
had enough of his own.

Outside in the backyard, a dog barked. Karina rushed
to the door, color flooding back into her cheeks. In a
flash, she was across the deck, crashing down the steps
to the lawn. "Get out of my tomatoes, Piper, you crazy
mutt!"

Daniel stepped onto the deck. The rain had stopped.
An exuberant and very shaggy cocker spaniel was running in circles around the scrap of lawn between the
deck and the garage. Karina ran after it, laughing now
and panting hard.

"Gotcha," she cried, and tackled the dog. Dog and woman went rolling on the damp grass, the dog's tongue lapping furiously while Karina twisted her head to avoid the slobbery onslaught. She finally knelt on the lawn, scratching the dog on the belly and muttering to it in puppy talk.

Daniel walked slowly down the stairs, his eyes roving over the backyard. In one corner, rows of tomato plants had been staked near the back fence. Between two front plants was a hole, freshly dug. His gaze went to the fence itself. Midway along the yard was a gap in a rotted board just big enough for a small dog to squeeze through.

"Piper is the neighbor's dog, I take it," Daniel said, coming across the lawn. He dropped to a squat and scratched the dog behind the ears, chuckling at the blissful look on the spaniel's face. "Nattie would go mad over this little fella. She misses her grandma's blue heeler."

Karina flopped back on her elbows on the lawn. "Didn't she have a dog of her own?"

"No. Nattie and I have lived with her grandmother for the past three years."

Karina sat up and plucked at a blade of grass. "I don't mean to pry, but—"

Ah, the inevitable questions about his wife. Daniel rose to his feet.

Karina got up, too, Piper leaping around her legs. "I'm sorry," she said. "Forget I said anything. Please."

He gazed at her, not smiling but not angry, either. Not anything. "Natalie's mother is dead."

"I'm sorry." Karina bent to push the dog away. She glanced up at Daniel and an odd expression crossed her face. "I...I hope you give your daughter lots of hugs."

Daniel blinked. Most women gushed about how sorry they were for the poor little mite. And for him. "Yes, I do, as a matter of fact."

"Good." Her lips curved in a smile as spontaneous and pure as the sunshine that was breaking from behind the parting clouds.

Daniel drew in a breath and gestured to the wooden building behind them. "Is, ah...is that the garage?"

"What? Oh, yes."

"May I see it?"

She hesitated. "Is there any point?"

"Perhaps I'll see that it wouldn't be suitable. Then I won't mind so much not being able to use it."

Her fine, black eyebrows lifted and she laughed. "That's a novel way of looking at it. Come on, then."

Daniel stepped inside as Karina flicked a switch and strips of fluorescent lighting brightened the interior. It was swept clean and was empty—except for a bright red Triumph Spitfire parked askew in the center of the four-square orderliness.

He glanced around. Plenty of space. More than adequate light, even for night work. A wooden work bench sat along one wall, while shelves lined another. There was even a high, wooden stool tucked under the bench and a corkboard attached to the wall. He walked over to the panel box and inspected it. Three-phase power—essential for some of his tools. The garage was perfect.

He nodded at the sports car. "Yours?"

Karina grinned. "Why should men with grey hair and potbellies have all the fun?"

"Why, indeed? Looks as if someone has done carpentry here before."

She nodded. "A friend used to make futon furniture

in here." She glanced sideways at him. "Guess your plan didn't work, huh?"

"Not exactly." He started to walk out of the garage, then stopped and faced her, his hands thrust in his hip pockets. "Look, I'm in a bind. I've got wood arriving from Melbourne any day and I want to get to work. How about at least renting me the garage?"

"You're importing wood from Australia? Isn't that a little strange when we've got about a zillion trees of our own in British Columbia?"

"The wood is special. What do you say? Can I use the garage?"

She went quiet for a long time, staring at the concrete floor. Daniel waited. One less stress in his life right now would be more than welcome.

At last she lifted her head and looked at him. "Would there still be room for Sammy?"

She had to be talking about the car. He noticed for the first time the chrome salamander snaking up the center of the hood in place of the traditional ornament.

"Sammy's small. There's room for both of us."

"In that case, okay."

He breathed out. "Great. Thanks." One down, one to go. Except he wasn't sure he still wanted to press the issue of staying until he found another rental. Not after seeing how upset she'd become in the kitchen earlier.

When they walked out of the garage, Piper was back in the tomato bed, head down, dirt spraying from his flying feet. Karina hauled him away from the plants, then crouched and held the dog's face so she could glare straight into his eyes. "Bad dog. No dig."

The spaniel twisted his muzzle this way and that in an effort to escape her scolding, but he didn't look particularly contrite.

Suppressing a smile, Daniel said, "When my tools arrive I'll fix the fence for you. Unless you've got a hammer and nails—I could do it right now."

Karina got to her feet, one hand firmly gripping the dog's collar. "Right *now?*"

He nodded.

"You mean you would fix the fence right this minute if you had the tools?"

What was she getting at? "Sure. Why not?"

"For one thing," she said, "there's a little matter of procrastination."

Daniel smiled. He very nearly laughed. It'd been a long time since he'd done that with anyone but Natalie. "Oddly enough, I've never suffered from procrastination."

Karina dragged the reluctant Piper back to the hole in the fence and pushed him through. "Well, try to cultivate some, because I don't want the fence fixed."

She stuck a small piece of wood against the hole and propped it there with a brick. "It keeps him out for a while," she explained, dusting off her hands and walking back to Daniel.

He shook his head. "He just lets you think that. Why not do the job properly?"

She looked at him as though he were crazy. "Then I'd never get to play with him."

"Of course," he murmured. "Why didn't I think of that?" He paused at the bottom of the steps so she could go up ahead of him. "If you like dogs so much, why not get one of your own?"

"And deliberately install another tomato excavator in my backyard? No thanks. Besides, dogs are long-term commitments." She reached the top of the stairs and regarded him thoughtfully. "But a budgie might be good. And I could teach it to talk.''

Daniel's eyebrows rose. Conversation with Karina took more turns than a tiger snake's tail. ''Er, right,'' he replied, and added a twist of his own. ''Isn't that a lot of tomatoes for one person?''

She led the way back inside the house, talking over her shoulder. ''Mama always had a tomato patch. I'm not much of a cook but I still follow her old Italian recipe for tomato sauce every year.''

''Does your mother live in Victoria?''

For a moment, Daniel didn't think she'd heard him. Without speaking, Karina took the kettle off the stove and walked to the sink to fill it.

''No,'' she said at last, very quietly. ''Not anymore.''

He was about to ask where her mother lived now when a thin wail came from above. ''Daaaddy!''

KARINA SAT AT THE kitchen table working on the logo for a friend's business card. The doctor had come and gone after diagnosing acute bronchitis and ordering Natalie to spend the day in bed. Daniel had filled a prescription for antibiotics at the local drugstore and given Natalie the first dose. He'd also registered with House Rentals Plus by telephone, proving conclusively that procrastination wasn't part of his vocabulary.

Now he was tidying up the kitchen while Karina watched covertly. She'd reminded him the cleaning lady was coming tomorrow, but he'd just shaken his head with a disbelieving smile and rolled up his sleeves.

As tenants went, Daniel would be a good one, she thought. He was neat and clean, but she could live with that. He was quiet; perhaps a bit too quiet, but that was probably a good thing. It meant he wasn't her type and therefore not a threat. He liked dogs; that was always a good sign. And he was reliable. Anyone who cared for his daughter so diligently had to be a responsible person.

On the other hand, she wasn't looking for a roommate. She'd been perfectly honest when she'd told Daniel she'd thought about it long and hard. Her rational as well as her emotional decision had been that she needed time to herself. That hadn't changed overnight.

Interesting how many muscles were employed in the simple act of washing dishes, she mused as she watched his movements. His arms flexed, which made his shoulders strain against his sand-colored cotton shirt. His torso twisted as he stacked the dishes beside the sink, causing a contraction of his denim-clad buttocks, which in turn tensed his leg muscles right down to the calves.

"You know," Daniel said, "there are so many eyes in this house I feel like I'm being watched wherever I go. Don't you find it a bit creepy?"

Karina put her head down and concentrated on the logo. "It never occurred to me. Mind you, I regard my creatures as friends. When they talk to me, I talk back."

Daniel pulled the plug, and the water gurgled down the drain. Picking up a hand towel that had been rolled into a ball and left on the counter, he dried his hands and hung the towel neatly on the oven handle.

"This bloke is a good conversationalist, is he?" He gestured to a luridly painted plaster gargoyle attached to the wall.

Karina laughed. "A bit of a complainer, but not bad."

Daniel shook his head, then glanced at his watch. "I'd better start looking for a hotel for the night."

"You and Natalie can stay here until you find a house to rent." Karina bit her lip, surprised at her impulsive offer. Hadn't she just decided she wanted him to go?

Frown lines creased Daniel's forehead. "You don't have to do that. The doctor said Nattie could be moved."

"I know." Karina sought a valid reason to explain her change of heart. And found none. She shrugged. "I would just feel better if you stayed. For Natalie's sake."

Still he hesitated, regarding her through narrowed eyes. "Just how capricious are you?"

She laughed. "Are you afraid I'll change my mind again?"

"Frankly, yes."

"Don't worry. Two or three changes on the same subject is all my brain can handle." She got up from the table and put out her hand. "Deal?"

He looked at it so long she thought he was still making up his mind. Then he wrapped his fingers around her hand and held it. "On one condition."

"What's that?"

"I can take down those cardboard palm trees from beside my bed. When I woke up this morning I felt as if I was in a commercial for suntan lotion."

Karina smiled. Daniel Bowen was sober, dull and ordinary. A model tenant and no threat at all to her equilibrium. Imagine not liking palm trees. "It's a deal."

He pressed her hand. The warmth from his fingers felt awfully good, and for a moment she wondered if she'd made a mistake. Then she remembered the palm trees. "What are you going to do now?" she asked.

He let go of her hand. The warmth in his gaze faded and the fine lines across his brow reappeared. "Call my brother."

# CHAPTER THREE

DANIEL WALKED INTO the kitchen the next morning and stopped short at the sight of Karina dressed for work. She looked like an ad for *Vogue* in her tailored suit jacket, slim black skirt and high-heeled shoes. Even her lively hair had been tamed into a smooth, dark chignon.

"Mornin'," he said, and laid an envelope stuffed with bills on the table. "Here's the rent for July—two rooms plus the garage."

Karina flashed him a smile. "Thanks. Can you wait till tonight for a receipt? I'm in a bit of a rush." She took a bite of toast and followed it quickly with a sip of coffee.

"No worries." Daniel poured himself coffee and noted the unconventional details of her outfit he'd missed at first glance; the tiny silver butterfly inserted into her hair, the rhinestone salamander that slithered up the lapel of her electric blue jacket and the dozen or so silver bangles that jingled up her arm as she lifted her cup to that splendid, curving mouth.

"Do you know anything about golf?" she asked.

He raised one eyebrow. "Golf?"

"Golf." Heels clicking on the linoleum, Karina deposited her cup in the sink and brushed the toast crumbs from her hands. "I'm entering a tournament next month and I don't have a clue how to play."

He shook his head. "I played a few times, years ago,

but never liked the game enough to bother learning properly."

She looked disappointed for a moment, then her smile was back, full force. "Never mind, I'll just ad-lib."

Daniel was pretty sure you couldn't ad-lib a game like golf. But if anyone could pull it off, he'd place his bet on Karina Peterson. She seemed confident enough to brazen her way through anything.

Karina gathered up her purse and briefcase. "Any word from your brother?"

"I left another message on his answering machine. He hasn't called back yet."

"Why don't you just drop in on him?"

Daniel sipped at his coffee. "He'll call today."

"If you say so." She glanced at Felix the Clock. "I'm late. See you tonight." She started off down the hall, still talking. "Jenny will be here..." Her voice trailed away.

"Who's Jenny?" he said, forced to follow her. Didn't this woman ever stand still and talk?

"The cleaning lady," Karina replied, going out the door. "She comes at ten. Help yourself to anything you want. Anything you can find, that is." She flashed her wide smile again and waved, keys and bangles jingling. "'Bye."

"'Bye." He almost leaned forward and kissed her. Such was the force of habit, even when habit was three years dead and gone. Even when habit had been formed by another woman. A totally different kind of woman.

By the time he pulled back, clutching his coffee cup a little too tightly, Daniel was alone on the step.

He hardly ever thought of Francine anymore, except with sadness for Natalie's sake and regret that anyone should die so young. He'd tried to be a good husband. As good as a man could be who hadn't loved his wife.

Daniel tipped back his head to drain the last of his coffee. Natalie would be waking soon. Going inside, he rinsed his cup and left it on the draining board. Then he made a tray of scrambled eggs and toast to take up to his daughter.

He knocked softly and opened the door. A rustle of bedclothes told him Natalie was stirring. "Mornin', Possum. Ready for some breakfast?" He set the tray on the bedside table and handed her a glass of juice and a pill.

"Yes, thanks. I'm starving." Natalie struggled to sit up in bed. She took the juice and chewed the cherry-flavored pill with relish. "Yummy."

"Don't get too used to these tablets," Daniel warned. "They're not lollies."

The antibiotics were having a positive effect, though. Her fever had gone down and her color was healthier. Another day and she'd probably be out of bed. Then he could get on with looking for a vehicle, setting up a bank account, placing ads in the local papers—

"Daddy, is Karina coming up to see me this morning?"

"No, darlin', she already left for work."

"Oh." The single word, the downturned mouth, expressed a wealth of disappointment.

He ruffled her hair affectionately. "You must be feeling better if you're getting choosy about your visitors. Do you want me to read you a book?"

Natalie brightened. "Read the one Karina left with me last night. It has dragons and everything."

Daniel picked up the book lying on the bedside table and read to Natalie while she ate her breakfast, keeping one ear open for the sound of the telephone. He finished the book and read two more, but still Brian hadn't called. Maybe he'd got in late last night and hadn't had a chance to check his messages. By this time of the morning he was probably at work.

Daniel closed the book. "Okay, Nattie, time for that bath you were too tired for last night."

The bathroom, like every other room in the house, was bursting at the seams with Karina's personality. Makeup and jewelry were scattered over the vanity, purple and blue hydrangeas erupted from a papier-mâché vase next to the tub, and a damp towel had been flung carelessly over the wicker chair in the corner.

Somewhere in the room, a top forty radio station pumped out pop music. Karina's taste in music, he'd discovered already, was as insatiable as it was wide-ranging. There was never a moment of the day or night when the radio or CD player wasn't on.

Daniel ran the bath, then started to hunt for the radio to silence it. There weren't many places to look and he found it quickly enough, a small transistor wedged into the lower shelf of the medicine cabinet. He turned it off with a wondering shake of his head. A man couldn't hear himself think around this house.

Peace restored, he helped Natalie into the bath and lathered shampoo through her straight blond hair. How was Brian going to react to seeing him again? he wondered.

The first few years after he and Francine had married, all Daniel's attempts at communication had been rebuffed. Later, there'd been too many moves, too many changes of address to keep up with. He wasn't much of a letter writer; nor, it seemed, was Brian. It'd been easier to let things slide, thinking someday he'd return to Victoria to visit his folks and patch things up.

He'd come back once, shortly after Natalie was born, but Brian had been away. Unavoidably, his father had said, but the troubled look in his mother's eyes had told a different story. Brian still hadn't forgiven him for eloping with his fiancée; not that Daniel blamed him. Why else would he have scheduled an extended trip, business or not, the month his only brother was home from Australia?

"Okay, kiddo, rinse time." He adjusted the water temperature and sprayed Natalie's head with the nozzle attached to the tap.

But the rivalry between Brian and himself had started long before Francine. Brian had always resented the fact that Daniel made the high school honor roll year after year. And he, himself, had certainly disliked the attention Brian received as captain of the football team and ace basketball player.

Okay, so they'd been jealous of each other as teenagers and rivals in love as young men. But they were brothers. Surely that was a bond that could never be broken?

"Look, Daddy, I'm a submarine!" Natalie submerged her face, bubbles roiling around her head as her legs thrashed the shallow bathwater.

"You're one sick chook, is what you are," he said when she emerged, gasping.

"I'm not a chicken." She pushed wet hair out of her face and drew herself up with great dignity. "I'm a little lady."

"Who told you that?" he asked with a grin.

"Grandma." Her small mouth drooped. "I miss Grandma. When are we going to see her again?"

His grin faded. "It might be a while, Nattie. We'll

give her a ring tonight, let her know we arrived safely. Come on, time to come out.''

He helped her from the tub and wrapped a big, fluffy towel around her shivering body. So sweet, so fragile, her little pixie face. Her blue eyes so serious. "You'll learn to like it here in Canada, sweetheart.''

"I guess so. But why won't Karina let us live here?''

"I don't know exactly,'' he said, rubbing her hair dry. "I suppose she likes living alone.''

Natalie pushed the towel back from her forehead, her fair brows pulled together in confusion. "But yesterday she had all those friends around.''

Daniel nodded, remembering the small crowd that had dropped in by ones and twos to drink coffee and yak the day away while Karina worked on her pig.

"Having friends over when you want company and having strangers living in your house are two different things.''

"We're not strangers,'' Natalie said. "We're us.''

Daniel laughed and hugged her tightly. "So we are, Possum, so we are.''

The telephone rang.

Daniel leaped to his feet. "Wait here,'' he told Natalie, and thundered across the landing to the stairs. He was halfway down when he remembered the extension in his bedroom and hastily backtracked. He dived for the receiver on the eighth ring.

"Hello?''

"Goodness, you sound as if you've been running. I forgot to tell you there's a tin of tuna in one of the lower cupboards if you get hungry. And there's always peanut butter, though I'm not sure how much bread's left. Sorry about the lack of food. I'm going shopping any day now.''

"No worries." Daniel sank onto the bed. He tried to imagine Karina scheduling artwork and organizing staff and failed completely.

"If you see Piper in the yard, would you do me a favor and chase him back through the fence?" she rattled on.

"Sure." Karina's voice had a musical quality he hadn't noticed when talking to her in person. For a moment, he considered asking if she would say hello to Natalie, then dismissed the idea. He could hear the click of computer keys in the background. Karina had more important things to do than talk to a child.

"You never did tell me if you had a hammer and nails," he said.

"In the basement— Wait a minute! Don't you go locking Piper out. Someday he'll learn not to dig up my tomatoes."

"I wouldn't bet my last dollar on it," Daniel replied. "All the spaniels I've known act as though they have a 'roo loose in the top paddock."

*"Pardon?"*

"In other words, not too bright."

"And I thought you were a dog lover. How's Natalie?"

"Improving." He heard a faint beep on the line.

"Can you hold a sec?" Karina said. "I've got another call." A moment later, she was back. "Sorry, gotta run. The boss has a bee in his bonnet about something. See you later." She hung up.

Daniel stared at the receiver, then slowly replaced it. For two whole minutes he'd forgotten to be disappointed the call wasn't from his brother.

The bathroom, when he returned, was empty, and a trail of watery footprints led to Natalie's room. He paused outside her door. She was sitting on the floor, wrapped in a towel, talking to herself. Or, rather, talking to Mrs. Beeton.

Daniel frowned. With difficulty, he restrained himself from interrupting the one-sided conversation. When was she going to get over her friendship with the invisible Mrs. Beeton? It had begun shortly after Francine's death and it worried him. It also made him feel somehow inadequate, though he knew he did the best he could. The simple fact was, the girl needed a mother.

Maybe he should have tried harder with that single mom he'd met at Natalie's kindergarten. But he knew he needed someone for himself, as well.

Someday he'd meet the right woman. But next time around he wouldn't rush into marriage until he was sure his love would last. He wanted it all—wife, lover, friend—for himself, for Natalie and for his children yet to be born. *Their* children, whoever she might be.

Natalie glanced around, saw him and smiled. "Can I have a scratch-back, Daddy?"

"Sure thing." Daniel smiled at the word inversion, something she'd done ever since she'd learned to talk. He helped her back into her pajamas and tucked her into bed, arranging the favorite blanket just so. "Do you want me to sing you a song?"

Silence. "No, thank you, Daddy," she said in a small polite voice.

He couldn't blame her. He was tone deaf and he never remembered the words.

"When our trunks arrive we'll dig out that tape of Mommy singing your favorite songs, okay?" They'd made the recording once when Francine had gone away on a business trip, and he was grateful for Natalie's sake that she would always have her mother's voice on tape.

He'd even made several copies in case the original wore out.

She brightened a little. "Okay."

He gently scratched her back and told her a story about when he was six and Brian was eight and they'd caught tadpoles in the old gravel pit up the hill from their house.

Soon Natalie's small back rose and fell in the regular rhythm of sleep. Daniel pulled her pajama top down, tucked the covers around her neck and went downstairs.

He wandered restlessly into the living room. What now? He couldn't sit by the phone all day. The house and its inanimate inhabitants made him claustrophobic, so he went through the kitchen and out the back door.

A furry black snout poked through the crack in the fence. Now there was a problem just begging to be fixed. Karina had told him not to board up the fence, but she obviously wasn't aware of the alternatives.

Whistling, Daniel strode back into the house. In the corner of the meals area, he found the door to the basement.

KARINA STEPPED OUT of her office, and an elastic band zinged past her nose. She glanced in the direction it came from and saw a shiny bald head duck out of sight behind an office divider.

"*Kevin,*" she admonished in her best authoritarian voice. The "boys," as she called her team of artists, got a little silly sometimes, but she cast a blind eye on most of their antics because they produced good work. And they were fun.

Tiptoeing through the maze of open-plan cubicles, she leaned over Kevin's divider and cocked the elastic above his hairless head, trying very hard not to laugh. He looked up, his blue eyes twinkling innocently above a full, black beard threaded with grey.

"I was aiming at Wally, Your Honor." Kevin held his hand over his heart. "I fired in self-defense."

"Sure, and I'm Annie Oakley." She let the elastic drop to his desk, then nodded at his rendering of a storefront with a penny-farthing bicycle done in neon lighting. "This is excellent."

Kevin smiled modestly and waved a stubby hand. "I used your suggestion about putting a kid on the bike. It made all the difference." He leaned back in his chair. "You're wasted in management, Karina. You're a better artist than the rest of us put together."

Karina leaned one arm on the top of the divider and rested her chin on her hand. "I do miss the hands-on aspect of designing...."

She straightened. No point in pining over the past. "But I can do more good for the department as art director. We'd never have got the new computers and graphics packages if I hadn't convinced Ross it would boost productivity." She nodded at Kevin's sign design. "Have you shown this to sales yet?"

"I was going to take it across a little later when I meet Jackson for lunch."

Karina raised her eyebrows a fraction.

"Or...I could go right now."

"Good idea." Karina rewarded him with a brilliant smile. "Then come and see me in my office. I've got a new project I want you to start on right away."

"Okey-doke." Smiling, Kevin snapped her a salute.

Karina turned to walk away, then stopped. "By the way, Betty's cousin, Daniel, and his daughter arrived on my doorstep on the weekend, expecting to rent rooms in my house."

Kevin's smile was replaced by a puzzled frown. "I thought you weren't going to rent anymore."

"I wasn't. But it seems no one let Daniel know."

Kevin's mobile face twisted. "Uh-oh. I screwed up again, didn't I?"

"Royally. The little girl's sick, and they've got to stay at my place till they find another rental." Seeing Kevin's contrite expression, she softened. "It turned out okay in the end. But do you happen to have Daniel's money order lurking around? I imagine he'll want it back."

"Sure thing." Kevin clapped his hands down his torso as though frisking himself for the money order. Not finding it, he began pulling out drawers and peering through his overflowing in-tray. "It must be around somewhere."

"Try your wallet," Karina suggested. "How are Betty and the baby doing?"

Kevin smiled broadly. "Just fine. We'll drop in next time we're out your way. I know Betty will want to catch up with Daniel and his little girl."

"Come over next week sometime. Natalie should be better by then." She turned and started to walk away. "I'll be in Ross's office if anyone wants me."

"Okay, boss."

Karina stepped briskly along the plush carpeted hall to Ross Preston's office, straightening her shoulders a little more with every step. Ross the Boss was the only sour note about her job. Sometimes she wished she possessed a tongue sharp enough to cut him down to size.

No small job, she thought as she caught sight of him through his glass-fronted office. His burly shoulders bulged above a tilted-back chair, and his surprisingly dainty feet were crossed at the ankle and planted on the windowsill. He was talking on the phone, but at her knock he swiveled around, grinned under his bristly orange mustache and motioned almost coyly for her to enter.

"Good morning," she said pleasantly, determined not to let his penchant for innuendo spoil her good mood.

Ross hung up the phone. "Karina! Always a pleasure." He leaned back in his chair with his arms crossed behind his head, exposing transparent sweaty patches beneath the armpits of his white shirt.

Karina gritted her teeth and lowered herself into a chair. Only Ross could make the word *pleasure* sound like a perversion. "What's up?"

"This." Lowering his arms, he picked up a sheet of paper and snapped at it with a pudgy forefinger.

Karina peered across the desk. The paper was a handwritten memo from herself to Ross, requesting a spot in the corporate golf tournament. "Oh, yes. I'd like to enter this year."

Ross slumped forward, elbows on his desk, a hangdog expression on his freckled face. "Karina, Karina, Karina. You know I'd give anything for you to come to Parksville for the weekend. We could have such a great time."

Her smile stretched tautly across her face. When she got her promotion she'd never have to smile at Ross Preston again. "Yes, I'd love to get to know your wife better."

"Tina never attends these things," he said with a dismissive wave. "The sad fact is, neither can you."

Karina's smile froze. "I beg your pardon?"

Ross held his hands palms up in a gesture of helplessness. "The tournament is by invitation only."

"I thought it was open to all executives employed by the Franklin Group of Companies."

"Other corporations take part, as well. But, yes, in a manner of speaking, you're right."

"In a manner of speaking? I'm art director. I should get an invitation. Right?"

Ross squirmed in his chair, reminding Karina of a small boy hiding his dirty fingernails at the dinner table. "What's going on here?" she said. "Don't tell me only male execs get invitations."

Ross laughed a little too heartily. "That would be discriminatory."

"Exactly." She stared him down. "Since SignCity doesn't discriminate against women, why didn't I receive an invitation?"

Ross pushed back his chair and began to pace the area behind his oak desk. "The first corporate cup was held over thirty years ago. In all that time, no woman has ever been invited to attend the tournament."

Karina laughed, though she was anything but amused. "Then it's definitely time one was."

Ross stopped pacing and leaned over his desk toward her. "Franklin is big on tradition."

"SignCity moves with the times," Karina retorted, quoting from the company brochure.

Ross shook his head solemnly. "If it were just our company, I'd go to bat for you. But dozens of other firms are involved. The invitations were sent out weeks ago. Everything is all arranged."

"I can't believe this." She laughed again. "Do you know what year this is?"

"Hey, I'm a nineties kind of guy," Ross replied, assuming an earnest expression. "But the old boys on the board, well..."

Karina was stunned. "You mean no woman has *ever* gone to the tournament?"

"Alice Whitehead from the Vancouver office finagled an invitation from someone in a subsidiary firm a few years ago."

"And?"

Ross shrugged. "She went, but I don't think she had a good time. Honestly, Karina, the tournament's just a guy thing. You know, locker-room humor, sweaty socks. It wouldn't be any fun for you."

Karina rose to her feet. "This isn't about fun, Ross. It's about power and keeping women from having their fair share."

Ross smiled at her. "Now, now, Karina. Don't take it personally. Look at you, you're art director. I wouldn't have given you the job if I didn't think you could handle it."

"You didn't *give* me the job," she replied. "I *earned* it."

"And a damned fine job you're doing, too. You make me look real good upstairs. I appreciate that."

Karina muttered a hasty goodbye and left his office before she gagged. *No wonder there are so few female executives at SignCity,* she thought angrily as she walked back to her own department. *They couldn't stomach their male counterparts.*

She had nothing against men. Some of her best friends were men. It didn't mean she wanted to *be* one. Or act like one. Or think like one. The thought of becoming like Ross was enough to make her violently ill.

Maybe she should do as Joanne suggested and start her own business. But the thought of working in isolation scared her. She liked being able to walk out of her office and toss an idea around with half a dozen people. She thrived in the creative, chaotic atmosphere of the art department.

At this stage in the game, giving it all away would be tantamount to giving up. She wasn't ready to give up. If Ross thought he could brush her off this easily, he and the board had a big surprise coming.

DANIEL GOT TO HIS FEET and brushed the dirt from his knees. Gathering up Karina's tools, he stepped back from the fence to admire his handiwork. He couldn't wait to see the look on her face when she saw what he'd done.

He climbed the steps to the deck and pushed open the back door to find a young woman sloshing water around the kitchen floor with a mop.

"Who are you?" she demanded, brandishing the mop. Her anxious gaze flicked from his face to the hammer in his hand.

"Daniel Bowen." He placed the hammer on the stove top. She was more a girl than a woman, with mouse brown hair and wide brown eyes. "You must be Jenny."

"Daniel Boone?" she said skeptically.

*"Bowen,"* he repeated. "I'm Karina's new tenant. She mentioned you were coming this morning."

"Oh." The girl looked less frightened but still suspicious. "Karina said she wasn't renting anymore."

"She made a temporary exception in our case because my daughter's sick."

"That sounds like Karina." Seemingly reassured, Jenny lowered her mop back into the bucket. "And *you* sound Australian."

Daniel went to the sink and started to wash the dirt off his hands. "I lived there for years but I was born and grew up here."

"What were you doing with the hammer?" Jenny asked, wringing out the mop.

"Fixing the hole in the fence."

She shook her head. "Karina's going to kill you."

"We'll see." Daniel picked up a towel and dried his hands. "Pretty hard yakka cleaning up around here."

Jenny leaned on her mop. "Yakka?"

"That's Australian for *work.*"

She grinned and resumed mopping. "I'm 'yakkaing' my way through university. I think Karina makes a bigger mess just so I can earn a few extra bucks. She's so great."

The corners of Daniel's mouth curved slightly. "She very generously left a heap of laundry in the dining room for you to iron."

"Great," Jenny said, mopping energetically. She glanced over her shoulder at him. "Do you have anything you want done?"

"I look after myself, thanks." He paused. "Do you know of a supermarket nearby that delivers?"

"There's a Safeway on Oak Bay Avenue. I think they deliver."

"Good. Do you know what Karina likes to eat?"

"Gee, I don't know.... Wait a minute. Pasta. She loves pasta. Her mother was Italian."

"So I've heard. I gather she used to live here, too."

Jenny nodded. "A long time ago. She's dead now."

Like the turn of a kaleidoscope, the pieces that made up the puzzle of Karina Peterson rearranged themselves to form a different pattern. Why hadn't she mentioned yesterday that her mother was dead? She'd gone so quiet. Was it possible her mother's death still affected her? He had a sudden vision of Natalie mourning her mother for the rest of her life, and a chill passed over him.

"I'll let you get on with your cleaning," he said, and

took the telephone and phone book into the living room. He made a list, dictated it to the clerk at the supermarket and was assured the groceries would be delivered within a few hours.

He put down the phone, satisfied. A nice meal was the least he could do to thank Karina for taking them in. From the looks of her cupboards and her slender figure, she could do with a good feed.

DANIEL HEARD THE front door open and Karina call "Hellooo" in a singsong voice just as he picked up the upstairs extension. He punched in his brother's number anyway. He'd probably just get the answering machine again.

The phone rang. Daniel sat on his bed and immediately stood again. *Brrring...brrring....* Anchored by the cord, he tapped his foot, shifted position and tapped the other foot. By the tenth ring he was ready to give up. Then he heard his brother say, "Hello?"

Daniel swallowed hard. "Brian."

"Hello? Who is this?" Brian's voice was brisk, tinged with impatience.

Daniel took a deep breath and gripped the receiver. Okay, so he was a little disappointed Brian hadn't recognized his voice. But after all, it was ten years since they'd spoken and his accent had changed.

"Brian, it's me, Daniel." Silence. "Your brother. I left a message the other day."

Another silence. "I got the message," Brian said finally. "But frankly, I couldn't think of anything I wanted to say to you."

Head bowed, Daniel pinched the bridge of his nose. He'd expected Brian to be cool at first but he never thought he'd hear such frigid dislike from his own brother.

"I don't know what you mean." Daniel spoke lightly, deciding to ignore Brian's tone. "We've got years of news to catch up on."

"Do you think you can waltz in here after what you did to me and carry on like nothing happened?" Brian said. "Think again, *Danny boy*."

Daniel sucked in his breath. He hated that nickname.

"I know what I did was wrong," he replied as evenly as he could. "Some might even say unforgivable. But we're brothers, and once upon a time we were friends. Can't we get together and talk things out?"

"Sounds fascinating," Brian drawled. "But I'm a busy man. I really don't know when I could get around to it."

"Pick a time," Daniel said through his teeth. "I'll be there."

"My, my, aren't we conciliatory? A bit late now, don't you think, Danny boy?"

"At least I'm making the effort!"

"You're wasting your time. I'm not interested in patching things up. As for our being friends when we were younger, whatever made you think that? So long, little brother."

"Brian, wait—!"

It was too late. Brian had hung up.

Daniel dropped the receiver with a clunk onto its cradle. He paced the room, anger and frustration building. He'd admitted he was wrong. He'd said he was sorry. What more could he do?

The sound of light footsteps on the landing made him glance up. Through the open door he saw Natalie fly past on her way downstairs in her bare feet.

"Natalie! Put your slippers on!"

No response but the receding thud of her steps on the staircase. Muttering under his breath, Daniel went to her room, found the slippers and hurried down the stairs. Dammit, he and Brian *had* been friends once upon a time.

Thinking of his brother, he almost tripped over Natalie. She was sitting on the floor in the hallway, poring over a clear plastic sheet filled with cartoon drawings and the name *Natalie* written in several different type faces.

"How many times have I told you not to go around in your bare feet?" He crouched beside her and jammed the sheepskin slippers over her toes. "Don't you know you've got bronchitis? And where did you get that? Put it back."

Natalie's bottom lip wobbled but she stuck out her jaw. "It was on the hall table," she declared, clutching the transparency to her chest. "It has to be for me. My name is all over it."

"That may be, but you wait till it's given to you."

"Aw, Daddy," the little girl wailed.

"*Natalie.*" Daniel waited impatiently until she did as she was told, then he stalked down the hall to the kitchen.

Karina stood at the kitchen counter, her hips moving in time to the music from the radio as she spread peanut butter over a slice of whole wheat bread. She glanced up as Daniel strode into the room with Natalie trailing behind.

"Hi, guys," she said with a big smile. Tossing the peanut butter knife into the sink, she took a clean one from the drawer and opened a jar of mayonnaise. Daniel watched, appalled, as she spread a large dollop of creamy white goo on top of the peanut butter. She folded it over and lifted it to her mouth.

Just before she sank her teeth into the bread, she said, "Just grabbing a quick bite before I go out. I've had the worst day imaginable. How was yours?"

# CHAPTER FOUR

DANIEL GAPED AT HER. Pans of food simmered on the stove. The table was laid for three. The spicy aroma of tomatoes and garlic filled the kitchen. And Karina was snacking on peanut butter and mayonnaise.

His day just couldn't get any worse.

"Daddy made dinner 'specially for you," Natalie informed Karina as she shuffled across the floor in her slippers.

"Shhh, Nattie." Daniel drew a deep breath and mentally counted to ten. "It doesn't matter. Anyway, I made it for all of us."

Karina stopped chewing and looked around, clearly noticing for the first time the full extent of his labors. "Gosh, I'm sorry. I already made plans." She reached for the phone. "I'll call and cancel."

"Don't be silly," he said roughly, and moved the phone out of her reach. He walked over to the stove and turned off the heat under the boiling pasta.

She came to the sink and peered around his shoulder as he emptied the contents of the pot into a colander. "Fettucini," she murmured regretfully. "My favorite."

Daniel carried on with his task, forcing himself not to look at her. She couldn't have known he'd go to any trouble over dinner. It wasn't fair to take out his anger at Brian on her.

Karina took another bite of the revolting concoction

in her hand. The aroma of peanut butter reached his nostrils, splitting wide the thin skin of his control.

He turned on her. "Peanut butter and *mayonnaise?*"

She smiled up at him. "I like it."

"Peanut butter is eaten with bananas." His voice rose over the grating sound of Bjork's vocal gymnastics. "Or jam if you're a child." He knew he was getting worked up over nothing, but at this moment, he really didn't give a damn.

"Oh, that's so boring." With a laugh and a careless flip of her hand, she walked away.

Daniel slammed the pot back onto the stove. So he was boring, was he? Just because he ate decent, regular meals? Or was it because he didn't like her stupid palm trees?

Into the thickening silence, Natalie piped up proudly, "Daddy fixed the fence for you, too."

Karina stopped short and whirled to face him, bangles jangling, wisps of dark hair flying. "You did *what?*"

Daniel held her gaze. "I 'adjusted' the fence."

She gave a snort of laughter. "I asked you not to!"

"Before you get your knickers in a knot, I'd advise you to take a look at what I did."

He might as well have been speaking to the fence itself. Daniel could almost see the angry rebuttal forming on her lips. To his surprise, instead of invective came another burst of laughter.

"Why do you do that?" he said.

"What?"

"Laugh when you're feeling angry?"

She obliged him with a scowl. "Don't try to change the subject."

"It's important." He crossed to the window and snapped off the radio. His blood pressure dropped immediately. "If this is one of your little foibles, I want to know about it."

"Little foibles?" Karina repeated, eyes flashing. "You make me sound like a neurotic housewife. You're angry, too, about dinner and trying not to show it."

"Yeah, I'll admit I'm a little ticked, but I'll get over it."

Her high heels clicking over the linoleum, she strode to the table and snatched up her purse. "Thank you for making dinner," she said, her voice tightly controlled. "And it really was nice of you to try and help by fixing the fence," she added, her voice softening slightly. "But please put the broken boards back the way you found them."

Daniel folded his arms across his chest, leaned against the counter and sent her a long, hard glance. He could explain exactly what he'd done to the fence, but why should he when she'd condemned his handiwork without even seeing it?

"I'm not touching it until you've had a look. Then, if you're not happy, I'll bash a hole big enough for a bull mastiff to walk through on its hind legs."

She clamped her lips together in a fixed smile, her blouse lifting as she drew a deep breath. "Okay. I'll look at it later."

She would get over it once she'd seen the fence, Daniel assured himself as he heard the front door close. But staying here, even temporarily, was clearly a mistake. Karina was used to a freewheeling lifestyle. Natalie needed stability and regular meals.

First thing in the morning, he'd check with the rental agency to see what progress they'd made. Then he'd look in the paper again. There had to be *some*place they could call home.

Wearily he straightened and moved away from the counter. A faint, sniffling sound drew his attention to Natalie. She was huddled in the corner, very still. Her small hands were clutching the belt of her robe and she looked ready to dissolve into tears.

"Nattie, sweetheart." Closing the distance between them, he knelt down and hugged her tightly. "What's wrong?"

Natalie's small frame trembled inside the circle of his arms. She began to hiccup. "K-Karina didn't even notice I was b-better. She didn't even say h-hi to me."

"Yes, she did, sweetheart, when we first came into the room." He pressed a kiss on top of her head, overwhelmed by his child's sudden, passionate need.

"She was l-looking at *you*," Natalie wailed accusingly.

"Now, Nattie," Daniel said firmly. "Karina had a bad day. You're not feeling a hundred percent, either. Come on, let's eat. I seem to recall fettucini is your favorite, too."

To his relief, she scrubbed away her tears and put her hand in his. He rose to his feet and led her to the table. If only all their problems were so easily fixed.

"I COULD KILL THAT MAN." Karina stabbed at the lemon twist on the rim of her glass of Cinzano until it fell to the table with a watery plop.

"Ross the Boss?" Joanne asked sympathetically. She took a sip of white wine and reached for the bowl of rice crackers the waiter had just deposited on their table.

"No, Daniel."

"Whoa! Back the executioner's truck up. Didn't you call me because you were upset about what happened at work?"

"I'll get to that in a minute. It wasn't even what he did—though that was bad enough—so much as the way he looked at me."

Joanne leaned across the table, holding her string of amber beads to her chest so they wouldn't drag in her drink. "Was it...sexual?"

"No." Karina jabbed at the fallen lemon twist with her straw. What really rankled was his comment about her laughing when she was angry. If he noticed things like that after only a few days, what else would he perceive about her? "It was more like...insolent."

"Insolent?" Joanne leaned back in her chair, biting her lip. "That sounds interesting. I wouldn't have thought he was capable of insolence."

"He's capable, all right." Karina signaled to the waiter for another drink. "Maybe he had a right to be annoyed, but how was I supposed to know he'd cooked a meal? Am I expected to be home every night from now on? I'm not used to this. I've always picked tenants who fit into *my* life."

"Knowing the state of your pantry, he probably thought he was performing an act of mercy. I think it's sweet of him."

"Of course it's sweet, that's the whole problem. If he's this nice, how can I ever kick him out?"

"You should hear yourself, Karina," Joanne said, a tiny, smug smile on her face. "One minute he's insolent, the next minute he's too nice. Admit it, you're crazy about him."

Karina crossed her arms over her chest. "That's ridiculous."

"*He* obviously likes *you*," Joanne persisted. "Why else would he go to all the trouble of making dinner?"

"To feed himself and his daughter," she said, refusing to believe otherwise. "If he really liked me, he wouldn't have tampered with the fence."

Joanne waved that away. "Men just like to fix things. It gives them a reason for being."

Karina sighed and leaned forward to rest her arms on the table. "Okay, so I'm overreacting. But it's time he and I worked out some ground rules. This sort of stuff is usually sorted out before tenants move in. Daniel kind of sneaked up on me."

"Not such a bad thing in my humble opinion. How's the kid?"

Karina's expression softened. "Getting better. I heard her in her room this morning, talking to her dolls. She's got one named Mrs. Beeton she chats to just like a real person."

Joanne smiled. "They're so cute at that age." Then the waiter arrived with another Cinzano and white wine, and she sighed as she took her glass. "I'm going to regret this tomorrow, but what the hell."

Karina removed her straw from her glass, sucked on it, then jabbed it in Joanne's direction. "Your problem is, you don't get out often enough."

"That's one of my problems," Joanne corrected her. "My main problem is a husband who's gone half the year doing fieldwork. He's home now, but only for a week. If it was another woman, I could fight it. But how do you compete with fish guts?"

Karina made a face. "Is Peter still doing fish guts?"

"Gut *contents,* I should have said. Apparently it's of vital importance to the salmon fishery. Something about food species and environmental damage."

"Why don't you go with him sometime? I'd help your mom with the kids. You could have a romantic weekend on the banks of the Nechako River...."

"Up to my bazookas in freezing-cold water counting stream insects? I don't think so."

"Where's your sense of adventure? Think of moonlight on rippling water...."

"Think of the black flies."

"Wind, whispering in the pines..."

"Grizzlies raiding your food supply."

"Sunrise over the mountain peaks..."

"Working from dawn till dusk, which in the northern summer is eleven o'clock at night. No, thanks. However, if I can talk Peter into a weekend at Whistler, I might take you up on the offer."

"Anytime. I mean it."

"Thanks. Now, tell me more about Daniel."

Karina moved her glass in watery circles around the table. "I think he's chomping at the bit to get started on his carpentry business. Because Natalie's sick, he can't even go to the bank, though he seems to have a wad of Canadian cash on him."

"Carpentry, eh? Does he do renovations? I'm dying to get our bathroom fixed up."

Karina shook her head doubtfully. "I don't think it's that kind of carpentry. I'll ask him. If I ever speak to him again, that is."

"Give him a chance. Now, what has Ross the Boss been up to?"

"Wait till you hear," Karina said, and explained about the golf tournament.

"Ross is such a creep," Joanne said when Karina had finished. "Any chance he'll relent?"

"No," Karina said. "He's too concerned with his own position to stick his neck out for me. Besides, the decision really is over his fat, round head. Since there's nothing in writing saying women are excluded, I have no way to fight the powers that be. Going as a guest of someone from a sister company seems to be my best prospect so far.''

She noticed Joanne's gaze drift to the other side of the lounge. "What are you tracking now, Jo?"

"That waiter over there with the cute buns."

"Joanne! You're a married woman."

"I was thinking of you, not me."

Karina sighed. "Give it up already."

"Come to think of it," Joanne said with a sly grin, "Daniel has a pretty nice derriere, too."

"Forget it," Karina replied, laughing. "He's on my hit list."

SHORTLY AFTER MIDNIGHT, Karina parked Sammy on the side of the garage farthest from the workbench and went into the backyard.

She flicked on the tiny flashlight attached to her key chain and tiptoed through the damp grass to the edge of the tomato patch. Even without the faint beam of the flashlight she could see that wooden boards covered the spot where the gap used to be.

Cursing under her breath, she stepped gingerly into the soft dirt between the tomato plants to take a closer look. It shouldn't be too hard to knock out the patched section.

Aiming the tiny light at the fence, she stooped to inspect Daniel's handiwork. What she saw made her catch her breath in surprise. Slowly she smiled. Her smile grew until it broke into a peal of laughter that rang out through the balmy summer night.

On the other side of the fence, Piper woofed excitedly.

KARINA BOOTED UP her computer the next morning with a flourish of her wrists that reminded her so much of a

flamenco dancer she stamped her heels in a rat-a-tat-tat.
While the computer whizzed through its warmup, she
punched in Joanne's telephone number.

Instead of beginning work as she usually did while on
the phone, Karina swiveled back and forth in her chair,
gazing absently out the window. She smiled to herself
and hummed the light, jazzy tune that had been playing
on the radio as she'd drifted off to sleep the night before.

"Hello? Karina?" A voice broke through her reverie.
"I can hear you humming. Speak, woman."

"Hi, Jo." Karina's smile became a grin. "You
wouldn't believe what he did!"

"Ross the Boss?"

"No, Daniel."

"It must be good from the sound of rapture in your
voice."

"He put a *door* in the fence where Piper's hole used
to be."

"A door?"

"It's got little hinges and a latch."

"Cute."

"I can open it and shut it anytime I want. I mean,
face it, spaniels aren't the brightest of dogs."

"Last week you swore he was a prodigy."

"I know, but no dog can resist a hole in a fence. Or
a garden full of fresh dirt."

"I take it Daniel's out of the doghouse, so to speak?"

"Oh, Jo, I feel terrible about the way I spoke to him.
I seriously underestimated his respect for my feelings."

"Not to mention his powers of lateral thinking."

"I wish I could make it up to him somehow."

"Make him a special dinner. On second thought, not
such a good idea. I know, take him *out* to dinner."

Karina's euphoria faded abruptly. Daniel was turning out to be not quite so ordinary as she'd thought. A date could be dangerous. "Gosh, Joanne, I don't know...."

"You could use the occasion to set those ground rules," Joanne suggested helpfully.

"Hmm. You have a point. That sort of thing should be done in a neutral atmosphere. But what about Natalie?" she said, feeling compelled to create obstacles.

"I'll baby-sit."

"Didn't you say Peter's going on another field camp soon? I'm sure you'd rather spend your last few evenings together."

"This is more important."

Karina sat up straight, pulling the cord taut. "We've been through this, Jo. Don't start matchmaking again."

"Karina, how could you think such a thing?"

In the background, a child began to wail. "No, you're not having chocolate milk on your porridge. Sorry, Karina, not you. Although, come to think of it..." Joanne's tone became faintly accusing. "Julie only started asking for chocolate milk on her cereal after you were over for breakfast two Saturdays ago."

"Gee, Joanne, gotta run...."

"Karina!"

"Yes?"

"Better give him plenty of warning."

"Naturally. Daniel's not the spontaneous type."

BUT WHEN IT CAME right down to it, Karina couldn't find quite the right moment to mention dinner to Daniel. The further they got from their standoff in the kitchen and her discovery of Daniel's handiwork, the harder it became to call the invitation either an apology or a thank-you—especially as she'd already done both.

The closer Saturday came, the more it started to seem as if she'd be asking for a date. She wasn't, of course, but he might think she was. At least until she explained. And explanations were always so embarrassing.

If only it would just sort of happen on the spur of the moment. She preferred spontaneous events, anyway. If you planned too far ahead, expectations tended to reach mythic proportions.

By the time Saturday morning rolled around she was convinced it was a disastrous idea. But when she called Joanne to cancel, Joanne wasn't home. How could anyone exist without an answering machine? Karina wondered as she hung up the phone after another fruitless attempt to contact her friend.

Now it was Saturday evening. Dinner was over and Natalie was upstairs getting ready for bed. Karina wandered into the living room, where Daniel was drinking a cup of coffee and reading a book. It was a thick, hardcover book, one she felt certain had very small print. The kind of book that gave her a headache.

Karina sank into a chair opposite and watched him from under her lashes while she flipped idly through an arts magazine. He certainly had interesting bone structure with that high-bridged nose and those prominent cheekbones. She liked the way his eyebrows peaked at the corners of his eyes, then drifted away in little wings to his temples. And his mouth curved up at the corners even when he wasn't smiling. And he didn't smile very often.

Why was she finding it so difficult to ask him out for the evening? She wasn't a shy person. And it wasn't as though she had any special feelings for him.

Daniel tucked a leather bookmark in the shape of a

gum leaf between the pages and got up. "Think I'll check on Natalie."

Karina glanced at her watch. Almost seven. Joanne was due any minute. Well, whatever happened after that would certainly be spontaneous.

Even though she was waiting for it, Karina jumped when the doorbell rang. "I'll get it," she called, and hurried past Daniel into the hall. No telling what Joanne might blurt out if he opened the door.

Daniel paused, his hand on the banister. One eyebrow disappeared into a lock of chestnut hair that had fallen over his forehead. "Big date?"

Breathless, she managed a nonchalant shrug. "Just Joanne."

Karina waited until he'd climbed the stairs and disappeared into Natalie's room before she opened the door. "Where have you been?" she exclaimed to Joanne. "I've been calling all day."

Joanne entered with her usual bustle of bags and layers of extraneous clothing. "We took the kids to Sealand and then for a pizza. All ready for your big night out with Daniel?"

"Shhh. I haven't asked him."

"What do you mean you haven't asked him!"

"I just couldn't. Anyway, it's too late now. Dinner is best for talking, and we've already had dinner."

Joanne shoved both hands into her hair and pulled it into a frizz. "Karina Peterson! Peter leaves the day after tomorrow, and I left him all alone tonight just so I could baby-sit. You get right up there and speak to Daniel."

"Come on, Joanne. You know you only offered to baby-sit because you're trying to matchmake. It won't work. Anyway, I can't think of anything to say at this late hour that sounds plausible."

"*You* at a loss for words? I don't believe it. Just tell him you're going out and you want some company."

"What if he gets the wrong impression? He might think I like him."

"What a catastrophe. Go."

"It's all very well for you," Karina argued in hushed tones. "He isn't your tenant. The fence incident is all but forgotten. Best to let sleeping dogs lie."

"Sleeping dogs. Very funny. What's the big deal? You've never had a problem asking anyone to go out before. It's not as if you're asking him to *marry* you."

"Will you keep your voice down? Go home. Peter needs you."

"Daniel needs *you*. Think about it. He's all alone in a new country with only a child for company. Do you think he wants to spend another night hanging around the house? Would *you*?"

Karina opened her mouth in denial, then shut it again. "Maybe that's what's making him so tense."

Joanne put her big straw bag down on the floor beside the hall table and started to peel off her jacket. "He's tense?"

"Yes. I assumed he was fretting over his brother, but maybe he just needs to get out. He's hardly put a foot outside the yard since he got here."

"See? That's it for sure."

Karina pushed back her hair with both hands and nodded. "Okay, I'll do it."

She ran up the stairs. Just as she cleared the landing, Daniel stepped out of Natalie's room. Karina pulled up short, her nose inches from his chest.

"Daniel! Hi. You're coming out with me tonight."

He gazed down at her with a quizzical smile. "Beg your pardon?"

Karina took a small step back and tried to ignore the uncharacteristic fluttering in her stomach. "I mean, would you like to go out? Get out of the house for a while?"

"I can't leave Natalie."

"Joanne will baby-sit."

Karina squirmed. Daniel was staring at her as though wondering how to say no as kindly as possible. "I meant to take you out to dinner as a way of saying sorry for our little blowup the other night," she continued. "And to thank you for fixing the fence the way you did. But I…well…I didn't quite get around to it. Say you'll come. We need to talk."

Daniel glanced at Natalie's door and back at Karina's animated face. She was right about needing to talk. And anything would be better than another night sitting around the house, brooding. Besides, Karina had seemed a little tense this week. If she wanted an escort, maybe he ought to be a sport about it.

"Okay. What did you have in mind?"

Karina's smile lit her eyes as she twirled away to her bedroom. "Let me surprise you."

DANIEL TILTED HIS JAW and ran the electric razor over his skin as he eyed himself in the bathroom mirror. Granted, Karina's excitement was infectious, but he was surprised at how much he was looking forward to going out with her.

His hand stilled. Was this a date? Nah, he thought, moving the shaver under his chin in short, quick sweeps. It was an apology or a thank-you. Neither was necessary but women were funny that way—they always wanted to even the score. Still, an evening out with Karina could be fun. Daniel began to whistle along with the transistor radio in the bathroom cabinet.

He'd finished washing up, changed his clothes and was chatting to Joanne in the living room when he heard Karina's footsteps on the stairs. Suddenly he found it impossible to focus on what Joanne was saying about primary schools.

He twisted in his chair for a glimpse of Karina. Then she came swinging through the arched doorway and his powers of concentration deserted him completely.

Her glossy, dark hair swirled around bare shoulders, and a short, flouncy skirt swished against her thighs. She came to a halt in the middle of the room, fiddling with the clasp on a silver charm bracelet and chattering excitedly.

"This is going to be great. You won't regret going out tonight, Daniel, I promise. Darn this clasp, I really must take it to the jeweler. I hope you're wearing comfortable shoes."

Daniel rose to his feet. Karina snapped the clasp shut and glanced up. He saw surprise flicker in her eyes and instinctively reached up to adjust the scrap of bright red fabric below his jaw. "It's a bow tie."

Karina laughed, a high, musical sound. "I can see that. I love it. It's so...debonair."

Daniel grinned. The woman had taste. Turning to Joanne, he said, "I'll call in about an hour to see if Natalie's okay."

"Don't worry about a thing," Joanne replied, making little shooing motions toward the door. "She'll be fine."

Daniel held open the front door and Karina floated past on a cloud of some delicious scent that reminded him of a tropical garden. "Comfortable shoes?" he said. "Are we going bush walking?"

# CHAPTER FIVE

"BALLROOM DANCING," Karina informed him as they picked their way through the ballroom of the Empress Hotel to an empty table beside the dance floor. She glanced at him as he pulled out her chair, watching closely for signs of bolting. Not everyone cared for ballroom dancing.

Across the vast, high-ceilinged room, the band was tuning up, a discordant medley of horns and strings interspersed with impromptu bars of Latin rhythms. Under the table, Karina's feet twitched eagerly in their blue satin pumps.

Daniel caught the attention of a passing waiter and ordered drinks, white wine for her and lager for himself. His gaze swung back to Karina. "Did you think I wouldn't like dancing?"

She smiled and shrugged, flicking her hair off her shoulders. "I didn't know. It seemed easier to keep you in the dark than hog-tie you and drag you here. Do you mind very much?"

"Not at all." He gave her one of his rare smiles, a tantalizing glimpse of white teeth against tanned skin.

Ground rules, she reminded herself. She was here to set ground rules. But before she could organize her thoughts, Daniel spoke again.

"You've seemed a little upset this week," he said. "I hope you're not still annoyed about the fence."

Karina laughed. "I love what you did with the fence. It's like something out of *Alice in Wonderland*." She fiddled with a coaster. "But if we're going to share living space for a while, we need to talk about arrangements and expectations."

"You don't want to be tied to meals or other domestic events," he said, leaning back in his chair. "I got the message the other night."

"It's just that my schedule is so erratic," she said quickly. "I often work late, or I go out for a meal with friends."

"You don't have to explain. I don't necessarily want to be tied to a routine, either. I cook because I enjoy it and because I want Natalie to eat properly. You'll find out when you have kids of your own someday."

Karina felt a familiar jab of annoyance. "Why does everyone assume that I'm going to have kids?"

His eyebrows rose. "Won't you? I got the impression you liked children."

"I do, but...I'm committed to my career."

"That doesn't preclude a family, surely?"

"Now you sound like Joanne." To her relief, the opening bars of a lively waltz began to filter through the ballroom, putting an end to the conversation. Karina glanced at the couples straying onto the dance floor and back to Daniel, her body already starting to move.

He rose from his seat. "Shall we?"

"Yes!" She led the way to a clear spot on the polished hardwood dance floor. Daniel caught her hand from behind, turning her to face him. He put his other arm around her waist and drew her closer.

Okay, so his face wasn't quite as ordinary as she'd thought when they'd first met. Interesting, intelligent and kind, yes. But not what you'd call handsome. Not the kind of face a woman saw in her dreams at night.

No sir, no way.

Around them people had begun to dance, but Daniel was still gazing at her, a slight frown on his face. With a stab of compunction, she realized maybe he didn't know how to dance.

"This is a waltz," she explained matter-of-factly. "You go forward one step and I go back—like so. To the side one step, and close." She moved as she spoke, pulling him along with her.

A tiny smile appeared at the corners of his mouth. She beamed back at him encouragingly. "I'm so glad you're not one of those men with a massive male ego who can't stand to be instructed by a woman. One, two, three, one, two, three... See? You're getting the hang of it already."

"I have a good teacher," he said, still smiling. They took a few more turns before he said, "Mind if I lead for a while?"

Karina nodded. She mustn't be patronizing. Men were men, after all.

Daniel raised their clasped hands a notch higher. His arm tightened around her waist. Suddenly his grip seemed both expert and possessive. He gave her the tiniest of winks.

Then he whirled her away across the dance floor.

Karina's astonished grin turned to a smile of delight as they whizzed past other couples, turning, turning to the lilting strains of "The Merry Widow."

He could dance! She laughed with pure pleasure. Boy, could he dance!

The waltz slid into a mamba. Then a cha-cha, followed by a tango. Karina had to work to keep up with Daniel as he led her in variations she'd never seen before. Through it all, the faint, enigmatic smile never left his face.

The band took a break and Karina and Daniel made their way back to the table. "Why didn't you tell me you could dance so well?" she demanded, laughing.

Daniel shrugged. "You didn't ask."

"And I thought I had you all figured out. Wait a minute," she said as he was about to sit down. "Your tie is crooked." She reached up and straightened it for him, conscious of the raspy warmth of his jaw where her knuckles brushed his skin. "That's better."

"Thanks." His eyes met hers.

She quickly took her seat. Daniel seemed different tonight, more dominating, more...physical. And his smile was positively lethal when he got around to it. If she *were* looking for a man...

"Where did you learn those moves?" she asked, striving for an offhand tone.

Daniel leaned back in his chair and crossed one ankle over his knee. "Francine and I were in the state championships three years running. Strictly amateur, of course."

"There's nothing amateur about those fancy dips and spins. I feel like a complete idiot." She held back her damp hair and fanned her neck with the makeshift ponytail.

"You're an excellent dancer. Plenty of natural rhythm." His gaze strayed to her bare shoulders. "You look warm."

Self-conscious, she let her hair fall. "Was Francine your wife?" She hoped he wouldn't think she was prying again, but she was curious about the woman.

He gave a curt nod, then glanced around the room.

"Never a waiter when you need one. I'll go get some water."

Karina watched him weave through the tables toward the bar. Darn, she'd done it again. Where did natural curiosity stop and prying begin?

Francine was probably blond like Natalie, with legs like Ginger Rogers. Karina imagined Francine and Daniel coming home after a night of dancing, laughing and talking as they climbed the stairs to their bedroom....

An icy drop of water splashed across Karina's bare arm as Daniel deposited a jug of ice water on the table in front of her. "The waiter's bringing more wine and beer in a moment," he said, and filled a glass for her.

"Thanks." She reached for her water glass and her fingers brushed against his. The touch brought her daydream flooding back, and she snatched her hand away. What had gotten into her, fantasizing like that about Daniel? Somewhere between the staircase and the bedroom the woman's hair had become dark brown like her own.

He drank deeply of his water, draining the glass. "Did you ever find someone to teach you golf?" he asked, lifting the jug to refill his glass.

Karina pushed her hair behind her ears, a few strands catching in her dangly silver earrings. "I'm not sure I'll be going to the tournament. It turns out only *male* executives are invited. Can you believe it?"

Daniel removed his jacket and leaned back in his seat, regarding her thoughtfully. "It sounded to me like you don't even play golf. Why do you want to go so badly?"

"It's not golf I want to play, but politics."

"Ah."

She took a sip of water. "You can't beat 'em if you can't join 'em."

"The question is, why do you want to?"

Karina traced swirling patterns in the film of condensation on her glass. The answer was simple. Without the prospect of a family to raise, she had nothing to mark her progress through life except rungs on the career ladder. That was enough. It had to be.

"When I started at SignCity," she said, "I was at the bottom of the pecking order. Last one hired, first one fired. I couldn't afford to be vulnerable to every economic downturn that came along, so I became the resident expert on computer graphics. That was eight years ago. These days I'm the one that does the hiring and firing."

The waiter appeared with their drinks. Daniel waited until he'd gone, then reached for his beer. "And now you want to climb even higher."

She sipped at her wine. "It's the logical next step." What else was there for her to do?

He gave her an odd look. "Somehow I never thought logic would be your guiding light."

She smiled. "Maybe I put that badly. I need a challenge or I'll stagnate." And a reliable income because she would always be on her own.

"That I can understand. Once I've mastered something, I like to move on to something new."

"In a way, I envy you, working for yourself," she said. "No one to answer to, no one stabbing you in the back, no one taking your ideas and getting the credit."

He shrugged. "I just prefer working on my own."

She shuddered. "I'd go bananas."

"Hire someone. Form your own company. There's got to be a happy medium. If you don't like what you're doing, try something else."

Karina smiled and shook her head. "I do like what

I'm doing. It's the system I can't handle. So far I've gotten ahead on my own terms, but I'm up against the big boys now. Sometimes I wonder if it's all worth it.''

''You mean,'' he said, one eyebrow lifting, ''being committed to a company that's not as committed to you?''

She made a face. He'd summed it up in a nutshell, and for once she couldn't think of a snappy comeback. ''I hate it when you do that.''

''What?'' he asked. ''Make a valid point?''

''No,'' she said, laughing. ''Shut me up so effectively.''

He smiled. ''I'm not trying to shut you up. I just can't help but notice certain inconsistencies in your life.''

Karina laughed again, unperturbed. ''That's all part of my capricious nature. Being consistent is boring.''

''No one could accuse you of that.'' He raised his glass. ''To inconsistency.''

''To surprises,'' Karina added, thinking of his prowess on the dance floor. She clinked her glass against his.

The music started up again and she was on her feet in an instant. ''How about showing me that fancy little twist in the lambada again,'' she said, pulling him onto the dance floor.

''Liked that, did you?'' he said. ''I came up with it myself.''

DANIEL CAME QUIETLY out of Natalie's room and shut the door. Moonlight streamed through the window above the stairwell, flooding the second-floor landing with silvery light. He heard Karina say good-night to Joanne and start upstairs.

She appeared before him, her blue dress looking dark

grey in the moonlight. He nodded at the door he'd just closed and put a finger to his lips. "Nattie's fast asleep."

Karina bent to slip off one shoe, then the other, and stood with them dangling from her fingers. "Thanks for coming out tonight."

"It did me good," Daniel replied. "And I enjoyed dancing with you." The faint music issuing from Karina's bedroom made him aware of the midnight quiet of the rest of the house. They were whispering so as not to wake Natalie, and it seemed to lend a clandestine air to their conversation.

"I'm glad we got everything sorted out," Karina said, but she made no move to go to her room.

"We didn't decide anything about meals."

"We can work it out tomorrow."

"There you go, procrastinating again. How about I cook enough for three and you can eat if you're here, or not, as the case may be."

"That's generous of you. I'll cook sometimes, too."

"Okay. Just give me some advance warning."

The shadows around her mouth deepened in a smile. "Why? So you can run out for a hamburger first? Believe it or not, I can cook when I put my mind to it."

He grinned. "I believe you, though millions wouldn't. I meant so I wouldn't start dinner. I'm not as easy as I look, you know."

"You're easy to get along with." She bit her lip, looking as though she wished she hadn't said that. "Did you ever get in touch with your brother?"

He pulled off the bow tie hanging loosely around his open shirt collar. "I talked to him."

"Great. Are you getting together with him soon?"

Daniel glanced away. "He's pretty busy right now."

Karina gazed at him in silence for a moment, then

crossed the landing to sit on the top step. "Come over here and tell me all about it." When he didn't move, she patted the floor beside her. "Come on. I can't stand up any longer. My feet are killing me."

He wasn't looking for sympathy, but her matter-of-fact tone was a powerful draw. For ten years he'd never confided in anyone. Suddenly he felt an overwhelming need to unburden himself.

He went and sat beside her on the step, breathing in the scent of jasmine that clung to her warm skin. With her rosy coloring and smile like sunshine, he'd always thought of her as a creature of daylight. But now, with moonlight silvering the smooth curve of her bare shoulder and shadows darkening her hair to black, she looked like a goddess of the night.

She touched his arm and the silver charms on her bracelet tinkled faintly. "What caused the feud between you and your brother?"

He leaned against the banister, half facing her. "Before I married her, Francine was Brian's fiancée."

"Oh!" Karina's eyes widened. "What happened?"

"It's a long story...."

"I'm listening."

"Brian was living in Vancouver at the time," Daniel began slowly. "I knew he was seeing someone, but we were all surprised when he announced he was engaged."

"Why surprised?" Karina stretched her legs along the step below.

His gaze dropped to her thighs, and for a moment his mind went blank. "Sorry, what did you say?"

Karina tugged her skirt lower. "Why were you surprised your brother was engaged?"

Daniel returned his gaze to her face. "Brian was always very popular with women. I expected him to play the field for years."

She shrugged. "He must have been in love."

"That's the obvious conclusion...."

"But?"

"I don't know. Sometimes he acted so offhand with her. Anyway, the weekend he brought Francine home to meet my parents, I came, too. They were all sitting around the living room having a drink before dinner when I arrived." He paused, recalling that fateful moment he'd walked through the door.

"I took one look at Francine—" He twirled the bow tie between his fingers, groping for words. "Maybe it was the way *she* looked at *me*, but I knew immediately something big was going to happen. I didn't know whether it would be wonderful or terrible. Turned out it was a bit of both."

"So it was love at first sight?"

Daniel was silent, considering how to answer. How could he describe his feelings at the time, tainted as they were with all that came after?

"I was attracted to her immediately but I tried not to show it because she was Brian's fiancée."

"And she was attracted, too?"

"Not openly flirtatious, but she kept looking at me when no one else was watching. I tried to ignore it...."

"But...?"

"I'd barely turned twenty-two. Francine was almost two years older and light-years more sophisticated. It was just friendly banter at first. I never intended to get serious."

He passed a hand across his forehead, wishing he could wipe the memories from his mind. At what point could he have stopped the train of events that had thrown all their lives off track? Would he do things differently now if he could? But then Natalie would never have been born. And that was unthinkable.

"That night," he continued, "Francine knocked on my door on the pretext of lending me a book we'd talked about at dinner. She was in her nightgown. I was half undressed. Brian's room was right next door but she didn't seem to care."

"What happened?"

"Nothing, really. She sat on my bed and we talked. I can't even remember what about—the book, most likely. But the thoughts going through my head should have been X-rated. I lay awake all night. The next day I took off before breakfast. I couldn't face Brian after what I'd been thinking about his fiancée."

Karina pulled her knees up and propped her elbows on them, cupping her chin in the palms of her hands. "So, how did you two eventually get together?"

"Francine came to Victoria on her own one day and looked me up. I was flattered, I can't deny it. We had lunch and walked around Beacon Hill Park till dusk, holding hands like a couple of honeymooners." He paused. "She didn't take the ferry back to Vancouver that night."

Why was he telling Karina all this? And what would she think of him when he was done? He contemplated glossing over the rest, but now he'd started he couldn't stop. If she thought worse of him for what he'd done, well, he'd just have to bear it.

"After that we saw each other every chance we could. I wanted to tell Brian about us, but Francine kept saying she should be the one to do it. Like a fool, I listened to her."

"Did she ever tell him?"

"No. Finally I couldn't stand sneaking around anymore; it made what we had seem so cheap. So I went to Brian and told him I was in love with Francine."

Daniel stared into the shadows, his cheeks burning at the memory of that humiliating scene. "He just laughed in my face. I was furious he didn't take me seriously. After that, I thought, why bother?"

"He must have been shocked when you two suddenly got married."

Daniel nodded. "Three days before their wedding was due to take place, Francine and I eloped. We sent him a telegram from Melbourne." He paused and ran a shaky hand through his hair. "Brian's never forgiven me or willingly spoken to me since."

Karina was silent. He heard only the faint rustle of her dress as she leaned her back against the wall. "I can see why he'd be angry," she said at last, then reached out to squeeze his arm. "But you mustn't feel so bad. It couldn't have been easy for you."

The understanding in her voice made him feel slightly less grim. At least Karina didn't despise him. "It wasn't. I had to choose between my brother and the woman I honestly believed to be my partner for life."

"Choices can be hard to make," she agreed quietly, tucking her hand back in her lap. "And consequences even harder to accept. 'Partner for life' has such a solid, dependable ring to it, yet it's so rarely true these days."

He nodded. "If Francine had lived, I doubt we'd be together now."

"What happened to her, Daniel? How did she die?"

"Leukemia. It happened so fast we hardly had time to adjust before she was gone. Natalie took it really hard. She was only three and couldn't understand why Mommy wasn't ever coming back."

The image of his tiny daughter's bewildered, tear-stained face floated in the darkness before him. His throat closed up and he went silent, remembering.

Then he glanced at Karina. Her head had dropped forward, her long, dark hair spilling over her bare arms and hiding her face. His hand hovered over her shoulder, not quite touching. "Karina?" he said gently. "What is it?"

She lifted her head, rubbing at the corners of her eyes with the heel of her hand. "Nothing. It's just…poor Natalie."

"I know. She's suffered so much. I worry about where she'd live if anything happened to me."

"Relatives?"

He locked his hands around one knee and shook his head. "Her grandmother in Australia is getting too old to look after a child. My parents head south every winter in their mobile home. Betty and Kevin have enough children of their own. The only person Natalie could go to is Brian. But he has to want that, too. I *have* to make peace with my brother. For Natalie's sake, as well as my own."

"Unless you were to marry again."

"I want to, when the right woman comes along."

Their eyes met for a flicker of a second before Karina looked away. Marriage, Daniel reflected, was one helluva conversation stopper.

Her face still averted, Karina began to hum softly to the faint music coming from her open bedroom door.

"Don't you ever turn that off?" he asked.

"I program it to go off long after I'm asleep." She covered a yawn with her hand and rose to her feet. "It's late."

Daniel rose, too, but he didn't want to say good-night. "One last dance?"

Karina looked up at Daniel, intending to tell him she was too tired. But the slanting crest of one high cheekbone shone in the moonlight, and the shadows made a mystery of the hollow at the base of his throat. Compelled by reasons she didn't want to examine, she nodded.

Daniel put his arm around her waist, drawing her to him. She started to pull back, but he held her firmly, nestling his chin next to her temple. Turning her face into the hollow of his neck, she breathed in his scent, cotton and warm skin with just the faintest hint of a woodsy aftershave. It seemed hard to believe that only a week ago she hadn't even known he existed.

They slow-danced around the landing, moving in small circles. Karina was aware of him in a way she hadn't been at the ballroom—the heat of his body, his thighs brushing hers, the firm pressure of his hand on her back.

"Thanks for listening," he said, his breath ruffling the hair at her temple.

She swallowed and nodded, not trusting her voice.

His hand moved on her back, and she could feel each of his fingertips like a tiny caress. Her breasts tingled against his chest; their lower bodies pressed together, moving sensuously to the music.

He was aroused. And so was she.

This was not good.

Struggling against instinct, she pulled back until her body no longer touched his. "Daniel?"

"Hmm?" His eyes were closed.

"There's another house rule I haven't mentioned."

"What is it?"

"The landlady never gets romantically involved with her tenants."

He opened his eyes and looked at her. "Why not?"

"It just doesn't work."

He stopped dancing and just held her. "Are you saying you don't like me?"

"I'm not saying that at all."

"Then what's the problem?"

"Living in the same house would be too awkward when the romance is over."

"Natalie and I are only staying here temporarily. Besides, how do you know it would end?"

"It just won't work," she insisted.

Daniel gazed back at her in silence, and now she wished for enough light to read his expression. Part of her, God help her, wanted him to override her arguments with a kiss. And more.

Instead, his fingers slipped away from her waist, brushing her bare arms as he slowly released her. "Good night, Karina."

"Good night."

Deprived of his touch, Karina fled to her room. She undressed, slipped beneath the covers and, shivering, tucked her knees up to her chest. The sheets felt cold after the warmth of Daniel's embrace.

Her bed, like her heart, was a lonely place.

# CHAPTER SIX

KARINA GAZED INTO Natalie's shining eyes and gently tweaked one pink cheek. "Natalie Bowen," she said in a large and important voice, "I hereby declare you healthy as a horse, strong as an ox and fit as a fiddle."

Natalie giggled and danced in a circle around Karina's latest papier-mâché creation, a prancing unicorn clothed in swirls of green and ivory, peacock blue and crimson.

"Can I help? Please?" The little girl plunged her bare arms elbow deep into the basin of paste.

"Hang on," Karina said. "You can help, but you have to do exactly as I tell you."

"I will, I promise." Natalie pulled a dripping strip of fabric from the basin. "Where should I put this piece?"

"Here, on the back." Karina guided her hands. "Smooth it down. That's right."

Natalie's small fingers worked diligently at flattening the fabric over the wire mesh. "Why does it have so many colors? Unicorns are supposed to be white."

"White is made up of all the colors mixed together," Karina replied. "And I like colors."

"I do, too," Natalie agreed, nodding vigorously. "Once I painted all my arms red and all my legs blue with the paints Grandma gave me for my birthday."

Karina suppressed a smile and resisted the urge to ask how many arms and legs she'd had at the time. "Was your dad impressed?"

"He was not."

Karina turned at the sound of Daniel's voice. Behind his attempt at a frown she could see a smile lurking. His collarless white shirt contrasted sharply with his tan, and the lightweight suit jacket over clean, pressed blue jeans gave him a casual business air. Under one arm he carried a large portfolio.

"Daddy!" Natalie cried and launched herself at him.

"Steady on, Nat. You're as sticky as a fly on a bushranger's back." He let the portfolio slide to the floor and grasped her by the arms. With her hands well away from his jacket, he gave her a quick hug.

One arm around his daughter, he glanced over her head at Karina. "Mornin'."

"Hi." Unexpected confusion brought heat to her cheeks. Dropping her gaze, she stripped the excess paste from the piece of fabric in her hand and concentrated on shaping the unicorn's spiral horn.

When she looked up a few minutes later, Daniel was at the table, pouring cornflakes into a bowl. The portfolio was propped against the wall at his side. *A carpenter with an art portfolio?*

"Come and have breakfast, Nattie," he said. "Now that you're better, we've got things to do."

"Karina made me some toast," Natalie replied. "I don't want to go to the stupid old bank."

"Now, Natalie. There's also a house for rent I want to look at."

"She can stay with me for a few hours," Karina suggested.

Daniel's gaze collided with hers and bounced away. "Aren't you working today?"

*Oh, great,* Karina thought. They got a little carried away while dancing and suddenly they couldn't even look at each other. "No, this year I decided to spread my vacation out by taking a few days off here and there."

"Thanks for the offer, but I need to buy Nattie some new shoes for school while we're out." He paused. "That toast wasn't covered in peanut butter and mayonnaise, I hope."

Karina turned indignantly, then noticed his amused expression. "Specialty items are restricted to the dinner menu," she replied with a grin.

He smiled back at her, and suddenly everything was all right again. They were friends and roomies.

"What have you got in there?" she asked, nodding at the portfolio.

Daniel scooped another spoonful of cornflakes. "Have a look."

Karina wiped her hands on a towel and went to clear a spot on the table, only to find it was already clean. She ought to be paying Daniel, she thought as she laid the portfolio flat and untwisted the string that held the two halves together. She opened it up.

Sketches of fine furniture met her gaze—dining tables, bureaus, chests, desks, beds. Beside each sketch was a photograph of the finished product. Elegant and unique, the designs would suit any style of decor, from rustic to sophisticated.

She turned to Daniel, astonished. "I had no idea! Are these all your designs?"

He nodded, his mouth full of cornflakes. Then he swallowed. "Design and workmanship. Didn't I tell you I made furniture?"

"No. I thought you did kitchen cabinets or something." She glanced back at the photographs. "These are works of art! What kind of wood is that?"

"Jarrah, mostly. That's red gum," he said, reaching across the table to point out a red-hued chest of drawers. "I shipped a container containing both types a couple of months before I left Melbourne. It should arrive any day."

Karina studied the photograph of a jarrah bed frame, admiring the smooth-grained wood and flowing lines of the headboard. The corners were rounded, yet the design, like all the others, looked clean and sharp.

"Now I see why you import your own wood," she said.

Daniel nodded. "I reckoned red gum and jarrah would be unique over here, especially since it's recycled from old woolsheds and warehouses. When I locate a source of local timber I'll incorporate it into my designs."

Karina pulled out a chair and sat down, leafing through the rest of the sketches. "You must have had a good business going in Melbourne."

"Not bad. The problem was, I got too big. And the bigger I got, the less I time I had for the woodworking. I still did the designs and a lot of the finishing, but it wasn't the same as putting my hands to raw timber and turning it into fine furniture."

Karina thought of her rise through the ranks at SignCity and nodded. "I know what you mean."

Daniel pushed his bowl away and poured a cup of coffee from the jug on the table. "In a way, my decision to come back to Victoria was opportune. A chance to sell up and start fresh. I'm going to show my portfolio around a few places, see if I can drum up some business."

She gazed at him with new respect. "It takes guts to start over. I'd like to place the first order with your new company."

Daniel paused while reaching for the blue-and-white creamer. "Seriously?"

"Yes. I've wanted to replace that old oak dining table for ages but haven't seen anything I like." She glanced back to the portfolio. "Till now."

"Fine, then," he said, looking pleased. "You could pick out one of these designs or I could do something new."

"Something new," she said. "I want my table to be one of a kind."

"Like its owner."

The quiet timbre of his voice and the intent look in his eyes jolted her into remembering the need for caution. Friends and roomies they might be, but there was a definite undercurrent of something more.

She closed the portfolio, once again avoiding his eyes. "May I have some say in the design?"

He sipped his coffee. "Just tell me what you like."

She could think of several answers for that one, none of them fit for Natalie's small ears. Grinning, she risked a glance at him. "I know you're not easy, and I suspect you're not cheap, either...."

His mouth lifted in a smile, and a spark appeared in his eyes. "You're darn right I'm not cheap."

Karina laughed. Was it her imagination or was he smiling more often lately? "Name your price."

"The unicorn, or another like it," he replied. "For Natalie."

Natalie, who had been industriously layering strips of fabric onto the unicorn's back, looked up, eyes wide. "Really?"

He nodded.

Natalie gave an excited bounce. "Goody!"

"That's not a fair exchange," Karina protested. "One

of your tables is worth far more than a papier-mâché unicorn.''

He shrugged. ''Nevertheless, that's my price.''

''Tell you what. I'll throw in a logo design and layout for business cards. You'll be needing new ones.''

''Done.'' He held out his hand to shake on the deal.

Karina put her hand in his. This time he didn't seem to notice the bits of paste that clung to her fingers. Palms linked, fingers clasped, his eyes held hers.

Then he pulled his hand away, absently brushing at the sticky bits. ''Natalie will like having something of yours when we find our own place.''

Karina stepped away, curling her fingers into her palm. Why did she keep forgetting they weren't staying? And why was she getting all moony-eyed over him all of a sudden? He'd think she was an idiot, telling him they couldn't be more than friends, then blushing and starting like a schoolgirl at the sound of his voice or the touch of his hand.

''So, where's this house you're looking at?'' she asked, forcing a casual tone.

''Out near the university. Sounds like a palace, but you know what real estate blurbs are like.''

''Well, don't take just anything. You're welcome to stay till you find something suitable.''

''Thanks,'' he said, and smiled at her again.

*Oh, boy.* ''How are you getting on there, Nattie?'' she said, turning to the girl. ''What a good job you're doing! Let's just smooth down this lump on his back a little. We don't want your unicorn to end up looking like a camel.''

The girl looked up at her with shining eyes. ''Is he really going to be mine? Really truly?''

"Absolutely. Can you think of a magical name for him?"

Natalie's face scrunched up as she thought. "I know! I'll call him Merlin."

"Perfect." Karina pulled a wet strip of cloth from the basin and laid it over the unicorn's nose.

"Karina?"

She glanced across at Daniel, who was stirring sugar into his second cup of coffee. "Yes?"

"I just had a thought about your golf tournament."

She perked up. "Oh?"

"Why not go as someone's guest?"

"I can't go with anyone from SignCity," she said, her shoulders slumping. "They're all married. It wouldn't look good no matter how innocent it really was."

"Then what about an executive from another company?"

"I thought of that. I've already talked to a guy I know at Westholm Foods, but he's taking his girlfriend. Then there's Jason Doncaster from our Vancouver office. But he broke his leg water skiing, so he's out."

Daniel rocked back in his chair, frowning. "Are all the companies taking part affiliated with SignCity?"

"No," Karina said, shaping the unicorn's nostrils. "It's pretty much a free-for-all. But I don't know any male execs outside the Franklin Group of Companies."

Daniel rose and took his dishes to the sink. Then he leaned one shoulder against the frame between the rooms and gazed at her.

She glanced at him. "What?"

"Whoever you get should be someone you can trust."

*Yes,* Karina thought, gazing into his trustworthy hazel eyes. Technically speaking, he was CEO of his own company, small as it was. Immediately she dismissed the idea. He'd never do it; he didn't play golf, and, of course, the tournament was by invitation only, unless...

"Ideally, your escort should be a friend," Daniel continued, and she noticed he was watching her closely. "Someone with your interests at heart."

He meant *himself,* she thought with a quickening of her pulse. Nope, still no good. After what she'd said last night, asking him to go away for the weekend would send exactly the kind of mixed message she wanted to avoid.

Then another idea occurred to her. "That's it!" she exclaimed. "Daniel, you're brilliant."

His eyebrows lifted into the shock of hair that fell across his forehead. "What are you thinking?"

"What you said just now about how my escort should be a friend. I know just the person."

He pushed away from the door frame. "You do?"

"Yes. An old high school buddy of mine recently joined the Calgary office. I know he's not married, because he just got divorced. I'll give him a call first thing Monday morning."

He took a step toward her. "I meant *me.*"

"You?" Flustered, she backed away. "Remember what we talked about last night?"

"I meant I'd come just as a friend." He held her gaze. "What are you so worried about, Karina?"

"Nothing. It's just..." She laughed. "Wouldn't we be a pair, two nongolfers like us? We'd spend all our time trying to hit our way out of sand traps and I'd never get my schmoozing done. Thanks, Daniel, but I'll call my friend in Calgary."

"Maybe you're right." His smile seemed strained.

"Excuse me. I'm going to give Brian a quick call before I go out."

Daniel plodded upstairs. So what if she hadn't taken him up on his offer? He didn't even like golf. Anyway, hadn't he decided last night to back off?

Opening his address book to Brian's number, Daniel sat on the bed and dialed. He waited, tapping his foot soundlessly on the dhurrie carpet that covered most of the polished hardwood floor. With the palm trees gone and only a set of framed Balinese batiks decorating the walls, he felt more at home in the spacious, airy room.

Brian picked up the phone on the second ring. "Hello?"

"Hi, Brian. It's Daniel."

"When are you going to get the message, Danny boy? I don't want to talk to you."

"Look, I know you have a right to be angry," Daniel said quickly before Brian could hang up. "Even Karina thinks so. But your niece doesn't deserve this kind of treatment."

"Karina? Who's Karina?"

"She's the woman I'm staying with," Daniel explained impatiently. "The thing is, Natalie—"

"What is she—three, four years old?" Brian asked in a bored drawl.

Daniel's jaw clenched. "She just turned six."

"Is that so? Tell me more about Karina. She must be a very perceptive lady to take my side in the matter."

"I never said she took your side—"

"No point splitting hairs. What's she like?"

What possible difference could it make to Brian what Karina was like? Daniel thought irritably. "She's a graphic artist. Very talented. Bright, bouncy—"

"Sounds like a rubber ball." Brian's interest seemed to fade.

It was the perfect opportunity to drop the subject, but somehow, now he couldn't. "She's nothing like a rubber ball," he said. "She's got beautiful eyes. And hair like a cloud at midnight." *A cloud at midnight? Where the hell had that come from?*

"You sound completely besotted, Danny boy." Amusement tinged Brian's voice. "Had her in the sack yet?"

"She's my landlady," Daniel snapped. "And a friend. That's all."

"Steady on, Sir Lancelot. I wouldn't dream of tarnishing the lady's honor. Look, I've got to run. Call me again next week. I might have a minute or two to spare."

Daniel slammed down the phone, but not before he heard his brother's derisive chuckle. Now Brian was playing games with him. Daniel was tempted to call him back and tell him what a jerk he was.

But knowing Brian, that was exactly what his brother wanted him to do; lose his temper, making it Daniel's fault their feud remained an open, festering sore. Well, Daniel had no intention of becoming a martyr to his brother's nasty disposition.

Then he remembered Natalie and he dropped his head into his hands. He would call again and again if necessary.

Not only for Natalie, though. For himself, as well, to right the wrong he'd done. Somewhere inside the supercilious bastard he'd helped create was his brother. Somehow Daniel had to reach him. Then maybe he'd find that small piece of himself that had been missing all these years.

He rose slowly and went downstairs, his footsteps

heavy on the carpeted staircase, an almost physical pain in his chest from the mixture of anger and guilt he felt toward his brother. In the doorway to the meals area he paused and jerked his head at Natalie. "Come on, Nattie. Sooner we go, sooner it's done."

"But, Daddy..."

"Now!" he barked, and turned on his heel. Meekly Natalie ran after him.

Seconds later Karina heard the front door slam. Fury welled up in her, a protective instinct for that blameless child and her agonized father. Something would have to be done about that brother of his.

She reached for the phone book on the kitchen table and started flipping through it. Abruptly she pushed it away, appalled at herself. What she was contemplating was interference on a grand scale.

Not interference, she argued with herself, *helping.*

*He won't like it,* a little voice in her head warned.

It's for his own good.

*He'll be angry, and rightly so.*

The end justifies the means.

*That's what the Nazis said.*

"Oh, be quiet," she muttered and opened the white pages.

There were three Brian Bowens in the book. The first lived across the Gorge in Esquimalt, home to the navy and most of the industry in the area. Intuition told her that wasn't Daniel's brother. She dialed number two and waited while the phone rang.

"Hello," she said when a man answered. "This may sound a little strange, but do you have a brother named Daniel?"

"May I ask who's calling?"

Those few words were enough to answer her question.

In spite of Daniel's slight Australian accent, the two men sounded almost identical.

"I'm sorry. You don't know me. I'm Karina Peterson."

"Ah, Karina," he replied more warmly. "The woman Daniel's living with."

"The woman Daniel and his daughter are renting rooms from," she replied. She was wrong. Daniel's voice was a little deeper, Brian's a little smoother. But still pleasant.

He chuckled. "I stand corrected. To what do I owe the pleasure of your call?"

"Daniel's told me so much about you," Karina said, improvising as she went. "I know he's longing to see you again after all this time away, but it's been difficult with Natalie sick. I wondered if you'd like to come for dinner one night. Say, this Saturday?"

"Saturday? Let me check my diary."

Karina twined the cord around her finger, waiting. He'd sounded a little surprised but not antagonistic. Maybe Daniel had blown things out of proportion. It was easy to do with siblings.

"Saturday would be fine," Brian said, coming back on the line. "I hope Natalie is better. It's been so disappointing not being able to catch up with them yet. I've been very busy at work lately."

"What do you do?" Karina asked politely.

"I'm sales manager for a British car dealership."

"Really? I've got a '78 Triumph Spitfire."

"Is that so? A great little sports car, the Spitfire. Of course, we deal mostly with Rolls-Royce and Bentley, but if you ever need parts, I'm sure I could help out."

"Super."

"My pleasure. Till Saturday, then."

"Till Saturday. About seven."

Karina gave him her address and replaced the receiver, pleased with herself. Brian seemed perfectly charming and genuinely interested in getting together with Daniel. Surely it must all be an unfortunate misunderstanding.

# CHAPTER SEVEN

"YOU DID WHAT!" Daniel shook his head in disbelief. Either he was losing his hearing or Karina had lost her mind.

"I invited your brother to dinner." Karina carried on calmly painting her toenails a bright copper color. "I thought you'd be pleased."

Daniel threw down his portfolio and the bundle of documents he'd collected at the bank and various government offices. Maybe he ought to be pleased but he wasn't. His only brother would barely talk to him, let alone agree to meet, yet he'd come running at the drop of a hat for Karina. Why?

He pushed aside the stirring of jealousy that sprang out of nowhere. It was absurd not to want Brian and Karina to meet, yet...

"You should have asked me first."

"Would you have said yes?"

"No."

"I don't understand you, Daniel. Brian seemed anxious to see you. Does it really matter that you weren't the one to make the arrangement?"

"That's not it at all."

"Then don't look a gift horse in the mouth." She stretched her leg and waggled her toes to dry the polish.

She *didn't* understand, Daniel realized. If Brian had

accepted so readily, he must have an ulterior motive. But she probably wouldn't believe him if he told her so.

"Do you realize you've done exactly what you didn't like me doing when I fixed your fence?" he demanded.

Her cheeks colored but she said, "Look how well that turned out. This will, too, you'll see. I thought I'd invite Joanne to even out the numbers. And, of course, Betty and Kevin. Is that okay with you?"

Daniel pushed a hand through his hair. She really thought she was helping him. "Sure, why not. The rest of you ought to be able to hold up the flagging conversation."

"Great. How did the house check out? Any good?"

"Wonderful. If you overlook the Hell's Angels living in the basement and the early Depression decor. Joanne was right, pickings are mighty slim."

He gathered up his papers to take them upstairs. "By the way, I talked to Betty earlier. She's going to be in town tomorrow with the kids. She said they'd all drop over after Kevin gets off work."

"Great. I haven't seen the baby since he was born."

Daniel turned to go, then paused. "Oh, and, Karina?"

"Yes?"

"Thanks, I guess."

She smiled. "My pleasure."

KARINA KICKED OFF her shoes and dropped her bag on the hall table. The faint whine of the power saw told her Daniel was in the garage, working. And since there was no sight or sound of Natalie, she assumed the little girl was out there, too.

Karina ran up the stairs. Betty and Kevin and their brood would be here any minute. She had just enough time to change out of her work clothes.

Sure enough, the doorbell rang as she was pulling on a pair of beige linen shorts. Quickly she buttoned up a fitted sleeveless shirt in dark purple and ran down the stairs to open the door.

"Hi, Betty! Kevin! And let's see..." she took a big breath "...Ryan, Gillian, Matthew, Cara and baby Alex. Come in! It's so good to see you all again."

The family trooped into the house, filling the foyer and spilling down the hallway.

"It's great to see you, Karina," Betty said, holding the baby carrier close to her chest. "Sorry to descend en masse, but the kids just had to meet their new cousin."

"Well, of course they did." Karina peeked through the folds of the blanket at the baby's tiny, pink face. "What a cutie! He's got your red, curly hair, Betty. And your ears, Kevin."

Kevin grinned and shook his head. "Poor kid. We'll have to get 'em fixed."

"Daniel and Natalie are out in the garage," Karina said, then turned to the jumble of kids who ranged in height from midthigh to neck-bending adolescence. "I can't believe how big you've all grown. Too big for soft drinks and chips, I'll bet."

Amid a loud chorus of nos, Karina laughingly led the way to the kitchen, trailing children like ducklings. As she entered, the back door opened and Daniel stepped inside. He saw his cousin and her family and his face creased in a wide smile.

"Betty. Great to see you." He hugged her, then broke away to grip Kevin's hand. "G'day, Kev. You've got a lot to answer for, mate."

Kevin rubbed the top of his head and chuckled. "You look like you're surviving, at any rate. How are you? It's been a long time."

"Too long. This is Nat—" Daniel glanced around. "Hang about, where's Natalie? She was right behind me a second ago." He retraced his steps and opened the door wider to reveal his daughter holding a toy koala by one paw.

He bent down and Karina heard him whisper, "It's okay, Possum. There aren't as many as it looks."

Natalie took his hand and shyly came forward. Daniel ran through the children's names for her, looking to Betty for confirmation.

"Pretty good," his cousin said, "considering Ryan was the only one born before you left for Australia."

"That's right. He was what, two or three when I left?"

"I was pregnant with Gilly, so he would have just turned three." Betty extended a small, blunt-fingered hand to Natalie. "Come here, honey, and show me your koala."

Natalie proudly brought forth the brown-and-grey stuffed toy. "His name is Blinky Bill."

"He's beautiful. And now you've got lots of cousins to play with, as well."

Kevin poked the tubby koala in the stomach with his forefinger. "Don't let this little guy eat them, though, eh? He looks like he's got an appetite."

Natalie giggled. "He only eats gum leaves."

"Speaking of food, we were about to get you kids something to eat and drink," Karina said. "Natalie, can you get the chips from the pantry?"

Natalie nodded and did as she was asked. Karina got out the soft drinks and poured the chips into a wooden salad bowl. Then she shooed all the children onto the deck. "Off you go and get acquainted."

Daniel, meanwhile, had popped the tops on a quartet of beers for the adults and handed them around.

"Brian's coming over for dinner on Saturday," Karina said to Kevin and Betty. "Will you two be able to make it?"

Kevin turned to Betty. "Isn't that the day your mother's coming in from Winnipeg?"

*"Moosejaw,"* Betty said, rolling her big green eyes. "She lives in Moosejaw."

"Moosejaw? When did she move there?"

Betty turned to Karina. "Honestly, I don't know how you put up with him at work. But he's right about my mother arriving that day. I'm sorry. I would have liked to see Brian."

Ignoring the glasses Karina had set out, Kevin took a swig of beer straight from the can. "Yeah. He hasn't been out to our place for what—?" He turned to Betty. "A couple of months?"

Betty nodded. "About that." Sounds of discontent emerged from the bundle of blankets at her feet, and the car carrier began to rock. She unclicked the straps and scooped up her baby. "Are you hungry again already, little one?"

Lifting one corner of her blouse, she positioned the baby and began to nurse. "Have you seen Brian yet, Daniel?"

Daniel took a long sip of beer. "Not yet."

"I was a little surprised you wrote to me instead of him when you were looking for a place to rent," she said. "Or are you two still not talking?"

"We're talking. Just not very nicely."

"Too bad," Kevin said. "The guy's a riot. Last Christmas he dressed up as Santa and handed out presents to the kids."

Daniel raised his eyebrows. "*Brian* did that?"

"He's great with the kids," Betty said enthusiastically. "Teases them unmercifully, and they adore him."

Kevin laughed. "The older kids caught on right away who was under the red suit and teased him about his paunch. I've noticed he's been working on it since."

"At least he didn't lose the Santa Claus outfit like someone else I know," Betty said with a pointed glance at her husband.

Karina laughed. "Oh, Kevin. Only you could lose a Santa costume."

"It's around somewhere," Kevin replied, pulling on his bushy mustache. "Which reminds me..." He dug his wallet out of his back pocket. "Here's your money order, Danny. Sorry about the mix-up."

"No worries." Daniel accepted the dog-eared slip of paper with a grin. "Glad to see you didn't absentmindedly cash it."

"You'll have to come out to the farm for Christmas, Daniel," Betty said. "The kids'll have a ball together."

"Sounds good. Are you still on that acreage out on the Saanich Peninsula?"

Kevin nodded. "With the falling-down farmhouse and the barn in constant need of repair. Still handy with a hammer and nails, Danny?" he added with a grin. "We've been saving up a few jobs, just waiting for you to come home."

Daniel smiled. "I'd be glad to give you a hand."

"You don't know what you're getting yourself into," Betty said, laughing. "But you're welcome to visit whenever you want." She took the baby off her breast and raised it to her shoulder where it promptly issued a loud burp.

Her beer growing warm in her hand, Karina leaned

against the counter and watched the three of them laughing and talking. Daniel's pleasure in seeing Betty and Kevin was obviously reciprocated. Soon he'd be reunited with his brother and he'd be part of a large, happy family.

Unlike hers. With Tom in Toronto and her father in Penticton, cards and telephone calls formed the only tenuous links. If only Mama hadn't died, they might not have drifted so far apart.

The sound of the back door opening made her glance around. Natalie entered, bearing an empty chip bowl. "That was fast," Karina said.

Natalie set the bowl on the counter and gazed shyly at Betty. "Can I see the baby?"

"Of course. We'll let your daddy hold him, then you can get a good look. Say hello to cousin Daniel and Natalie, Alex," Betty cooed to her baby as she handed him to Daniel.

Daniel took the infant and nestled him in the crook of his arm. The sleeves of his faded denim shirt were rolled up to the elbows, and the baby looked tiny, pink and fragile against his strong, tanned forearm. A tender look crept into his eyes, and he smiled gently as he touched the baby's nose with the tip of a callused forefinger.

Little Alex's rosebud mouth lifted in a smile. Natalie laughed delightedly. "Oh, Daddy, can I have a baby brother?"

"Maybe someday, Possum."

She stroked the baby's tiny, curled fist. "When?"

Daniel laughed and shook his head. "Someday. I promise."

And he would keep that promise, Karina thought. Any lingering ideas she might have had about getting involved with Daniel were banished. The man was a natural father. He deserved a family.

Daniel glanced up at her. "Do you want a go, Karina?"

"Me? Oh, yes." She reached for Alex, and her bare arm brushed Daniel's as she slid her hand beneath the tiny bundle.

"Don't be nervous," he said, his breath warm on her cheek.

"I've held lots of babies." But she was trembling by the time they'd completed the delicate transfer of the baby from one pair of arms to the other.

She held Alex upright, close to her face, her fingers splayed behind his head for support. "Hello, Alexander the Great. How's my guy?"

She gazed into Alex's tiny, perfect face and breathed in the soft scent of talcum, mother's milk and new baby. Bittersweet longing stabbed through her. Then he smiled at her, and such a rush of pleasure filled her heart that she laughed softly.

"Amazing what power you little nippers have," she murmured, and stroked his satiny cheek.

She felt Daniel's gaze on her and glanced up to see him leaning back in his chair, watching her intently.

"He's absolutely beautiful, Betty," she said, and handed Alex carefully into the other woman's arms. Then she turned to the others and added brightly, "Is anybody else hungry? Since it's my night to cook, what do you say we order pizza?"

KARINA HUNG the spare leash Piper's owners had given her on its hook by the back door. She stepped inside the kitchen, exchanging the fresh morning air and the chirping of birds for the aroma of freshly brewed coffee and the sound of Daniel and Natalie laughing. Their happy voices made her smile even though she didn't know what the joke was.

"Hi, Nattie," she said. "You're looking better every day. I see you've got a peanut-butter smile. Is it as good as Vegemite?"

Natalie giggled. "It's messier. Can I play with Piper after I wash up?"

"I don't see why not. We'll just knock on his door and ask him, shall we?" She brushed a hand lightly across the girl's head, the smile lingering on her face as she watched Natalie run off.

She glanced over at Daniel. "Hi."

His eyes seemed to be waiting for hers. "Mornin'. I thought you'd gone to work."

"No, I got up early and took Piper for a walk in the park," she said, pouring herself a coffee. "Since there's a lull at the office, I thought I'd take another day off."

"Good. I'm going to work on the design of your table after breakfast. You can put in your two cents' worth if you like."

Karina smiled and reached for the sugar. "I'd love to."

Daniel eased his long legs out from behind the table and carried his dishes to the counter, where she stood stirring her coffee. Then she felt his hand in her hair and glanced up, startled.

"You've got enough twigs in here to build a bird's nest," he said, pulling one out. "Looks like Piper took *you* for a walk."

She gave a husky laugh and ducked away from him, brushing at her hair with her hand. "A bowl. I need a bowl," she muttered and stooped to rummage in the bottom cupboard.

"Joanne called," he said, going to the coffeepot and pouring himself another cup. "She said to tell you she'll bring a dessert tomorrow."

"Great. I was hoping she would." Karina straightened, clutching a cereal bowl in her hands. "Are you sure you're okay with this dinner thing?"

"No worries."

*"No worries,"* she repeated. "What does that mean exactly? That *you're* not worried or that *I* shouldn't worry about you?"

"Both." He crossed to the fridge and took out the carton of milk. "By the way," he added, pouring some in his coffee, "is it true you put chocolate milk on your cereal?"

"Joanne has *such* a big mouth." Karina stalked to the fridge, pulled open the door and gestured inside. "Do you see any chocolate milk in here?"

"No, but then, I did the shopping last week." He handed her the carton.

"It's not as if I make a habit of it," she said grumpily, flooding her cornflakes. Then she smiled. "It's not bad, though, once you get used to it."

He laughed out loud. "Just don't show Natalie that particular culinary delight if you don't mind. I'm going out to the garage to get started. Will you be long?"

"Just as long as it takes to down a bowl of cereal."

He was still laughing as he went out the door. She made a face at his back. Such a nice laugh for such an irritating man.

It was the fastest bowl of cornflakes she'd ever eaten.

THE GARAGE WASN'T all hers anymore, Karina thought, walking through the door into Daniel's workshop.

At the bench, Daniel leaned over a sheet of drafting

paper illuminated by a goosenecked lamp. Spread around him were the tools of his trade: rulers and pencils, compass and calculator. Farther down were vises and hammers, nails and sandpaper. The mentholated scent of gumwood shavings mingled with the odors of glue and linseed oil.

He'd taken over her garage and her life with his tools and his way of fixing things she never admitted were broken because then she'd have to deal with them. She ought to mind, but somehow she didn't.

She joined him at the bench, conscious of the snug fit of his faded blue jeans and the way his cotton shirt stretched across his shoulders. "Very professional rendering," she said, examining his sketches of the top and side view of a dining table.

He nodded without looking at her. "I studied architecture for a while."

"Really?" she said, glancing at him with raised eyebrows. "Why did you quit?"

"I moved to Australia."

"Oh." *Francine.* Her gaze slid back to the drawing.

"I probably would have quit anyway," he said, leaning an elbow on the bench and gazing up at her. "I found I got more satisfaction from creating the wooden models of my designs than I did from working with pen and paper."

Again Karina felt a spark of kinship. "I know what you mean. It's a good feeling to see the tangible results of your ideas. I hardly ever get that from my work anymore. Maybe that's why I do so much *papier-mâché.*"

His gaze drifted from her eyes to her mouth and back again. Disconcerted, she glanced back to the drawing on the workbench. "The table looks very long."

"Eight feet. It's a little wider than usual, too, but I

measured your dining room and it should fit nicely. Since you like to entertain, I reckoned you'd want a table you can bring a crowd to.''

She smiled. ''However did you guess?''

He grinned and tapped his temple with the end of a pencil. ''I have amazing powers of deduction. What do you think of the corners?''

''I like them,'' she said, tracing the elongated octagon with her finger. ''They're different.''

''I plan to use some jarrah beams salvaged from an old woolshed in Western Australia. They'll give your table great character.''

''Sounds wonderful. I can't wait to see it finished.''

Daniel straightened away from the bench and his bare forearm brushed hers. Somehow she'd edged closer to him without noticing.

''About these legs...'' she said, forcing her attention back to the table. ''I like them, but I wonder if they could be angled like this...?'' She picked up a pencil and lightly sketched over Daniel's drawing.

''That would look good,'' he admitted. ''But there might be a problem with stability. You can't have too great an inward angle. How about this instead...?'' He took the pencil out of her hand, and with broad, sure strokes, sketched an alternate design.

Karina watched, fascinated by his hands. His fingers carried the odd scar from nicks that had healed. Lean but muscular and tanned by the Australian sun to a light reddish brown. Even more interesting than their appearance was the way they moved, as though they were capable and clever. Which, of course, they were.

''Yes!'' she said, turning to him when he'd done. ''I love it.''

His clear hazel eyes reflected her pleasure as he gazed

back at her, silent and smiling. She thought briefly about auras and wondered why she'd never believed in them before. What else could explain the thickening of the air around them, the sensation that she could feel him even though they weren't touching?

Then his eyes grew intent, his mouth lost its curve and she knew with a breathless sense of the inevitable that he was about to kiss her. She had a split second to retreat...but she didn't.

Slowly Daniel bent his head, closing the space between them. Their lips touched for the very first time.

"Daniel," she murmured against his mouth, her heart pounding. "We agreed not to get involved."

"Shhh. Don't talk."

He cupped his hands around her jaw, his callused fingertips caressing the soft hollow behind her ears. All her objections faded in the immediacy of lips against lips, breath mingled with breath.

Her arms slid around his waist, and his shirt felt smooth and warm beneath her fingers. She inhaled his clean, male scent. Her lips parted, and she tasted him in a warm, moist fusion of tongues.

Then the thing she'd longed for practically all of her life finally happened.

Time stopped.

Just like that. No movement, no space. Only a warm glow that started in her heart and spread to every reach of her soul. A glow that had no beginning and no end.

A glow reflected in Daniel's heated gaze when she finally broke away, drawing in air on a long gasp.

That first breath, like the tick of the second hand on Felix the Clock, moved her back into the present. Into a world that kept spinning, no matter how much she wanted it to stay still. Into a fragment of time that couldn't last, no matter how much her heart yearned for it.

"Daniel." It was agony to move apart from him.

"Don't run away," he murmured. "It was only a kiss." With his fingertips, he lightly touched her lips.

A sensual shudder ran through her and she heard his own sharp intake of breath. Only a kiss, indeed.

She drew back another step. Just because he kissed her didn't mean he wanted to marry her. But the path they were treading like eggshells could only lead to a dead end. For Daniel's sake, as well as her own, she couldn't let this go any further.

"I wonder what Natalie's up to," she said, edging farther away. "We should check on her."

"She'll be all right for a minute."

"I've got a lot to do today," she said, avoiding his eyes. "I'm thinking of setting up a study in that extra room in the basement. I used to rent it out but I could use it myself if I installed a computer with a modem and a fax machine." She took a deep breath, aware she was talking too much, too fast.

Daniel stepped closer and put his arms around her waist. He held her loosely, his chin resting on her head. "What are you so afraid of, Karina? Tell me."

She shook her head mutely against his chest, barely breathing. The comfort of his embrace was almost as seductive as his kiss. She longed to tell him of the pain in her heart, but nothing anyone could do, not even Daniel, could ever make things right again.

She pushed him away for the second time, avoiding his questioning gaze. "Please. I've got to go."

# CHAPTER EIGHT

KARINA SWUNG DOWN the hall toward the kitchen, humming softly to the music in her head. At the doorway, she paused. Daniel was standing in front of the fridge studying the calendar, unaware of her presence. His hair, damp from the shower, was slicked back off his forehead. His freshly shaven jaw looked shiny and tanned.

She fingered the tiny salamander brooch that curled up the lapel of her dress. They'd hardly spoken since yesterday's encounter in the garage. Would he be as nervous as she felt?

Surely not. It was only one little kiss between friends. A spur-of-the-moment thing. Hadn't she been wishing Daniel was more spontaneous?

But friends had no business kissing like that. Their relationship had to return to a strictly platonic level, *immediately*.

The thing to do was act as though nothing had happened. So, head high, a deliberate swing in her step, Karina sauntered into the room.

"Good morning!" She crossed to the table, leaned over and flipped on the radio. Dixieland jazz filled the sunny room.

"Mornin'." Daniel's smile was both genuine and uncomplicated as he nodded at the radio. "Bill Bix I like."

Karina let out a silent sigh of relief. Daniel was a

mature individual. He wouldn't let a little thing like a kiss ruin a good relationship.

"You're very intent on that calendar," she said, helping herself to coffee. "Something important coming up?"

"I'm registering Natalie for school at Oak Bay Primary the week after next. We've got an appointment to meet her teacher."

"Oh? Have you found a house?" She wasn't sure if she was pleased he'd be nearby or disappointed he'd be leaving.

"Not yet, but I've decided to concentrate my search on this area. I like the older houses and established gardens. Being near the water is nice, too."

"I still remember my first day of school," Karina said, stirring in sugar and milk. "For some reason I thought I'd learn to read and write that first day. After all the excitement of getting new pencils and erasers, I was terribly disappointed."

Daniel chuckled. "I'll warn Natalie not to expect too much." He glanced back at the calendar. "That's an interesting hieroglyph marking August eighth. Does the date have some special significance?"

For a moment, Karina had trouble breathing. She dropped a fourth spoonful of sugar in her cup and stirred so hard the coffee slopped over the side. "Oh, that," she said, trying to sound casual. "It's just my birthday."

A drying lock of hair fell across his forehead as he turned his head to glance at her. "Your birthday? Are you having a party?"

"No." Karina popped a piece of rye bread into the toaster and reached for a knife from the drawer. She stared at her distorted reflection in the shiny chrome surface of the toaster, willing him to drop the subject. Any second now, he'd ask why not.

Questions and concern; she couldn't handle it. She hadn't wanted to rent in the first place. Why hadn't she stuck to her guns? Her thoughts had become so confused lately. She felt all the old grief of her mother's death, as well as fear of what was in store. Plus something new. A sort of regret. But for what?

"You don't sound very excited about it."

Karina forced herself to look at him and immediately wished she hadn't. His hazel eyes seemed to burn right through her. With a shrug, she glanced away. "It's just another day."

Daniel circled around her, his gaze piercing the curtain of hair that fell across her face. "I've only known you a few weeks, but somehow that doesn't sound like you. I'd have thought you'd have a huge party with lots of people and loud music. Dancing, decorations—the works."

Abruptly she pushed past him to the fridge. "Where'd you get that idea?" she said, searching for the cherry jam.

He gave a short laugh. "I can't imagine. You're like an open book...in a foreign language. So what *are* you going to do?"

Her toast popped. Karina pulled it out. "I haven't decided yet." She glanced sideways to see him studying her, a puzzled expression on his face.

"Trying to choose between a party or a night on the town?" he said. "Between a restaurant and a take-away?"

"*Out,*" she corrected, seizing the chance to change the subject.

"I beg your pardon?"

"It's called take*out* here, not take-away." She loaded her toast onto a plate, picked up her coffee and went to the table. Daniel wasn't stupid. Surely he could see she didn't want to talk about her birthday.

"Whatever." He pulled out a chair and sat down opposite her, still gazing at her. "The lingo will come back quickly. Already I almost feel as though I never left."

"Are you staying in Canada permanently, then?"

"That's the plan. But…well, we'll have to see." Daniel picked an orange out of the fruit bowl and began to peel it.

"You mean, see if your business gets off the ground?"

His gaze dropped to the orange in his hand. "I was thinking of Natalie. She's born and bred an Aussie. And she really misses her grandmother."

"That would be hard. And I can imagine how her grandmother must feel. But kids are resilient. Natalie will be happy wherever you are."

Daniel's face clouded. A continuous circle of peel dangled from his long fingers as he methodically went round and round the orange.

"Something wrong?" Karina asked.

"No." Then he sighed. "Yes, there is. It's Natalie…. She still hasn't got over losing her mother."

"Daniel—" In spite of her resolution to keep her distance, Karina reached out and touched his arm. The breath swelled in her throat until the words had to be pushed out. "She never will."

He went still, his gaze rising to meet hers. The long strand of orange peel broke free under its own weight and dropped, unheeded, to the floor. "What do you mean?"

Karina forced herself to go on. "She'll learn to live with the pain, but she'll never really get over it."

"Never?"

"Never."

Brassy, breezy, Dixieland jazz filled the silence between them.

Daniel bent to pick up the orange peel. "This is first-hand knowledge, isn't it?"

She nodded. "My mother died of breast cancer when I was thirteen." Her toast sat cooling on her plate, her appetite vanished.

"I'm sorry," he said softly. "You were right on the brink, so to speak. Your mother must have been quite young when it happened."

Karina heard the *thump-whoosh* of her heart. Felt the blood burning through her veins. "She was thirty-two."

He paused for the space of a heartbeat. "How old are you going to be next month?"

"Thirty-two." It was barely a whisper.

"I see." He was silent for a bit. "Is your father still alive?"

"He retired to Penticton a couple of years ago." Rolling her shoulders to relax them, she added, "Funny, eh? Most older people come to Victoria to retire."

"I guess you don't see him very often, then."

"Even before he left, I never saw much of him."

"Why not?"

She shrugged. "I don't know."

Daniel gazed at her intently. "Yes, you do."

Karina picked up her slice of toast and immediately put it down again. "He never really got over Mama's death. All through my high school years, he was so distant, like he was on another planet. I think—" Her voice broke.

Daniel gently pressed her hand. "Go on."

She swallowed hard. "I think I remind him too much of *her*. It seems to hurt him to be around me. So..." she drew a shaky breath "...mostly I leave him alone."

*"Damn."* Daniel rose and crossed the room to gaze out the window above the stove.

Slowly the breath seeped from Karina's bursting lungs. Thank God he hadn't tried to comfort her. She might have broken down completely.

"Every year on my birthday," Daniel said, still inspecting the backyard, "I make a point of doing something I've never done before. It's like a resolution to always go forward in life. Experience new things."

"Is that why you pull up stakes so easily?"

He spun around and looked at her. "Leaving Melbourne wasn't easy. I had my business, my friends. Natalie had her grandmother. But it doesn't hurt to try something difficult now and then if you've got a good reason for doing it."

Karina picked up her toast and took a bite. Getting through this birthday was going to be one of the hardest things she'd ever done, but it wasn't as if she had a choice. "So what kinds of things do you do on your birthday?" she asked.

"Last year I went rock climbing. The year before that I went on an archaeology dig with the university. I've been to a roller derby and a lecture by a nuclear physicist. It doesn't have to be exciting or daring. Just different. Something that lets you know you're alive and kicking."

Karina smiled. How could she ever have thought this man dull and boring? "I like the sound of that."

"You should try it." He leaned against the counter and crossed one leg in front of the other. "Since I'm something of an expert on the birthday adventure, I could help you plan."

"You could?"

He nodded. "I'd even go along if you want."

"You would?" She wasn't sure how she felt about that. It all sounded a little *too* appealing.

"I guarantee you won't regret it," he said. "Another party or another restaurant meal will always come along, but who knows when you'll get the nerve to go bungee-jumping again?"

Karina burst out laughing. "Bungee-jumping! No way! Even I'm not *that* crazy."

"What then?"

"Mmm, let's see." Karina looked to the ceiling for inspiration. "Chocolate pasta?"

"There's no such thing!"

She laughed at his expression. "Yes, there is, but I'll settle for dinner in Rome."

"Will Joanne baby-sit?"

"Of course. Hey, I know! How about dressing up as clowns and performing on the Johnson Street bridge at rush hour?"

He gave her the look he sometimes gave Natalie when she asked for something totally outrageous. "Choose that and you're on your own, darlin'."

"I was afraid of that," she said, shaking her head. "No staying power."

Karina's laughter lapsed into a smile, her gaze resting warmly on Daniel. This could work. They might actually become friends now that they were over yesterday's foolishness. Daniel would be a good friend to have. He seemed to know the exact degree of pragmatic cheerfulness required to lift her spirits.

But even as she gazed at him, the friendly sparkle in

his eyes turned to a darker gleam. Maybe things weren't quite as free and easy between her and Daniel as she'd hoped. She didn't want him to care for her. It was bad enough she couldn't be in the same room as him without being aware of every move he made.

"Maybe this isn't such a good idea, Daniel. I won't be very good company on my birthday this year."

Daniel pushed himself away from the counter and crossed the room to stand in front of her. Gently, he lifted her chin, his eyes grave and kind, the flame of desire banked. "You're not going to spend your birthday alone."

Karina gazed at him mutely, overwhelmed by emotions she couldn't begin to name. Sometimes she felt so *right* with him, as though life would go on forever in a haze of domestic bliss. Other times, like now, he touched her too deeply, and all her demons rose up to haunt her. She couldn't bear to ever hurt him.

The doorbell rang.

"I wonder who that could be?" she said, and started to pull away.

Daniel grabbed her by the shoulders and held her fast. "Promise me you'll at least think about it."

"I...yes, okay, I'll think about it."

He let her go and she hurried down the hall. If only he knew—she thought of little else *but* her coming birthday. Still, as she reached for the door handle, she made up her mind to try to think about something fun instead. Something she could do with Natalie to ease the girl's loneliness.

DANIEL CAME DOWN the stairs, glancing at his watch for the tenth time in the past half hour. So Brian was fifteen minutes late. No big deal.

He paused in the hall, listening to the muffled sounds of laughter that meant Karina and Joanne were still closeted in the kitchen. Karina had insisted on cooking dinner on the grounds that Daniel should be free to concentrate on his brother. He'd agreed in the end, but after experiencing several of Karina's "dinners," Daniel was grateful Joanne was there to lend a hand.

In the living room, Natalie was leaning over the back of the sofa, her small rump waving in the air as she craned her head at the bay window watching for her uncle. Her hair had been fashioned into two sleek French braids, thanks to Karina, and she wore her favorite summer dress of pink pineapples on a black background.

"Feet off the sofa, young lady." Daniel caught her by the waist and swung her to the ground.

"It's him!" Natalie exclaimed just as she was pulled away. "He's here!"

Daniel glanced out the window. A silver Jaguar had pulled up at the front gate and a stocky, fair-haired man was getting out. Daniel wiped damp palms against his denim-clad thighs.

A week ago he would have flung open the door and gone to meet his brother, but the phone calls of the past two weeks had taught him caution. Suddenly he was glad Karina was there to back him up. She was so good at talking to people she would surely put them both at ease and smooth over any unpleasantness with her unfailing good humor.

Natalie showed none of her father's reservations. She ran to the door and yanked it open. But when Brian stepped onto the porch, her excitement dissolved into shyness, and she ducked behind Daniel's legs.

Face-to-face with the brother he hadn't seen in ten years, Daniel was made forcibly aware of the passage of time. Brian's blond hair had turned to gray at the temples, and faint but permanent lines creased his forehead.

A profound sense of loss came crashing down on him. They'd missed out on so much—all the milestones of each other's adult lives, the successes, the setbacks, the hopes, the dreams....

Unable to speak for the constriction in his throat, Daniel stepped forward, hand outstretched. Brian merely gazed coolly back at him.

Daniel froze in midstride, his hand dropping awkwardly to his side. "Come in." He turned and led the way to the living room.

The doors to the dining room slid open. Karina and Joanne came through on a wave of laughter and the aroma of chicken and exotic spices. Karina's smiling face registered surprise, then pleasure at the sight of their guest.

"You must be Brian," she said in her lilting, laughing voice. "I'm Karina and this is Joanne." She turned to Daniel. "Why didn't you tell me he'd arrived?"

Before Daniel could speak, Brian extended his hand, a huge smile creasing his face. "Old Danny boy forgot his manners for a moment. I guess we'll forgive him for that." Laughing now, Brian put his arm around Daniel's shoulder in a parody of brotherly love.

Daniel stared at him, speechless.

"Pleased to meet you, Joanne," Brian continued without a pause. "And Karina! Danny's description of you didn't begin to do you justice."

Karina's surprised gaze flicked to Daniel. He smiled and gave a little shrug. Then he frowned as Brian reclaimed her attention with a prolonged handshake that seemed to involve all four of their hands and a great deal of smiling.

Brian drew Natalie into the circle, crouching down to gently tug on one braid. "So this is my long-lost niece, Natalie. My, my, you're a grown-up girl already." He reached inside his jacket pocket and pulled out a small, brightly wrapped parcel. "Here's a little start on all those birthdays and Christmases I've missed."

With a squeal of delight, Natalie tore open the wrapping and uncovered a small box containing a bracelet of shiny red and blue stones. She slipped it on her wrist and gazed at her uncle with adoring eyes. Karina and Joanne looked down at the pair with soppy smiles.

Daniel wanted to punch his brother's face in.

"WINE FOR EVERYONE?" Karina asked a few minutes later as she entered the living room with glasses clutched in one hand and a bottle of Italian white in the other.

Brian and Joanne were together on the sofa, while Daniel had taken one of the wing chairs. Karina thought Daniel's expression seemed a little strained, but she put the thought aside and perched on the edge of the other chair.

Amid a chorus of assent, Natalie's small voice piped up. "I can't have wine. I'm just a kid!"

Everyone laughed. "Will orange pop do, Miss Bowen?" Karina asked.

Natalie nodded graciously. "Yes, thank you. I can get it myself." She ran off to the kitchen.

Daniel looked pleased at his daughter's polite little speech. Brian gave him a wink. "Well, Danny boy, at least you've managed to instill manners into your child. You must have done something right."

"Natalie's a beautiful child," Karina said quickly. "She's a credit to Daniel."

Daniel's irritated gaze left his brother, and he flashed

her a smile of thanks. Joanne's interested glance flicked from brother to brother.

Karina set the wine bottle on the coffee table and attempted to extricate the glasses from between her fingers, laughing as they stuck to her skin and clinked dangerously. Daniel started from his seat to help, but Brian, who was closer, leaped to her rescue first.

One by one, Brian removed the glasses and set them on the coffee table. His unblemished fingers lingered under the tips of hers. "What lovely hands you have."

Karina felt her cheeks glow. After hours spent scrubbing away ink stains and shaping and polishing her nails, it was nice to have her efforts noticed. She glanced at Daniel, wondering if he'd seen the improvement, too. But Daniel's frowning gaze was fixed on the wine bottle as he drove the corkscrew into the cork with a force that seemed excessive.

"It's a wonder Natalie has any manners at all," Brian said, grinning. "You should have seen Danny as a teenager. He'd say the rudest words imaginable at Sunday dinner just to shock our grandmother."

Daniel glanced up. *"Brian."* His voice carried a distinct warning.

Karina's nerves prickled. Brian only smiled and lounged against the sofa, one arm resting along the back. Daniel sat on the edge of his seat, his jaw tight, his gaze fixed on his brother's lazy smile.

Ignoring him, Brian carried on with his story. "Danny would put this look on his face like butter wouldn't melt in his mouth, turn to Granny and say, 'Pass the effing potatoes, please.' But when he came to *that word* he'd drop his voice so only she could hear."

Brian laughed, and Karina and Joanne chuckled along with him. "My little brother was so-o-o bad." He leaned across and punched Daniel playfully on the arm. "Eh, Danny boy?"

"If you say so," Daniel replied quietly.

Karina's laughter slowed. Joanne covered her smile with her hand. Brian's eyes danced. A tense silence fell over the room.

Karina forced a bright smile. "You sound positively angelic compared to what *my* brother used to get up to," she said to Daniel. "I can't even repeat some of the things he did. Have you got that bottle open?"

"What? Oh, yes." Unwrapping white-knuckled fingers from around the neck of the bottle, he transferred it to his other hand and reached for a glass. He filled it halfway with a deep gold Frascati and passed it to Joanne.

"Brian," Daniel said without looking at his brother, "I'm sure Karina and Joanne aren't interested in hearing us talk about the good old days all evening." He poured another glass and passed it to Karina.

She reached for the drink and was shocked to see his eyes opaque with anger and the curving lines of his mouth flattened with pain. Sure, Brian was teasing him, but all brothers did that. Nobody thought the worse of Daniel for his boyhood pranks.

"I didn't come here to quarrel, Danny," Brian said. "And I certainly didn't intend to embarrass you in front of your friends." He held out his hand. "Forgive me?"

Daniel gazed silently at his brother but made no move to take his hand. Karina held her breath. *Why wouldn't he shake?*

Slowly, Daniel reached out. Karina started to laugh in relief. She broke off with a gasp as Daniel placed a glass of wine in Brian's outstretched palm.

"Cheers," Daniel said. He filled his own glass and raised it in a mocking salute.

Brian's eyes widened. His mouth fell open. He threw his head back and laughed. "Oh, he's a sly one. A real rogue."

"What's a rogue?" inquired a small voice at Karina's elbow.

"Oh, Natalie! You startled me." Karina had forgotten the little girl, she'd been so quiet until now. "Did you get your pop?"

"Yes, thanks. What's a rogue?"

"Oh, it's just a sort of...scoundrel." Karina could see by Natalie's puzzled expression this word was no better. "Like a bad guy but in a joking kind of way."

Natalie shook her head, obviously confused. "Daddy's not a bad guy. Why would Uncle Brian say that?"

"He didn't, not really. Oh, Nattie, it's hard to explain. Why don't you ask your dad about it later?"

She knew this was a cop-out, but how could she explain adult innuendo to the child when she herself didn't fully understand what was going on between Daniel and his brother?

Natalie skipped off to her father, and Daniel pulled her onto his lap. Joanne began telling a funny story about something her youngest child had said to the mailman.

Karina sipped her wine and studied the brothers. Brian was handsomer by conventional standards and wore expensive clothes, but she found Daniel's casual good looks more attractive. If only he would lighten up. He had a sense of humor. Why didn't he use it?

"Don't you agree, Karina?" Brian said, appealing to her.

She sat up. "I'm sorry, what did you say?"

"I said, you can't beat British-built cars for engineering excellence."

She smiled. "I don't know. My Sammy's a little temperamental. But he's also a lot of fun, so I live with the repairs."

"How about you, Daniel?" Brian turned to his brother. "In the market for a new car? I could get you a good deal." He winked at Karina.

"Thanks, Brian." Daniel spoke stiffly. "I've already bought a small pickup to use for work."

"Not that secondhand Japanese job parked out front?" Brian said, laughing.

Daniel glowered.

"I was driving past your showroom the other day," Karina interjected quickly. "I presume Bowen's British Autos on Blanshard is yours?"

Brian nodded. "Drop in next time you're going by."

"Thanks, I may do that. I noticed you could use a new sign out front."

"Watch out, Brian," Joanne warned him with a smile. "You're about to be wheeled in for an overhaul. I've seen Karina go into a restaurant for a meal and convince the owner to completely revamp the exterior of his building, including a brand new neon sign by SignCity. Which vastly improved the place, of course."

"Is business so slow that you have to go looking for it, Karina?" Daniel asked.

She flashed him a smile, pleased he'd relaxed enough to join the conversation. "Not at all. It's just that wherever I go, design ideas pop into my head and I blurt them out. Our sales department doesn't know whether to make me an honorary member or shut me down for unfair competition."

"Daniel told me you were a graphic artist," Brian

said, leaning forward. "I didn't know you designed signs."

"That's right." She sat back in her chair and crossed her legs. "SignCity Neon is the biggest neon sign company in the country. And the best, if I do say so myself."

"I don't doubt it. But neon doesn't quite fit the Rolls-Royce image."

"Don't be too sure. Neon can be very classy if you do it right. Picture this...." Gesturing with her hands, she began telling Brian her ideas for his sign. Vaguely she noticed Joanne murmur something to Daniel and the two of them leave the room.

When she had finished, Brian pursed his lips. "What you're describing doesn't sound bad. Not bad at all."

"Excuse me, Karina," Daniel interrupted, poking his head through the doorway. "Joanne wants to know where you've hidden the cinnamon."

"Goodness, are you in the kitchen again?" She turned apologetically to Brian. "I promised I'd take care of dinner, and here I am yakking away...."

Daniel cast a quick glance at his brother. "It's all right."

Karina jumped to her feet and pulled Daniel into the living room. "No, it's not. I need to prove I can concoct something other than peanut butter and mayonnaise."

She left the room to the sound of Brian's laughing voice followed by Daniel's sardonic murmur, and mentally patted herself on the back for getting Daniel together with his brother at last.

In the kitchen, she found Joanne forking through the couscous while Natalie kneeled on a chair and industriously grated carrots all over the table.

Karina rooted through the spice jars in the cupboard

next to the stove for the cinnamon. "Sorry about that, Jo. I got carried away talking shop."

"I noticed." Joanne glanced up. "He's nice, isn't he?"

Karina's gaze flicked to Natalie before answering. "Yes," she said cautiously. "I mean, what's not to like?"

"Exactly. On the other hand, siblings' relationships are like marriages. Outsiders never know all that goes on below the surface."

"True, I guess. Here's the cinnamon." She lifted the lid on the Moroccan chicken and tipped the spoon to her lips. "You were right, it needs a dash more.

"What I don't understand," she added, "is why You Know Who is so uptight." Karina glanced at Natalie again, but the girl was engrossed in scraping up bits of carrot from the far reaches of the table. "What's His Name seems so genuinely amiable. To hear You Know Who talk, you'd think he hated his guts."

"Are you talking about Daddy and Uncle Brian?" Natalie asked suddenly.

Karina rolled her eyes at Joanne, then glanced back at Natalie. "Yes." She didn't believe in lying to children, but neither did she think further explanation would serve any useful purpose. "Wow, what a lot of carrots you've grated. How about sprinkling them in the salad for me?"

"Okay," Natalie said cheerfully, and scooped up the pile with both hands.

Joanne dipped a spoon into the chicken and tasted the sauce. "Perfect." She dropped the spoon in the sink and turned to Karina with a grin. "It's showtime."

As soon as Daniel was certain Karina was out of hearing, he set his glass down hard on the table and faced his brother. "What the hell are you playing at, Brian?"

"Why, Danny, whatever do you mean?" His blue eyes widened.

"I mean, what's all this 'forgive me' crap? Every time I've called you, you've been cold and distant, if not downright offensive. Now suddenly you're slapping me on the back like the best of buddies. And don't give me that innocent expression. It's as calculated as the rest of your act."

Brian shook his head sadly. "Danny boy, I was just trying to be friendly. We've had our differences in the past, but we're still brothers."

Daniel took a deep breath and counted to ten. Was it remotely possible Brian had had a complete change of heart and sincerely wanted to be friends? He doubted it very much.

"Besides," Brian continued, "I didn't want to embarrass you in front of your lady friend by playing the nasty big brother."

"She's *not* my lady friend." Daniel got to his feet and paced the short distance to the stereo system. He flipped through the CDs without seeing them. "And why did you tell them it was me who said that to Grandma?"

"What's the matter, Danny boy? Afraid of tarnishing your image? Come on, it was just a little joke. You could have told them the truth."

Daniel threw him a look that could have withered the entire north Queensland rain forest. And should have devastated Brian, too, except he was so damn cocky.

"Well, maybe you're right. It would have looked a tad petty." Brian put his hands behind his head and leaned back on the couch. "Made a good story, though, didn't it? Put you in the limelight."

"You're the one who always wanted to be in the lime-light." Daniel slid the CD drawer shut and strode over to Brian. "Why did you really come here tonight? I'd hoped it was to see me and Natalie, but now I wonder if you didn't come just to meet Karina."

"You do me an injustice, little brother," Brian replied. "Though I must admit, when I heard Karina's voice on the telephone I was curious to see what such an enchanting-sounding creature looked like."

A chill went down Daniel's spine. "Forget it, Brian. Karina's not for you."

"Why not? You've taken great pains to assure me you're not interested—though I suspect that's a case of protesting too much."

"How would you know? You haven't seen me in years."

"You forget," Brian said quietly. "I've seen you in love before."

Daniel went still. What he'd felt for Francine hadn't been love. But how could he say so to the man who'd lost his future wife to Daniel's passing fancy?

"I'm not in love with Karina." The words seemed to stick in his throat.

"I'd hardly blame you if you were," Brian said. "She's a beauty, all right."

Daniel bit back his anger at Brian's casual remarks. He felt protective of Karina, though he knew she wouldn't thank him for it. He felt possessive of her, although he had no right to be.

"She isn't interested in getting involved with any-one," he said. "She's devoted to her career."

Brian laughed. "Hey, little brother, just because you struck out doesn't mean the rest of the team has to stay on the bench."

Daniel's hands clenched impotently around thin air.
"I'm warning you, Brian, stay away from—"

KARINA CAME DOWN the hall to the living room to call
Daniel and Brian for dinner, but the sound of their voices
slowed her steps. Though their words were indistinct,
there was no doubt they were arguing. It must be about
Francine. Quickly, she retraced her steps partway, then,
loudly humming a fragment of *The Barber of Seville*,
she carried on without pause through the passageway
into the living room.

"—Karina!" Daniel finished furiously.

"Karina!" Brian exclaimed with hearty gladness as
his gaze swept over Daniel's shoulder to meet hers.

Brian's brow was so smooth and his smile so broad,
she could have sworn she'd been mistaken in thinking
she'd heard his voice raised in anger only a moment ago.

Or had it been Daniel's voice?

Daniel swiveled to face her. Karina felt a jolt of anguish at the tense, unhappy expression in his eyes.
Maybe this little dinner party hadn't been such a good
idea. Maybe it would have been better if they'd thrashed
things out on their own, without the added strain of having to be polite around her and Joanne. Not to mention
Natalie.

"Dinner's ready," she said, and slid open the heavy,
paneled doors that connected the living and dining
rooms.

The table, painstakingly set that afternoon by Natalie,
gleamed with Karina's royal-blue-and-white china and
Mama's handblown Italian wineglasses. Overhead, the
papier-mâché ladies circled. Wildly colorful and fla-
grantly impossible, they stirred gently in the light air
caused by Joanne's energetic bustling to and fro from

the kitchen with dishes of fragrant, spiced chicken and steaming couscous.

Brian's jaw dropped when he saw them, and Natalie giggled at her uncle's astonished expression. "They're flying spaghetti pickers, Uncle Brian," the little girl explained. "Karina made them."

Brian shook his head wonderingly. *"Spaghetti pickers?"*

Karina grinned. "I made them for a friend to hang in her Italian restaurant. The venture folded before it even opened, so here they fly, forever searching for the elusive spaghetti bushes."

"Elusive or mythical?" Daniel said, an edge to his voice.

"It's just a joke," Karina replied, wondering at his mood. He seemed brittle and unhappy despite Brian's friendly overtures. "Sit down, everyone, please."

She was half afraid there'd be a scuffle for seats, but to her relief it was settled quickly, with Daniel at her side and Brian directly across from her. Joanne sat across from Daniel, and Natalie took pride of place at the head of the table.

Joanne raised her glass when they were all seated. "I propose a toast to Daniel's first big contract in his new business."

Karina glanced at Daniel, startled. Surely one dining table didn't constitute a big contract.

"I haven't had a chance to tell you," he said to her. "I dropped into a home-furnishings shop in Oak Bay Village the other day with my portfolio. They called back this afternoon saying they'd take as many pieces as I can produce."

"That's wonderful. You're on your way." It *was*

wonderful. And childish of her to feel disappointed because he'd told Joanne first.

Then she noticed Natalie squirming in her chair and looking hungrily at the untouched food. "What are we waiting for?" she said. "Let's eat."

Brian was the perfect dinner guest, Karina thought afterward as she laid her knife and fork across her empty plate. He'd kept Natalie in stitches with his teasing, likewise Joanne with his friendly banter. To herself, he'd been charmingly attentive. Maybe he was a trifle too sure of himself, but that was easy to forgive.

Daniel alone had been on edge throughout dinner, constantly alert to Brian's every word and expression. Yet even with Daniel...no, *especially* with Daniel, Brian had been nothing but warm and friendly.

"Kar-ina!" Joanne called to her from across the table. She glanced up. "Sorry?"

"Brian was just saying how much he likes to golf. Maybe he can give you some pointers."

Karina sat up and looked at Brian. "You're a golfer!" Beside her, she sensed a surge in Daniel's tension level.

"I play most weekends," Brian replied. "Are you interested in the game?"

"It's a long story...." Karina proceeded to relate the tale of her career aspirations and how they hinged on attending the corporate tournament.

"My dear Karina," Brian said expansively when she'd finished. "I'm attending that tournament myself. I'd be delighted if you'd come as my guest. What do you say?"

"I'd love—!" She caught herself. How was Daniel going to take this? Would he feel slighted that she'd go with his brother and not him? Surely he'd realize she was only doing it for her job and not because she wanted to be with Brian.

Quelling her excitement, she turned to Daniel. "What do you think?"

# CHAPTER NINE

"WONDERFUL," Daniel assured Karina, hoping his smile didn't looked as strained as it felt. *Wonderful?* It couldn't be worse if she'd announced her intention of touring hell with Lucifer as her personal guide.

He glanced across the table and caught the flash of triumph in his brother's eyes. A second later, Brian's expression changed to one of benevolent goodwill as he gazed at Karina.

Rage coursed through Daniel out of all proportion to the circumstances. He *was* glad Karina had got her wish. But why did it have to be Brian who'd granted it?

He felt Karina's fingers, soft as eiderdown, on the back of his hand. He turned toward her, expecting to see the same troubled expression that had clouded her dark eyes all evening whenever she'd looked at him.

But, no, she was smiling gently. With a nod, she indicated his daughter, who was drooped sleepily over her half-eaten dinner.

Daniel rose. "Come on, Possum. Time for bed."

"I'm not tired," Natalie protested, yawning. But she allowed him to sweep her into his arms, and she snuggled her head against his shoulder.

"Say good night, Natalie."

"Good night, Natalie." She giggled drowsily.

"Good night," Karina and Brian said together.

"Good night, Natalie," Joanne said. "Don't forget Julie's birthday party next week. It's dress-up."

Daniel paused in the doorway. "Dress-up?"

"Don't look so worried," Karina said with a laugh. "I love doing costumes. Fairy princesses are my specialty."

Daniel nodded his thanks and carried Natalie upstairs. Karina was so good to them, he thought, ashamed of his fit of jealousy. And she always managed to make it seem as though they were doing *her* a favor.

Karina rose and began to clear the table, conscious all the while of Brian watching her. She waited until Joanne had taken a load to the kitchen, then turned to him with a puzzled smile. "What?"

He spread his hands in a gesture of helpless admiration and silently returned her smile. *Uh-oh,* she thought. This golf weekend could get sticky if she didn't do a little preliminary groundwork.

"It's really nice of you to take me to the tournament, Brian," she said, gathering up the cutlery. "I'd like to do something for you in return."

Brian shook his head. He rose and began helping her stack the dishes. "Don't even think of it. It'll be my pleasure."

"No, I mean it. I'm going to design a new sign for your dealership. No obligation—take it or leave it. But if you decide to take it, I'll knock the design costs off the project."

"That's very generous, Karina, but truly, it's not in the least necessary."

Karina gave him a big smile. "Oh, but it is. You see, before tonight I considered hanging out at the local Chamber of Commerce to nab an unsuspecting golfer.

This is so much better. A stranger might get the wrong idea about the weekend…if you know what I mean.''

Brian's eyes twinkled. "I know what you mean. Men can be such *animals*.''

Karina laughed. Everything was going to be all right, after all.

Brian moved around the table, picking up plates as he went. When he reached the spot where she stood piling cutlery into an empty casserole dish, he rested the plates on the table, his shoulder almost touching hers.

"I'll be the perfect big brother," he said. "I'll teach you golf and fend off inconvenient admirers. Did I mention I was on the fencing team at university?" He picked up a butter knife and made a minilunge past her ear. *"En garde.''*

Laughing, she leaned backward and brandished a salad fork. "Just don't stab my boss until he's put my promotion in writing."

Behind her, Daniel cleared his throat.

Karina spun around. "Daniel! You startled me.''

"Always remember to watch your back," he said, and strolled over to inspect the small collection of books lining the top shelf of the wall unit.

Brian uttered an amused grunt. She glanced back to see him gazing intently at Daniel. His brow was furrowed, but his mouth turned up at the corners, the tip of his forefinger pressed against his lips as though to prevent an incipient smile from broadening.

"I think I'll make coffee," she said. "Then we can have some of Joanne's cake. Triple chocolate delight, guaranteed to give you a coronary before you're fifty. No, stay right there," she added quickly when both brothers started to come to her assistance. "I'll bring it into the living room."

"Whew!" she exclaimed as she strode into the kitchen. "This is the weirdest evening."

Joanne looked up from the sink, where she was rinsing plates. "What's going on now? Are they duking it out in the living room?"

"Not yet, but I wouldn't be surprised if they ended up in the proverbial parking lot before the evening's over. I hope your chocolate cake will mellow them out."

"It'll weigh them down if nothing else. They won't be able to move quickly enough to damage each other."

Karina and Joanne looked at each other and laughed.

"I thought Daniel was going to pop Brian one when he invited you to the tournament," Joanne said.

Karina scraped off the side plates and handed them to Joanne. "Something deep and dark is simmering beneath the surface, that's for sure."

"Passion!" Joanne said in a theatrical whisper, her eyes widening.

"Revenge!" Karina whispered back, creeping up on Joanne with arms raised and fingers dramatically outstretched. Abruptly she lowered her hands. "Hang on. Brian's the one who should be seeking revenge, not Daniel."

"Oh, right." Joanne went back to stacking dishes. "He must have been pretty ticked when Daniel ran off with his fiancée."

Karina nodded as she poured ground coffee into the filter. "Who wouldn't be? But from what Daniel said, he and Francine weren't happy for very long."

She crumpled the empty coffee package and threw it into the garbage. Then she paused, kettle in hand, and listened. "It's awfully quiet out there."

Joanne straightened. "With kids, that's usually a sign of trouble."

"But they're two grown men."

"Yeah," Joanne agreed. "They'll work it out amicably."

Karina looked at Joanne. Joanne looked at Karina. "We'd better get out there," they said in unison.

Karina gathered up the dessert tray and, with Joanne hard on her heels, hurried back to the living room. To her surprise, the emotional temperature, far from approaching boiling point, was positively subzero.

Brian sat sideways on the sofa with the newspaper spread out in front of him. Daniel stood at the bookcase, thumbing through an ancient volume of Dostoyevsky left behind by one of her tenants. The brothers had their backs to each other, and the air between them was thick with animosity.

"Who's for cake and coffee?" Karina asked cheerily, creating a determined clatter with plates and cups.

The cake worked for a little while. Appreciative sounds issued from every mouth. But as the cake disappeared, so did all semblance of conversation. *Isn't this pleasant,* Karina thought, pressing her fork onto her plate to pick up the crumbs.

The emotional roller coaster they'd been riding since Brian had walked through the door had ground to a halt, yards from the finish. She had no more chatter, no more smiles, and from the look on Joanne's tired face, even her endless stream of quips had dried up. The silence of the brothers reigned supreme.

At last Joanne put aside her plate and stood. "I'd better go, Kar. If I'm not back by midnight, the baby-sitter will turn into a pumpkin and my kids will turn into mice." She went into the hall to retrieve her purse and coat. "On second thought, maybe that's not such a bad idea. I could put them in a cage and just give them a little food and water occasionally.''

Karina managed a chuckle, more out of loyalty than genuine humor. ''Thanks for all the help, Jo.''

''No problem.'' Joanne turned in the doorway. ''Nice to meet you, Brian. See you again, Daniel. No, don't anyone get up. 'Bye.''

Karina saw Joanne out. When she returned, Daniel was gathering up the coffee cups. ''Don't worry about those,'' she said.

With a shrug, he picked them up anyway and headed for the kitchen.

Brian rose. ''It was a wonderful dinner, Karina. I'm so glad to have met you.'' He moved toward the front door and took his jacket off the hook on the foyer wall.

''You're not going without saying goodbye to Daniel, are you?''

Brian shrugged, an eerie echo of Daniel's gesture minutes before. ''I don't think Danny's in the mood for family reunions tonight. You say goodbye for me. Please.'' He took both her hands in his and squeezed them lightly. ''I'll be in touch. Okay?''

Karina nodded helplessly. ''Okay.''

When he'd gone, she stalked down the hall toward the kitchen, her fury at Daniel growing with every step. She pushed open the door. He wasn't there. She went to the dining room. Not there, either. He couldn't have gone upstairs without her seeing him. The garage, then.

Sure enough, the back door was ajar, and from the deck she could see a solitary light burning in the low building at the back of the yard.

He was at the bench working on a drawing when she banged open the door. A muscle in his jaw jumped, but he didn't look up. In the glow of the gooseneck lamp, his profile looked as inflexible as the lengths of scarred red wood that had arrived that morning and lay stacked against the wall.

"Couldn't you even say good-night to your brother?" she said, storming into the room. "You finally get together and you treat him like some sort of...of... pariah."

Daniel's head jerked up, and he straightened away from the bench. The thin metal ruler he held between his hands bent under pressure. "Don't waste your time fretting over Brian, Karina. This evening was a farce from start to finish. The big-brother act is all for show."

Karina laughed compulsively and began to pace back and forth across the garage, hugging her arms around her waist to ward off the chill night air. "How can you say that? He was perfectly charming. He was great with Natalie, and *she* obviously adored him. He tried to make friends with you and you snubbed him."

Daniel slapped the flat side of the ruler on the bench. "He set out to make you like him and he succeeded. He wants you to think *I'm* the one who's being unreasonable. And it worked—I can see it in your face."

Karina stopped short and stared incredulously at him. "Daniel Bowen, I think you're jealous!"

His eyes sparked, green lights glinting among the amber. For a split second she saw something else there, as well, something primal and dangerous she'd never imagined could be part of Daniel.

He flung the ruler onto the bench, where it landed with a tinny clatter. Body rigid, hands clenched, he moved toward her. Rooted to the spot, she waited, electrified.

He didn't stop until the tips of his shoes nudged the toes of hers. With his face scant inches away, the memory of yesterday's kiss hung in the air between them.

Air charged with a chemistry they could neither acknowledge nor deny.

"My brother has nothing I want," he said, his voice low and harsh. "Nothing." He spun on his heel and disappeared out the door into the night.

KARINA SAT AT the kitchen table trying to concentrate on Daniel's business cards instead of wondering if he was avoiding her. He'd been back from visiting his parents in Campbell River for two days now and she'd hardly seen or spoken to him. Of course, that could also be because *she* was avoiding *him.*

She'd been wrong to interfere, she could see that now. Well, from now on she'd butt out. Daniel was perfectly capable of sorting out his own problems. First he had to *acknowledge* them, but that wasn't her responsibility, either.

She was so absorbed in her thoughts she didn't notice he'd entered the room until he sat down at the table opposite her and the faint, woodsy scent of his aftershave made her look up.

"Hi," she said, and wondered what was coming.

"I owe you an apology," he began stiffly. "I ruined your dinner party."

"It's not me you should be apologizing to."

Daniel's expression hardened. "I'll be damned if I'll apologize to Brian."

Karina put down the pen she'd been using and chose another from her set, one with a finer point. "You just apologized to me for a far less serious reason."

She began to rule a narrow border around Daniel's company name, Bowen's Fine Furniture. "Are you going to feud for another ten years?"

Daniel tossed down the spoon he'd been playing with. "I don't want to talk about it."

She shrugged as though she didn't care, but she was disappointed in him. "It's your life. I'm sorry I interfered. It won't happen again."

"Look, just because I won't apologize doesn't mean I'm giving up on Brian. I'm going to drop in on him after he gets home from work. Maybe without an audience, he and I can cut through the BS and work out our differences."

There was hope for him yet, Karina thought. She chose a favorite shade of rich, red-brown for the border on his card. "I'm sure you can."

His brow cleared. "I need to ask you a favor."

She lifted her head, giving him her full attention. "What can I do?"

"Look after Natalie for a few hours. I'd rather not take her to Brian's with me."

"No problem. I'll take her grocery shopping, then we'll make dinner. It'll be fun."

"She's not used to eating late," he said, the frown reappearing. "Six o'clock is her usual dinnertime. She should be in bed by seven-thirty. No junk food or she'll be bouncing off the walls."

Karina lay down her pen and stretched her cramped fingers. "*Relax.* I can handle it." She spun the card around to show him what she'd done. "What do you think?"

He gazed at it a moment, then glanced at her. "It's good. I like it." He pulled it closer and studied it further. "I really like it. How did you know what a woolshed looks like?"

"You can find almost anything on the Internet."

"Is that so? Anyway, getting back to Natalie—she's

meeting her teacher tomorrow. I want her to be well rested.''

Karina smiled indulgently. Daniel was behaving like a typical nervous parent overprotecting his offspring. ''She'll be fine,'' she assured him. ''Don't worry about a thing.''

''LOOK, NATALIE, a fabric store.'' Karina tugged on the girl's hand to slow her headlong race down the sidewalk. ''Let's pop in here for a minute. We can get some material to make you a costume for Julie's party.''

Natalie bounced up and down in front of a large display of fabric rolls. ''Goody! I want to be a fairy princess.'' Then her little face puckered. ''Shouldn't we get the groceries first? Daddy always says we have to do our work before we get a treat.''

Karina laughed and waved her hand, silver bangles jangling merrily. ''That's an admirable sentiment and you should stick to that rule—most of the time. But making a fairy princess costume is very complicated. We have to decide all sorts of things, like whether your wand should be silver or gold, or if there should be sequins on the bodice or tiny pearls. How could we make important decisions if the ice cream was melting in the back of the car?''

''Gee, I guess we couldn't, but...'' Natalie had that glazed look Karina sometimes noticed on Daniel's face when she was trying to convince him of something.

''We've got plenty of time,'' Karina assured her. ''Don't worry about a thing.''

DANIEL GLANCED AT his watch with growing impatience. Six-thirty. He'd been sitting on this park bench across the road from Brian's apartment building for more than an hour.

He hoped Karina wouldn't wait dinner for him. And that she'd get Natalie to bed on time if he wasn't back. Maybe he should give her a call to remind her.

Rising, he walked a dozen paces in either direction along Dallas Road. Expensive homes and apartment buildings lined the scenic drive along the waterfront but there wasn't a phone booth in sight.

He resumed his seat on the bench and leaned back, eyes closed. Thoughts of Karina drifted through his head, the scent of her perfume mingling in his memory with the smell of sawdust. It wasn't the fight over Brian that occupied his mind, but the kiss they'd shared.

How they'd connected. Tighter than a dovetail, hotter than an arc light. He could still feel the softness of her hair as it drifted like heavy silk between his fingers. Could still see the troubled look in her eyes as she'd pulled away from him.

He might have bought her story about not wanting to get involved with a tenant if he wasn't so certain there was more to it than that. For instance, why didn't she have a boyfriend? A woman who looked like she did, who was as smart and funny and warmhearted as she was, ought to at least have a boyfriend.

Unless she was getting over one. But if so, why wasn't she all droopy and depressed?

Maybe it had to do with her coming birthday. The fact that her mother had been thirty-two when she'd died obviously held significance for Karina. Was *she* afraid of dying? So afraid she wouldn't let herself fall in love? Surely not. Karina *was* a bit capricious, but that didn't make her totally irrational.

Women could be funny about birthdays, but he didn't

think that usually happened until they hit forty or fifty. As though a few wrinkles or grey hairs mattered. As far as he was concerned, the older a woman got, the more interesting she became. More confident, more at ease with herself. More beautiful.

Was it possible for Karina to become more beautiful than she already was? Now there was an interesting conundrum....

Daniel sat upright with a jerk. A silver Jag had just pulled into the curb in front of the apartment building across the road. Shielding his face from the sun, he watched Brian get out of the car and go through the glass doors into the lobby.

He waited another ten minutes to give Brian time to settle in, then he crossed the road and found his brother's name on the directory. His hand hovered over the intercom button. What if Brian refused to let him in? No point taking a chance.

Daniel waited until a couple came out engrossed in conversation and slipped in through the open door.

Up the elevator, down the wide, carpeted hall he went, glancing at the numbered doors until he found Brian's apartment. He knocked. No answer. Shifting his feet impatiently, he lifted his hand to knock again.

The door swung open. Brian held a tumbler of dark amber liquid in his hand, and his eyebrows lifted in faint surprise. Daniel braced himself for harsh words.

Brian gave him the once-over, his lips pursed thoughtfully. Then he turned and walked back into the apartment. "Like a Scotch, Danny?"

"Thanks, I would." Daniel followed Brian inside.

At a side table in the living room, Brian dropped ice into another tumbler and poured out a healthy swig of Scotch. Daniel glanced around, surprised by the art deco furnishings and abstract paintings that adorned walls of deep Chinese red. Somehow he'd expected a lot of chrome and black leather furniture. But then again, most of his ideas about Brian were ten years out of date.

"Nice place," he commented as Brian handed him his drink. A triple, by the look of it.

"I like it. Bottoms up."

Daniel raised his glass in a brief salute and took a sip. The scotch, smooth and expensive, slid down his throat and warmed his empty stomach.

"Have a seat." Brian lowered himself into a chair and gestured to the sofa opposite. "We got off on the wrong foot, didn't we, Danny?"

Daniel sank onto the scallop-backed sofa that was covered in a dark paisley not unlike Karina's pig. "Maybe I was a little hotheaded—" He stopped, studying Brian's bland, good-natured face suspiciously. Was this some kind of trap? He wasn't going to give anything away until he knew where Brian was headed with this.

Brian leaned forward, his hands spread in a gesture of reconciliation. "I was out of line with those stories about the old days. I'm sorry, Dan, I really am."

"Why did you do it?" Daniel asked, still wary.

"I guess I was getting back at you for...Francine. We never really had it out over her." Frowning at his drink, Brian swirled the glass and set the ice tinkling.

Daniel gave a short laugh. "You mean it would have been better if we'd settled the matter with a fistfight? We still could."

Brian shook his head. "Not a chance. I've got twenty pounds on you, but they're pounds of lard, not muscle. No, I'd rather just put the past to rest. Let bygones be bygones. What do you say, Danny boy?"

"Sounds good to me." He was so pleased, he managed to ignore the hated nickname. Pleased but cautious. Feeling like Charlie Brown wondering if Lucy would whip the football out of reach before he could kick it, Daniel put out his hand to shake on it.

Brian took his hand and gripped it hard. A smile spread across his ruddy face. "I've been waiting for this moment for a long time."

Daniel grinned back. "I have, too."

Slowly, Daniel released his brother's hand, still hardly daring to believe in the change that had come over Brian. But there was no one else around to impress or mislead with a false show of brotherly love. He had to be sincere. Unless he had some hidden agenda....

Daniel dismissed that thought. Brian had simply had second thoughts about his hard-line approach. Hadn't he, himself, come here today prepared to bend a little? *Take Brian's gesture of peace at face value,* he told himself. *All that matters is that we're friends again.*

Daniel leaned forward, his drink cupped between his hands. "I drove up to see Mom and Dad this week. They're doing really well. Dad catches chinook salmon by the boatload, and Mom's busy canning them—when she's not planning their next trip, that is. They're going to Arizona in November—"

"I know." Brian rose abruptly and went to the side table. "I saw them last month. Before that, in March. In fact, I've seen them hundreds of times in the past ten years."

"Of course." Daniel sipped his scotch, chastened. "Mom asked me how we were getting along. She and Dad will be happy to hear we're on speaking terms again. Maybe next time we could go up together."

Brian glanced at him. "Freshen your drink?"

"I'm fine." Daniel watched his brother load his crystal tumbler with more ice while studiously ignoring Daniel's remarks. Was Brian afraid of losing face? Or showing too much emotion? Maybe it was better not to rush things. They couldn't just wipe out a decade of estrangement in an hour.

But they could chip away at it.

"Say, Brian, how about a little game of one-on-one someday? There's a high school with an outdoor basketball court not far from Karina's."

Brian set down the ice tongs and picked up the decanter. "Now there's an idea," he said, flashing a grin sideways at Daniel. "I haven't whupped you in ages."

Daniel felt the sting but he grinned back. "You always did run circles around me on the court, you old bastard."

Brian laughed. "That's because you never practiced." He poured the Scotch. There was a faint cracking sound as the warm liquid hit the ice.

Daniel shrugged. "I'm into sports more now—tennis, swimming, basketball. Keeps me in shape." He didn't bother to add he'd taken them up once Brian was no longer around to make him feel inadequate. "I guess I've changed."

Brian's smile faded as he subjected Daniel to silent scrutiny. "You've changed, all right, Danny boy," he said, a catch in his voice. "You're a grown man. A father. Damn lucky son of a bitch if you ask me." He turned away, placing the decanter unsteadily on the table.

Daniel stared back, guilt gnawing at his gut. If he hadn't taken Francine away from Brian, his brother might be the one with the child. The thought of not having Natalie pulled at Daniel's heart, fierce and sharp. If Brian felt a fraction of that...

He rose and put a hand on his brother's shoulder. "It's not too late, Brian. You're only, what…thirty-six? Plenty of time to marry and have kids."

Brian shrugged his hand away. "I'm getting old, Danny boy, set in my ways. But maybe…" He turned to Daniel, a spark in his pale blue eyes. "Do you believe in love at first sight?"

Karina's image flashed into his mind. "No," he said a little too quickly.

"Then you *have* changed," Brian said, eyeing him curiously. "Wasn't that how you and…Francine got together?"

Daniel hesitated. His reaction to Francine had been more like lust at first sight. But was there any point in adding insult to injury by giving Brian an accurate picture of the past? Every time his brother said her name he sounded as if he were in pain.

"Yeah, it was pretty much instantaneous." *A flash in the pan.* "I'm sorry about the way things turned out, Brian. Really sorry."

Brian gazed at him for a long moment, nodding slowly. "I'm not surprised you took to her right away. Francine was one hot babe. Although what she ever saw in *you* that *I* didn't have, I never could figure." Tilting his head back, he took a large swig of Scotch.

Daniel gripped his glass hard. He wouldn't ruin their truce by taking offense. To be fair, he'd wondered the same thing at the time. Brian had been the golden-haired boy in high school, and university had only enhanced his reputation. As captain of the basketball team and a track star, he'd attracted the prettiest and most popular girls in the school.

All that was ancient history. "So, what about that spin around the courts?" Daniel said. "Saturday morning?"

Brian's eyebrows rose. "Didn't Karina tell you? She and I are going golfing Saturday morning." He came forward and slapped Daniel on the shoulder. "You don't mind, do you, Danny, old boy? You did say she wasn't a girlfriend."

Daniel stared at him. Karina had refused to get involved with him, yet she'd made a date with his brother. It was only golf, he told himself. Not even something Karina liked to do.

"Mind?" Daniel replied, almost choking on the word. "Why should I mind?"

"I thought maybe you had designs on her yourself," Brian said, his gaze fixed on Daniel's face. "I wouldn't want to poach in your territory. Tell me to back off and I will."

What could he say? Whatever *his* feelings might be, Karina had let him know loud and clear that she wasn't interested in a romantic relationship. If the same applied to Brian, his brother would find out for himself. There was nothing to gain by staking a claim on Karina. And a hell of a lot to lose.

"We're just friends," he said at last. "Go for it."

# CHAPTER TEN

"TURN AROUND, Natalie, so I can see your wings properly."

From her perch on top of the coffee table, Natalie obediently spun on her tiptoes, spreading her arms in glee. Excitement dabbed her cheeks with pink, and her blue eyes sparkled. She looked like a tiny doll on top of a music box, and it made Karina laugh to see her so happy.

"Daddy's going to be so surprised!" Natalie chattered excitedly. "He's never seen me be a fairy princess before."

Karina laughed. "He'll be thrilled. You look absolutely beautiful. Whoops, your right wing is slipping. Hang on while I sew it back into place."

Natalie stood as still as a six-year-old fairy can stand, jiggling slightly in her nearly new, pink satin ballet slippers. The slippers were a real score, Karina thought as she made tiny, neat stitches through the silver gauze wing. They'd found them in a thrift shop next to the fabric store, along with the star for the top of the fairy wand.

"Are you liking it here in Canada, Natalie?" Karina asked through a mouthful of pins.

Natalie judiciously tipped her head to one side. "It's okay. I like your house." She turned her head and Karina could see her pixie face in profile. "I like *you*."

Her heart swelled until it felt too big for her chest. "Thanks," she managed to say casually. "I like you, too."

"And Daddy?"

Her response was a little slower in coming, but she replied, "Sure, I like your daddy, too."

"Good. 'Cause I asked him when I could have another mommy and he said when we both fell in love with the same person. I told him I wanted it to be you."

Karina almost choked. "What did he say?" She wasn't sure she wanted to know the answer, but to be forewarned was to be forearmed.

"He said you didn't want to fall in love." Natalie's round, blue eyes shone with curiosity. "Why not? Don't you want to wear a pretty white dress and have flowers in your hair and live happily ever after?"

"Gee, Natalie, all that sounds great, but there's more to marriage than the wedding day. Things don't always work out the way you expect or hope." Letting Daniel kiss her was even more irresponsible than she'd thought, Karina realized. Natalie could get hurt, too.

"If you change your mind, can I be a flower girl and wear my fairy costume?"

"Mmm," Karina murmured noncommittally, suppressing a smile. She jabbed the needle into a thick knot of fabric at the base of the wing and pushed hard.

Natalie's tummy growled. Karina winced as her conscience and the needle pricked her at the same time. They never had got around to grocery shopping. That tin of tuna was probably still in the cupboard, but it was a bit late to make a casserole now.

She tied off the knot and got to her feet. "Hey, Natalie, ever tried tuna-and-peanut-butter sandwiches?"

Natalie made a most unfairylike face. "Yuck!"

"Maybe you're right. Have another corn chip."

The little girl plunged her hand into the bag of chips on the coffee table. "Daddy never lets me eat snacks before dinner," she said, munching happily.

Karina's conscience gave another twinge. She'd promised to have dinner ready, and here it was... She glanced at the clock on the stereo.

Oh, no. Twenty minutes to eight.

"Come on, Nattie. We'd better put away this stuff and get you something decent to eat."

Spilling crumbs down her sequined bodice, Natalie crammed a last handful of chips into her mouth. "Mrs. Beeton wants Daddy to get married again, too," she confided.

Karina began picking scraps of fabric off the floor. "Ah, Mrs. Beeton. We'll have to make her a special dress for the wedding. Whenever that is," she added hastily. She'd forgotten for the moment there wasn't actually going to be a wedding.

"Mrs. Beeton doesn't need a dress," Natalie replied. "She wears heavenly rain-mints."

"Heavenly raiment?" In her surprise, Karina dropped a spool of thread and it rolled away under the sofa.

Natalie nodded. "Anyway, it doesn't matter what she wears, because no one can see her except me."

Karina got down on her hands and knees to retrieve the thread. "Isn't Mrs. Beeton a doll? I heard you talking to her in your room."

Natalie sighed with the exasperation of an intelligent child confronted with an unbelievably thickheaded adult. "Mrs. Beeton is an *angel*. Can I move now?"

"Whoa! Hold on there, Nattie. Mrs. Beeton is an *angel*?"

The girl nodded. "After Mommy died, Mrs. Beeton came down from heaven to look after me."

Stunned, Karina fell silent. The child's eyes were not alight with fantasy now. They were sober, pragmatic and tinged with a sadness that seemed far too great for her six years.

Karina searched Natalie's solemn little face, wishing she could say something to ease the child's pain. Wishing she could comfort her, let her know she wasn't alone in her suffering. But the thought of opening her own badly healed wound by telling Natalie about Mama made her heart recoil.

"Your daddy looks after you," she whispered at last, ashamed of her weakness. Though her words were true, they denied the gut-wrenching need the child had for her mother.

Natalie nodded, her mouth drooping at the corners. She turned her wand disconsolately in her fingers. Karina gazed at her sorrowfully. If only she could wave that magic wand and wish Natalie's mother back into existence. Why couldn't she say something, anything, that would help Natalie understand and accept her mother's death?

But how could she? She had little understanding and no acceptance in her own heart.

"You know what, Nattie," she said with a gentle smile. "Whenever I feel sad, I sing a silly song. It really works. Listen." She began to sing, "'Way down south where bananas grow, a bee stepped on an elephant's toe....'"

To her relief, a tiny smile appeared on Natalie's face.

"'The elephant cried with tears in his eyes...'"

Natalie's smile widened at Karina's exaggerated actions and grimaces. Encouraged, Karina got to her feet and grasped the girl's hands, spinning her around in a circle.

"'Pick on someone your own darn size!'"

Brandishing her wand, the girl marched up and down while Karina belted out the chorus.

"'Boom, boom, ain't it great to be crazy? Giddy and foolish all day long. Boom, boom, ain't it great to be cra-zy!'"

Natalie collapsed in a heap of giggles. Laughing along with her, Karina gathered her into a big hug and swung her around and around.

All at once she noticed they weren't alone.

DANIEL STARED AT Karina and Natalie, his troubles with Brian banished by shock. The living room looked as though a cyclone had hit. Snippets of muslin and satin were strewn everywhere, and drifts of the frothy material extended into the dining room. Scattered sequins winked up from the dark blue carpet along with bits of thread, bent coat hangers and lengths of ribbon and lace.

His gaze swept back to Natalie, taking in her flushed cheeks and wings knocked awry. And Karina. She might well look guilty, he thought, his mouth tightening. Natalie should have been in bed half an hour ago.

"Daddy!" Natalie leaped off the table and ran to his arms. "Look at the beautiful costume Karina made me." She pulled away again and capered around, springing on and off the coffee table like a baby goat.

"Get off the coffee table, Natalie."

"Karina said I could."

"*Get off the coffee table.*" He turned to Karina. "I didn't think I'd be this late," he said stiffly. "I hope you went ahead and had dinner without me."

"Er..." Karina's voice trailed away.

From the corner of his eye he saw her kick a corn-chip bag beneath the table.

"We haven't had dinner yet," Natalie chirped. "Do *you* like tuna-and-peanut-butter sandwiches, Daddy?"

Daniel grimaced in disbelief. "No dinner?" He looked at his watch. "You've been eating something, though, haven't you, Nattie?" He caught the girl as she swung by and stooped to inspect the yellow crumbs that dusted the front of her costume.

"Corn chips!" Natalie whirled out of his grasp. "'Way down south where bananas grow...'"

"I'm really sorry," Karina said quickly, sweeping fabric scraps off the floor and into her arms. "We got carried away. I'll make her a sandwich or something."

"'A bee stepped on an elephant's toe...'" Natalie sang blithely on, waving her magic wand.

"A sandwich?" Daniel repeated. "Surely you can do better than that with the groceries you bought?"

"'The elephant cried with tears in his eyes...'"

"Shh, Nattie," Karina said. "Not now. Your daddy's upset."

Instead of placating him, Karina's conspiratorial whisper fueled his anger. First, she hadn't told him about her golf game with Brian. Now she was siding with his daughter against him, making *him* look like the bad guy. Deep down, he knew he was judging too harshly, but at this moment, he was pretty much fed up with Karina Peterson.

"*I said,* what about the groceries?"

Karina shifted her glance back to him uneasily. "We didn't make it to the store on time."

Daniel squeezed his eyes shut and saw red. "What do you mean, you didn't—"

"'Pick on someone your own darn size!'"

"Natalie!" he bellowed. "Get upstairs and into your pajamas right this instant."

Natalie stopped singing abruptly, a stricken look on her face. She ran past him out of the room and up the stairs.

He turned to Karina. "You promised me you'd look after my daughter. That meant giving her dinner and tucking her into bed, not singing goddamn nursery rhymes till all hours of the night."

Karina let out an inappropriate burst of laughter. "I said I was sorry."

"I'm glad you think this is funny, because I don't. Sorry doesn't change a thing."

"Lighten up, Daniel," she said, not sounding sorry anymore. "It's not the end of the world if she doesn't eat on time for one night. She was having a ball till you came in doing your irate-father act."

"I've got a right to be angry. She was having a ball, all right. Bouncing off the walls. I *told* you that would happen if she didn't have a proper dinner."

Suddenly Natalie barreled back down the stairs, her pajama top only half buttoned. She pushed past Daniel and flung herself in front of Karina. "Don't yell at Karina. She's my friend and I love her."

"Oh, for Pete's sake!" He reached for his daughter, but she dodged away.

Dropping to her knees, Karina gathered Natalie into her arms. "Your father has a right to be angry, honey. I screwed up."

Fuming, Daniel watched impotently as Karina soothed Natalie. He couldn't help but notice the tenderness on Karina's face and his child's adoring response. And why shouldn't she be adoring? Karina had brought laughter and fun into her life. *And mine,* he thought, cursing himself for his misplaced anger. Did a missed meal really matter so much?

"Come on, Natalie," Karina said. "I'll make you some French toast."

"I'll do it." Daniel's voice was rough with emotion as he reached for Natalie's hand. He'd intended his words to be conciliatory, but Natalie burrowed deeper into Karina's arms.

Karina glared at him over Natalie's small blond head. "For heaven's sake, what difference does it make who feeds her?"

At that, the sobbing child wriggled free. "I'm not hungry!" Pushing away from both of them, she dashed out of the room and up the stairs. A second later, her door slammed shut.

Karina, her cheeks flushed and her mouth set in a grim line, silently began to gather up more scraps of muslin and lace.

Weary of it all, Daniel rubbed the back of his neck. "It's my fault for expecting too much. You couldn't know how important it is for a small child to get regular meals and plenty of rest. How could you? You're not a mother."

To his astonishment, Karina, who'd held up to his angry onslaught like a soldier, suddenly slumped as though he'd hit her. Tears welled in her eyes, spilled over and coursed down her cheeks.

"Daniel Bowen, you're an absolute pig!" Dropping the armload of fabric, she pushed past him and ran from the room.

Daniel stared after her in shocked silence. Overhead, her door slammed and he flinched. Now what had he done?

His stomach growled with hunger and his brother's

Scotch curdled his insides like acid, but he walked straight through the kitchen and out the back door. *Tuna-and-peanut-butter sandwiches, for crying out loud.*

He entered the garage, giving the hood of Karina's red sports car a frustrated thump with his fist as he went past.

Pieces of her dining room table were propped against the wall waiting to be put together. He ignored them and crossed to a steamer trunk tucked beneath the work bench. Lifting the heavy lid, he reached in and pulled out a large box wrapped in felt. He placed the box on the bench and threw back the wrapper.

Daniel ran his fingers over the smooth, black-brown ebony wood, admiring the way the lamp's beam brought out glints of auburn from deep within the grain. It reminded him of Karina's hair.

Once or twice he'd caught a glimpse of her dresser through her open bedroom door. Invariably, a pile of bracelets and necklaces spilled out of a pitifully inadequate pink container. A jewelry box, he'd decided, would make the perfect birthday gift.

He swung a leg over the high wooden stool and scooted it closer to the bench. Reaching for a fresh sheet of sandpaper, he started to rub the long edge of the piece of wood that was to become the lid. It was painstaking work, making small items, and he rarely did it. He wasn't entirely sure why he was doing it now.

Letting Natalie get close to Karina had been a mistake. Though how he could have prevented it, living in the same house, he didn't know. In hindsight, it was no wonder she'd bonded so quickly; Karina was a natural with children.

Soon his fingers and the lid were covered with fine dark dust. He prided himself on being a good communicator but he'd failed miserably tonight, letting his rivalry with Brian get the better of him. Images from the night of the dinner party came back with agonizing clarity. Karina's voice saying, *"Brian is perfectly charming,"* Karina's smiling eyes gazing into his brother's...

She'd said she didn't want to get involved with anyone. Maybe what she'd really meant was she didn't want to get involved with *him.* She was so kindhearted she might have merely wanted to save his pride.

Brian could give her something she needed. Daniel didn't think for a second she would deliberately use anyone, but common interests often led to stronger emotions. And if there was an attraction there to begin with...

The thought of Brian and Karina together made him grip the sandpaper hard between his fingers. Thousands of tiny grains of silica bit into his skin.

Pushing the thought from his head, he rasped at the hard black wood as if he could reduce his feeling of déjà vu to dust along with the rough edges of the jewelry box. That his brother was infatuated with Karina wasn't hard to understand—Daniel was equally infatuated.

But were his feelings for her strong enough to justify tampering with Brian's happiness *again?* He wanted her, there was no doubt about that. He liked her enormously, no question there, either, despite what had happened tonight. He admired her, respected her....

Was that love?

The thought of competing with Brian over a woman was unpalatable. He'd lived with the consequences of winning once before and it hadn't been worth the prize. But, then, the prize hadn't been Karina.

Daniel slid off the stool and paced the length of the garage to the open door. Looking out and up, he could see the light in her bedroom window. As he watched, her silhouette appeared behind the drawn curtains. His breath caught in his throat as she raised her arms and drew her dress over her head.

He turned away, his heart pounding.

KARINA LEANED AGAINST the door she'd just slammed shut. Eyes closed, she took in great gulps of air, forcing her tears under control. Tears couldn't make Daniel take back his words or change the truth of them.

It *was* true: she wasn't a mother. How could she know what a child needed, really? Oh, she was very good at playing with children; she'd had plenty of experience with Joanne's kids. She knew what they liked, how they thought. Sometimes she suspected that was because she was still a bit of a kid herself.

But her feelings toward Natalie were different. Something in the little girl struck a chord so deep it sometimes seemed as though she were reliving her own childhood. So much life and laughter, fun and silliness. Karina smiled at the memory of Natalie standing on the coffee table, singing at the top of her lungs.

Nattie was good at drawing and artwork, too. Daniel deserved a lot of credit for encouraging the girl's creative energy to bloom and grow. She'd never seen such an imaginative child—

Karina pushed away from the door. Should she speak to Daniel about Mrs. Beeton? Did she have the right? After tonight, he might not want her to have anything to do with Natalie.

No, surely he wouldn't be so unkind. But maybe he wasn't worried about Mrs. Beeton. *Was* it a worry? Or was it perfectly natural?

Karina remembered how she'd sunk into a fantasy

world for a while after Mama died. A world where
Mama magically reappeared and they were all happy
again. Of course, she'd known all the time it couldn't
really happen. How much of what Natalie pretended did
she think was real? Did it matter?

Karina wandered restlessly over to her dresser and
halfheartedly tried to tidy her jewelry box. She might
not be able to solve the problem of Mrs. Beeton, but she
could, she *must* deal with her own behavior. She rarely
lost confidence in her abilities, but tonight she had.

When Daniel had reminded her of the importance of
giving Natalie dinner on time, she'd thought he was just
being overprotective. But what if he'd seen something
lacking in her? Something that made her incapable of
handling the mundane but essential aspects of child care,
like proper food and rest. He'd worried but he'd trusted
her anyway.

And she'd let him down.

Karina jammed the lid on the jewelry box and pushed
it away, its contents still jumbled, like her thoughts. She
reached for a folding pewter frame, half hidden behind
a ceramic oil lamp.

Her mother and father on their wedding day. Her
mother smiled out of the photo, darkly beautiful in heavy
ivory satin. She held a bouquet of deep red roses the
color of her lips and the fainter bloom on her cheeks.

*Mama, I'm a failure.*

The idea came out of nowhere. Caught by surprise,
hot tears pricked the backs of her eyes. With a sharp
intake of breath, she blinked them away, but she couldn't
stem the agonized thoughts that crowded her mind.

*Yes, Mama, you heard me right. I was only half grown
when you died. You never finished teaching me. Look at*

*me now. I can't cook, I can't clean. I can't even take
care of one little girl.*

Sometimes she felt as if she'd never grown up. Never
*would* grow up. A chunk of her life was missing, the
part where she was supposed to follow her mother's
footsteps into womanhood. Instead, she'd made the jour-
ney with no one to guide her, blindly muddling through
the long years from thirteen to thirty-two.

*But you run a whole art department,* a voice in her
head protested. *You're one of the best graphic artists
around. You know the business like nobody else. Not
only that, but everyone likes you. People give their best
for you.*

Karina pushed the voice away. None of that was
enough if she wasn't capable of committing herself to a
man and bearing his children.

She folded her arms around her waist and hugged herself hard. For a little while today she'd been able to
pretend Natalie was her own daughter. It had been such
a good feeling, so full of joy. So *right.* Like the way
she'd felt in Daniel's arms.

Two fat tears squeezed out of her tightly clenched
eyes and rolled down her cheeks. It frightened her how
good the two of them made her feel—Natalie greeting
her with a hug and a kiss, the sound of Daniel's power
saw making a man's place in her home. For the first
time in what seemed like forever, she felt part of a family. She'd never realized until now how deeply lonely
she was. Or how big the gaping hole in her life that
friends and work just couldn't fill.

Sadly she folded shut the wedding photo and replaced
it on the dresser, then crossed to the window to peer
through the sheers. Cool night air curled through the

small space at the bottom of the window where she'd wedged it open with a hairbrush.

The light was still on in the garage. Daniel was out there now. Karina pulled down the blind and turned away.

A multicolored silk shawl with a long crimson fringe lay draped over the back of a chair. She wrapped it around herself, breathing in the scent of gardenia that was more memory than fragrance. And thought of the last time she'd seen her mother wearing it.

It was after Mama had been diagnosed but before all the really bad stuff started. They'd sat at the table in the meals area one sunny winter afternoon drinking cup after cup of milky tea and going over old photos. Mama was writing dates and names on the back.

She'd started by telling Karina about her childhood in Italy and ended up recounting every funny thing she could remember Karina doing as a child. Some of it had sounded pretty stupid, but Mama had laughed and laughed.

Karina spun on her heel and paced. She should stop remembering now. She felt the warning tightness in her chest, the pricking behind the eyes. She tried to think of something else, but the memories wouldn't disappear. Her mother's image, dark eyes alight and teasing, wouldn't fade....

Desperate, Karina reached for the radio beside her bed and turned up the volume. The ringing tones of a steel band blasted out at her. But even that wasn't enough to escape her thoughts. Forcing her mouth into a soundless O, she blew. Nothing happened.

Heart pounding, she licked her dry lips and blew again, her hands over her ears to shut out the sound of her mother's laughing, loving voice.

A thin, cracked whistle squeaked past her lips. With a rush of relief, she gasped for another breath. Tunelessly at first, then louder, more melodic, she blew until she was whistling in time with the music. Blanking her mind from taboo thoughts of warmth and love and happiness.

Slowly Karina began to breathe normally again. Now she could feel the Caribbean beat right inside her chest, drowning out the pathetic thumping of her heart.

Safe inside the cocoon of music, she flung off the shawl and pulled her dress over her head. Then she crawled into bed to lie curled on her side, arms tucked into her chest, eyes squeezed shut against the darkness.

# CHAPTER ELEVEN

ON THE CLIFF TOP golf course at Gonzales Point, Karina paused to admire the view. Across the Strait of Juan de Fuca, the Olympic Mountains soared, their white peaks etched against the clear blue sky.

With an effort, she dragged her gaze back to the small white ball on the tee in front of her. Planting her feet firmly, she adjusted her grip and waggled the club experimentally.

"Keep your arms loose," Brian coached. He'd already teed off at the men's platform, and his ball had gone zinging out of sight down the fairway. "Now, raise the club, ready to swing."

Karina dutifully did as he said. Club poised on high, she peered down the fairway, trying to remember everything he'd told her about wrists, elbows, knees.

"Ready?" he said. "Swing!"

She swung the club downward. *Whack!* The golf ball soared into the air, sailed down the fairway....

And landed thirty feet away.

"It's okay," Brian assured her as he jogged out to retrieve the ball. "Happens to everyone. Now if this were a *real* game, you wouldn't get another chance unless your co-workers are so chauvinistic they'd offer the little lady another turn."

"I doubt it," Karina replied. "Not that I'd take it even

if they did. I've got to compete fair and square or I'll lose all credibility.''

Brian replaced the ball on the tee. ''This time, keep your eyes on the ball as your club connects with it. Think of it as your boss's head if that helps.''

Karina laughed. Her smile faded as she realized whose head she'd like to be whacking a couple of hundred yards down the fairway. She wasn't trying to make Daniel jealous, but he might have looked a *little* put out when Brian had come to pick her up.

Instead he'd nonchalantly poured Brian a coffee and said how nice it was for Karina to have an expert teach her the game. He'd even come to the door to see them off, cheerfully bidding her to have a good time.

Focusing on the ball at her feet, Karina adjusted her grip. It had been almost as though Daniel were officially handing her over to his brother, for heaven's sake. He'd kissed her once and regretted it. Well, that was fine. More than fine, it was great.

''Karina?''

Shaking the hair out of her eyes, she glanced over her shoulder at Brian. From his quizzical expression she realized she must have been glaring at the ball for some time.

''Sorry.'' She swung her club back, high above her head. Nobody kissed *her* and regretted it. Down came the swing and—*thwack!*—the ball went flying.

''Fantastic!'' Brian gazed down the fairway, one hand shading his eyes. ''I can't even see it. You're going to knock 'em dead at the tournament.''

Karina turned to grin at him. She was actually having fun. Brian tended to be a little condescending, but for the most part he was good company, and he certainly knew golf.

Swinging her club over her shoulder, she joined him for the walk to find their balls. With his caddy trailing behind him, Brian looked every inch the serious golfer from his white cleated shoes to the pale blue polo shirt that perfectly matched his eyes.

He laid his hand lightly on her shoulder, and a faint echo of the attraction she felt for Daniel prevented her from ducking away.

"I hope you don't really believe what you said about everyone competing fair and square," he said.

She glanced sideways at him and was surprised to see he was serious. His hand began to feel heavy on her shoulder. "I said *I* would compete fairly. I'm not naive enough to think everyone does."

"Good," he replied with a nod. "Like Daniel said, you've got to watch your back. Just when you think people are playing by the rules, wham, somebody sneaks up from behind and sticks a knife into you."

Karina frowned at the note of bitterness in his voice. He wasn't talking about golf, or even business. He was talking about Daniel and what had happened with Francine. But she was *not* going to interfere again, so she just said, "Sometimes circumstances overwhelm even the best of us."

Brian directed his gaze ahead. "People create their own circumstances centered around personal gain. You can't trust anyone."

This was too much. She bent to tie a shoelace that didn't need tying, and when she straightened, her shoulder was free.

"I disagree," she said. "How people treat you is a reflection of how *you* treat *them*. And if you're too busy watching your back, you can't go forward, let alone mend fences."

He cast her a faintly sardonic smile, then continued up the fairway. "In high school," he went on as smoothly as if he weren't changing the subject, "I was good at sports but Daniel was always the popular one with the girls."

An image flashed through Karina's mind of Daniel as a lanky teenager casually leaning against a row of lockers, hands in his back pockets as he smiled his slow smile at some sweet, young thing. She nodded. Yes, she could see that.

Brian cast her a brief, assessing glance. "Sometimes it seemed as though he had all the prettiest girls eating out of his hand. He was always the smart one, you see. Girls like that."

"Come on, Brian," Karina protested. "You're an attractive man. You must have had plenty of girlfriends." It seemed to her the two brothers should have complemented each other rather than compete, but she had enough experience with her own brother to know that siblings didn't always see things logically.

Brian smiled, charming and modest. "You're sweet to say so. But I was involved in so many sports I didn't have as much time as he did to cultivate a social life."

"Did you resent Daniel for that?" Karina asked, wondering where all this was leading. She glanced ahead for her golf ball and thought she could see it lurking at the edge of the fairway a hundred yards or so away.

Again the tiny smile. "How could I help it? But we were friends, too. So I hid it as best I could." Brian looked up at the sky and sighed. "When I met Francine, it was love at first sight. I'd gone away to Vancouver to attend university and I was glad Danny had decided to stay in Victoria. You see..."

Karina glanced at his troubled expression. "Go on."

"I was afraid she'd take one look at Danny and leave me for him." Brian suddenly strode off to the right. "Here's your ball. A nine iron would be best for this shot."

Karina hurried to catch up. "Thanks," she said, taking the club from him. "Which way is the green?"

Brian pointed her in the right direction and she hit the ball, less successfully this time. She was more interested in hearing Brian's version of the story than in improving her handicap. But Brian fell silent as they walked over to his ball. There, he took his time sorting through his clubs and testing his swing. At last he raised his club and, with a short, sharp smack, sent the ball up and onto the green.

They walked off again in search of Karina's ball. "Daniel told me he met Francine at your parents' house," she said, unable to contain her curiosity any longer.

"That's right. I brought her home to meet the family once we were officially engaged. I was so happy she'd actually accepted me." A frown appeared on his brow. "I don't know if I've ever been quite that happy again."

Karina's ball rested a scant inch inside a sand trap. Brian pulled a club out of his golf bag, but instead of handing it to her, he gripped it hard with both hands.

"Even the prospect of running into Danny didn't faze me. But the moment he walked into the living room and I saw him look at Francine, I knew he was going to make a play for her."

"That must have been dreadful!" Karina exclaimed. "I can't believe Daniel could be so insensitive." Whose story came closer to the truth, she wondered, Daniel's or Brian's?

Brian's mouth twisted into a grimace. "Sorry if I've

destroyed any illusions you may have had about him. I'd hoped he'd changed over the years, but when we met at your house, well…he was just as antagonistic toward me as ever."

*That* was certainly true. "Francine obviously wasn't worth your heartache if she could fall in love with someone else so easily."

"That's what I tried to tell myself. But Danny can charm the birds out of the trees when he puts his mind to it."

His gaze became assessing again. Karina shifted uncomfortably. He was probably trying to figure out just how charmed she was herself.

"He's a nice guy," she said. Feeling a flush creep up her neck, she bent her head and nudged at the ball with her toe.

"Ah, ah, ah," Brian remonstrated gently. "Play it where it lies." He handed her the club. "Try to give it some lift."

Karina nodded, swung, hit the ball and managed to bury it deeper in the sand. "Shoot."

Brian came round behind her. "May I?" he murmured. Before she could answer, he'd reached around her waist and clasped his hands over hers.

His breath tickled the back of her ear and his heavy aftershave clogged her nostrils, making it difficult to breathe. Brian swung their arms back and up. She felt awkward and claustrophobic, as though trapped in someone else's body. She gave up trying to concentrate on the game and simply let him make the swing, resisting the impulse to wriggle free the moment the club made contact with the ball.

"Wonderful," Brian said, still holding her in his arms for the follow-through.

Karina kept her eyes on the ball, though it had long since stopped moving. Gently she tried to pull away, but his grip tightened and he turned her in his arms to face him. His eyes were very blue and filled with an admiration she suspected had nothing to do with her golfing ability.

Before she had a chance to draw back, he was kissing her, his lips cool and moist. Time didn't stop; it didn't even slow down. It was simply unendurable. Struggling, she raised her hands and pushed on his chest to create a space between them.

"Ah, ah, ah," she said, waggling a finger under his nose. "We agreed this was a business arrangement."

Brian released her with an expression of regret. "Is it because of Daniel?"

"No." She spoke too quickly, then cursed herself for sounding unconvincing.

"Because I thought perhaps you and he..." Brian's gaze probed relentlessly.

"No," she repeated, impatient now with his prying. "We're just friends."

In silence, they walked the rest of the way to the putting green. Brian's ball rested halfway between the hole and the edge of the closely trimmed circle of grass.

Karina watched Brian line up his shot. He took an experimental swing to one side of the ball, then raised his arms for the final stroke. Something about his attitude toward Daniel didn't quite mesh with the facts.

"So, Brian, do you still hate Daniel?"

Strangled sounds of a colorful nature issued from Brian's mouth as his ball zipped past the flag a foot wide of the mark. His naturally florid complexion turned a darker shade of red.

"Karina," he said, coming up to her and putting a

hand on her arm, "I don't hate Daniel. He's my *brother*."

"But you said—"

"I said I *resented* him. A very different thing from hate. Very different."

"Maybe I overstated the case."

"Besides, that was all in the past," Brian declared, giving her arm a little squeeze. "Now I want nothing more than to regain Daniel's trust."

Karina's eyes narrowed slightly. Brian seemed just a little too earnest. And surely it was Daniel who needed to regain his brother's trust? "Why didn't you try to get in touch with him all those years?"

Brian shrugged. "At first I was too angry. Later, when I'd cooled down, he, or I, made one move too many and we lost contact. I could have got his address from my parents, but I guess I was just too proud."

Karina nodded. That tallied with Daniel's story.

She turned away, feeling suddenly weary. Lately she was spending too much time at the office trying to stay out of Daniel's way. The early mornings and late nights were catching up with her.

Raising her arms in a prolonged stretch, she gazed upward, tracking a soaring bald eagle across the blue bowl of the sky. Abruptly she dropped her arms, pinpricks of excitement making goose bumps on her bare skin.

She knew how she wanted to celebrate her birthday.

KARINA ROCKED BACK in her office chair, enjoying the look of surprise on Ross Preston's face. It made him resemble a startled hedgehog.

"You're going to the golf tournament?" he exclaimed, jumping to his feet. With nowhere to pace in her cluttered office, he quickly sat down again, causing the guest chair to creak in protest. "But that's imposs—I mean, how did you manage that?" His small eyes narrowed to slits.

Karina waved her hand airily. "A friend of mine happens to be going and invited me along as his guest. *And* he's giving me golf lessons so I'll be able to keep up with you boys."

"Well, that's just fine, Karina. Just fine." Ross pushed a pudgy hand through his porcupine hair and got to his feet. "May the best man—ha, ha, *person*—win."

Karina smiled graciously and accepted his insincere good wishes with a mocking lift of her eyebrows.

*She already has, Ross, she already has.*

Karina's sense of victory lasted only until Ross ambled out of her office. Then she sank into her computer chair, oddly deflated. She was losing her appetite for the battle. Or maybe the battle didn't seem worth the effort anymore.

Just then, a frizzy blond head peered around the door. Karina spun away from the computer. "Joanne! What are you doing here?"

"Taking you to lunch." Joanne dropped into the guest chair Ross had just vacated. "Am I exhausted! I've been shopping all morning for Julie's party. Hats, streamers, balloons, paper plates, napkins... You wouldn't believe the junk. Of course, Julie wants everything decorated with pictures of some cartoon superbimbo that looks like a cross between Barbie and Attila the Hun."

She burrowed in a large plastic bag and brought out a package of colorful paper plates. "Look at that. I swear it's Pamela Anderson on steroids. Karina, you made a wise decision not to have children. They bleed you dry."

Karina managed a tight smile. "It's worth it to see them happy, isn't it?"

Joanne shoved the plates back into the bag. "Yeah. Don't mind me. I'm just complaining, as usual." Then she glanced at Karina in surprise. "Don't tell me you're coming around to the idea of having kids?"

Karina turned back to the computer screen. "Of course not." She positioned the mouse on the curving line of a hot air balloon, clicked and pulled. Instantly the balloon grew a bulge in its side.

"Darn," she muttered. "Now it's turned into a pumpkin." She pulled the line of the balloon back in with the mouse, adjusting it until it looked just right.

Joanne leaned over to look at the screen. "What's this, a sign for a sporting goods store?"

Karina shook her head. "It's an invitation to my birthday celebration."

Joanne sat up in her chair. "You're having a party after all! Oh, Karina, I'm so glad. What a fabulous idea. I'll make you a cake and some appetizers—"

"Slow down, Jo." Karina saved the image on the screen and turned to her friend. "I'm not having a real party. Not one with people and cakes and things, anyway. It's Daniel's idea of a birthday celebration."

"Daniel? Does this mean you two are back on speaking terms? From what you said about your costume-making session with Natalie, it sounded like things were pretty tense around your house."

"They are. The funny thing is, I don't think it's just about keeping Natalie up too late without her dinner."

"I'll bet he's annoyed that you're playing golf with Brian," Joanne said. "And that just proves how much he likes you."

Karina shook her head. "When Brian came to pick

me up, Daniel acted like he couldn't care less. Now, he— Oh, never mind. I don't know what's going on these days.''

Joanne shrugged. "Then don't worry about it. Tell me more about this birthday celebration.''

"Daniel's idea is for me to do something on my birthday I've never done before. You know, keep life interesting.''

"Your life isn't interesting? Tell me another one.''

"It is, but... I've been having a problem dealing with this particular birthday because, well, you know....'' Karina pushed a hand through her hair. "Anyway, I thought of something I've always wanted to do—hot air ballooning.''

"Ballooning! Fantastic!'' Joanne stretched out her long legs, and her parcels fell over like dominoes.

"In a way it'll be a gift for my mother, as well. She had a fear of flying. Maybe she'll look down on me from wherever she is and see it isn't so bad after all.''

"You'll have a great time,'' Joanne said, propping up her bags again. "I've always wanted to go ballooning myself.''

Karina scrolled through the list of type faces until she found the one she wanted, and began to type in the invitation. "Good, because you're coming. The balloon can hold four people besides the operator—you, me, Daniel and Natalie.''

"I'd love to. But wouldn't it be more fun if I took care of Natalie, and you and Daniel went alone?''

"No, it would not,'' Karina said firmly. "Quit it, Joanne. Daniel and I are just friends.''

"But he kissed you. He wouldn't have kissed you if he wasn't interested.''

Karina groaned. Why had she ever told Joanne about

that day in the garage? "Well, he's been avoiding me ever since. And that's fine by me, because anything else is just too complicated."

Joanne shook her head. "*Life* is complicated, Karina. Get used to it. Now, how about lunch? You can tell me all about your golf date with Brian."

Karina shut down the computer and reached for her purse. "It wasn't a *date.*"

Ignoring her, Joanne carried on with her flight of fantasy. "You'll have the two of them fighting over you before it's over, see if you don't."

"The last thing I want is for Daniel and Brian to fight over me."

"But it's so exciting."

"*Joanne...*"


"THE WINGS AREN'T sparkly enough," Karina said, gazing critically at her handiwork. Julie's party was less than an hour away and she wanted Natalie's costume to be perfect.

Daniel lowered the newspaper with a rustle and gave the wings a cursory glance. "They look fine to me," he said, and went back to perusing the Want Ads.

"Yes, but you're no expert on fairy princesses. We've established that."

Karina reached for the tube of glue. She and Daniel had achieved a shaky truce on the subject of costume design, with Daniel agreeing to give Karina free rein as long as Natalie didn't miss any more meals in the process.

Which was okay by her, Karina thought, daubing more glue on the wings. From now on she would stick to what she knew best. "Where's Natalie?" she asked, glancing at Felix the Clock.

"Brushing her teeth." Daniel folded the paper neatly and laid it aside with a stifled yawn. "Not a single house for rent in Oak Bay this month. And I even hung out at the *Victoria Times* building at dawn with the rest of the desperadoes."

"Gee, that's too bad." She cast him a sympathetic glance.

He was silent a moment. "Karina?"

"Mmm?" she replied, tapping the end of a vial to sprinkle flecks of gold glitter randomly over the gauze.

"There's something I've been meaning to ask you."

Karina looked up, mildly surprised. Daniel didn't usually preface his speech with pointless remarks. "What is it?"

He leaned forward, elbows on the table, and rubbed his thumb around the rim of his coffee cup. "Why didn't you tell me you were going out with Brian last Saturday?"

She blinked. So Joanne was right. The golf date *had* bothered him. Laying the vial of glitter on the table, she searched his eyes for a clue to his state of mind.

At that moment a shriek came from the second floor. Daniel jumped to his feet. "Natalie!"

Karina ran after him as he raced up the stairs. Natalie banged open the door of the bathroom, her fairy skirts billowing, her blue eyes wide.

Daniel gripped her by the shoulders, halting her head-long flight. "Nattie, what is it?"

"I'm sorry," she wailed. "All I did was flush some tissues, then I was going to go pee, but the water came *out* of the toilet instead of going down." She burst into tears. "I didn't mean to!"

"It's not your fault, Nattie," Karina said. She stood on her tiptoes in the bathroom doorway and leaned across the spreading water to pull a towel off the rack and throw it onto the floor.

"Stay out of the way, Nattie," Daniel ordered. "I'll see if I can fix it."

"But, Daddy," Natalie cried, her legs writhing together. "I need to go!"

"Just hang on."

Karina skated the towel over the floor with her feet, soaking up the water. "Hand me another towel," she said as Daniel appeared in the doorway. "I *did* tell you."

"What?" He passed her a towel. "Oh, you mean Brian. Have you got a plunger? Or a plumber's snake?"

"The plunger's behind the toilet but we won't need it. This has happened before. Don't worry, I can fix it." She shuffled over to the vanity and pulled a wrench from the bottom shelf.

Before she could use it, Daniel picked up the plunger and went to work on the toilet. "It's not that I mind you seeing him," he continued. "You're a—"

"I told you, I know how to fix this," she interrupted, alarmed at the ripples in the full toilet bowl caused by Daniel's energetic plunging. "It happens all the time."

"—free agent," Daniel concluded, clearly not listening. "Damn, something must be stuck down there."

"Free agent?"

"Yes. You have a perfect right to see whomever you please. In fact, Brian is probably just your type—outgoing, interested in art...."

*Free agent?* How could that be when her heart was hopelessly bound to Daniel's? "What makes you think something's going on between Brian and me?" she demanded. "And how dare you presume to know what kind of man is my *type?*"

"Did you say you have a snake?"

"Just exactly what's bothering you?"

"Da-addy," Natalie wailed. "I need to go *badly*."

Karina glanced at Natalie, hopping about the landing, and bit back a smile. She didn't quite fit the image of a delicate fairy flitting from tulip to columbine, but she was the cutest little improbable being Karina'd ever seen.

"I know, sweetheart," Daniel said to his daughter through clenched teeth. "I'm working on it as fast as I can."

He glanced up at Karina, a streak of dust smeared across the bridge of his nose and down his cheek. "You want to know what's bothering me? I think you didn't tell me because you assumed I couldn't take it. You thought I'd be jealous."

Impatiently Karina shook her head. "He called me at work on Thursday. That night I went out for dinner with some of the guys from the department and didn't get home till late. But on Friday night I mentioned our golf date to you. I'm absolutely positive I did. Well, practically positive."

"You don't have to explain," Daniel muttered, and thrust down hard on the plunger.

Water poured over the rim of the toilet onto the floor. Karina leaped back onto the sodden towels. "Would you let me get in there for a second? If you didn't want an explanation, then why bring it up?"

"*Da-addy!*"

"Hold on, honey," Karina said, reaching out to give Natalie's head a quick caress. "When your daddy's finished messing around, I'll have this fixed in a jiffy."

Daniel straightened abruptly. "Maybe one of your neighbors has a snake."

She jammed her hands onto her hips and glared at

him. *"You're not listening to me!* We don't need a snake! And I wasn't trying to hide anything."

The instant the words were out of her mouth, she wondered if they were really true. Maybe subconsciously she *had* avoided the subject for fear the news would deepen the rift between Daniel and his brother. She saw Daniel's mouth tighten and knew he'd seen her uncertainty. *Damn.*

An agonized moan from Natalie galvanized her into action. Shouldering Daniel aside, she hefted the wrench in her right hand. "Excuse me."

"You can't fix it with *that.*"

Ignoring him, Karina crouched down and tapped out the rhythm of an old tune on the pipe. "'Shave and a haircut, two bits—'"

"That won't work," Daniel said scornfully. "You need to get down past the *S* bend and unblock it."

"Trust me," she replied. "I know this toilet like…like I know this toilet."

"I'm telling you—" He broke off as the standing water in the porcelain bowl let out a loud gurgle and swirled down the pipe. He stared at her incredulously. "How did you do that?"

"I told you, this has happened before. I hit upon the solution—if you'll pardon the pun—quite by accident. Works every time. It must be the specific vibrations set up by that tune."

Daniel rolled his eyes. "It's a fluke, is what it is. You should get a plumber in to find out what's causing the blockage."

"I just fixed it!"

"Yes, but for how long?" His mouth twisted sarcastically. "Oh, I forgot. You're not into long-term solutions."

"Ouch. Is that the thanks I get—"

"Da-addy!" Natalie cried, hunched over in distress. "Can I go now?"

"Of course, Nattie," Karina said. "We'll get out of here right away." She pushed Daniel out of the bathroom before her, scooping up wet towels as she went.

Shutting the door behind her, she smiled at the sound of tiny staccato footsteps followed by a tinkle and an audible sigh of relief. Karina gave herself a mental pat on the back, partially vindicated for her shortcomings as a surrogate mom.

Downstairs Daniel went to the kitchen sink to wash his hands. "I'm still going to call a plumber," he said to her. "You can't leave a thing like that for long or you'll end up with real problems."

"But—"

"I'll pay for half the bill."

"It's not the money." She opened the door to the basement and heaved the towels in a long arc down the stairs to land neatly in the laundry basket at the bottom.

Daniel's eyebrows disappeared into the lock of hair that fell over his forehead. "You're unbelievable, you know that? A real nutcase."

"I am not a nutcase. I'm capricious, remember?" Karina joined him at the sink and rubbed soap over her hands. "And, Daniel, you've simply got to stop being so paranoid about Brian. I did not intentionally keep my golf date a secret."

Daniel dried his hands with brooding thoroughness. Finally he sighed. "All right. I guess I knew that, deep down. You're not deceptive and you have nothing to hide. Do me a favor and forget what I said."

Karina stared at him. Two minutes ago he'd mistrusted and maligned her. But she accepted the towel he held out to her and began to dry her hands. Maybe it would be better to forget his accusations. "You never did tell me how your visit to Brian went. Are you two any closer to sorting things out?"

Daniel leaned against the counter. "We're getting there. We talked about Francine and—" He paused abruptly. "Brian didn't come right out and say all was forgiven but he's willing to let bygones be bygones."

Karina started to throw the towel on the counter, thought better of it, and hung it neatly on the stove handle. "That's great. So, why don't you look happy?"

He shook his head, frowning. "Brian doesn't forgive and forget that easily. Once, when we were kids, I accidentally broke a model car of his. He held a grudge for years."

"So? What's that got to do with now?"

Daniel pushed away from the counter. "I just can't get it out of my head that he's got a hidden agenda."

Meaning *her?* She wasn't stepping into that one for all the noodles in China. "I'll forget everything you said in the bathroom on one condition."

"What's that?"

"*You* forget about calling a plumber."

Daniel turned to face her, hands on his hips. "What kind of condition is that? There's no connection between the toilet and your relationship with Brian."

Karina raised an eyebrow. "The connection is between the toilet and your *interpretation* of my relationship with Brian."

"But— Oh, all right. We'll let it go at that—*for now.* Just tell me one thing. What do you have against plumbers?"

"Nothing. But if the toilet is fixed properly, my technique might not work the next time it floods."

His eyes widened. "Karina," he said in a strangled voice. "That doesn't make a particle of sense."

She would have tried to explain it to him, but her eye caught the movement of Felix's longest hand as it ticked from one minute to the next. "The party!"

She ran off down the hall. "Hurry up, Natalie. It's almost time to go," she yelled from the bottom of the stairs. "Do you need any help?"

"I'm all right," Natalie yelled back. "Are my wings done?"

"They're almost dry. Come on down when you're ready and I'll pin them on."

"Okay."

Karina hurried back into the kitchen. Daniel's arms were crossed over his chest, and disapproval glared like neon from his eyes. She straightened her shoulders. "Now what?"

"I've spent the best years of my life trying to get that girl not to yell through the house."

"Oops." She tried hard not to laugh and very nearly succeeded.

A resigned expression came over his face. "Never a dull moment," he muttered, rubbing the back of his neck. "When does she have to be there?"

"Twenty minutes. I'll drive her over."

"Thanks, but there's no need."

"I know the way."

"You've done so much already." *Too* much, his expression implied, but she saw the smile that lurked behind the frown.

"I know," Natalie piped up from the doorway. "I'll fly over."

Daniel laughed. "Okay, Tinkerbell. Get your wings

on.'' He glanced at Karina. ''Come on. Let's get our fairy princess to the ball.''

Karina led the way down the hall. ''And we'll let bygones be bygones?''

''Okay by me.'' Opening the front door, he smiled his slow smile at her.

He had more than one way of shutting her up, Karina reflected as she sailed through the door after Natalie. And that smile was particularly effective.

# CHAPTER TWELVE

THE ALARM CLOCK radio clicked on and an old Beatles tune dragged Karina from a deep slumber. Blinking the sleep from her eyes, she noted the pale light of dawn, the birds chirping....

*Oh, no.* Pain wrapped around her like a blanket, and dread weighted her limbs to the bed. It was the morning of her thirty-second birthday.

*"Go forward in life,"* Daniel had said. She thought of the vow she'd made last night to be more consistent with her breast exams. Well, this was the right time of her cycle to check. And the doctor had drummed into her the importance of learning the feel of healthy tissue.

She raised one arm behind her head and cautiously reached for the underarm. As her fingers moved over her skin, gently pressing in concentric circles, her heart began to palpitate.

What if she found another lump? What if this time it was malignant?

She could still remember the day Mama had been given the final prognosis. Could still see Mama's hollow, frightened eyes when she'd looked at Karina knowing she wouldn't live to see her daughter grow up.

She finished checking the first breast and went on to the second, trying not to think of the long, pain-filled months during which they'd watched Mama's laughter fade and the music in her die.

A cold sweat had dampened her forehead by the time she lowered her arms in relief. Nothing, thank God. It was over for another month.

But she still had to get through the day. Karina hugged both arms around herself and rolled over, burying her face in the pillow. The logical side of her brain scolded her for being a ninny. The child in her cried out for comfort that would never come. If only she could slip into a dreamless sleep and wake up next year....

Humming to block out her thoughts, she shut her eyes and pulled the quilt tighter around her shoulders. She'd fallen into a light doze when she became aware of a persistent tune in her head—*Up, up "and awaaay..."*

Her eyes snapped open. Today she was riding in a hot air balloon.

Throwing back the covers, she rose and went to the window to open the blind. The sheer curtains lifted in a light breeze that carried the scent of the deep red roses beneath her window. The sound of robins chirping in the old maple out front filled her with an unexpected sense of well-being.

It was a good day to be alive.

She dressed quickly and quietly, wondering at the silence in the room next to hers. Then she remembered Daniel saying he would let Natalie sleep in as long as possible. She'd been so excited about the balloon ride she'd stayed awake long past her bedtime the night before.

Karina crept past Natalie's room. Through the half-open door she caught sight of the little girl's sleeping figure sprawled across the bed. One bare ankle peeked out from beneath the covers.

*Our fairy princess.*

He hadn't really meant it, of course. At least not the

way it sounded. But just for a moment, Karina wished
it was true.

She lingered on the landing, gazing wistfully at Natalie's tousled blond head. The girl's mouth curved suddenly in a smile that was so like Daniel's it made her
heart skip a beat.

Nattie stirred and Karina turned to run lightly down
the stairs, pausing at the bottom to glance down the hallway. Daniel was at the kitchen sink, filling the kettle.
Quietly she went into the living room and stood in front
of her mother's portrait.

Ageless, timeless, Eleanora Rossellini Peterson shone
like a rare pearl amid the eclectic bric-a-brac Karina had
collected over the years.

Karina's lips moved silently, as if in prayer. *God bless
you, Mama. I love you. I'll try to be strong today, for
your sake.*

Eleanora's midnight-dark eyes gazed back at her, her
faint smile as silent as an enigma.

Karina sighed and walked down the hall to the
kitchen.

Daniel looked up from pouring ground coffee into the
filter. "Mornin'," he said. "Sleep well?"

"Wonderful."

"You sure?" he persisted, his eyes searching her face.

"Yes!" She smiled to reassure him. Crossing the
room, she pushed back the curtains at the window over
the table. The crystals hanging from the curtain rod began to swing, and rainbows danced over the walls.

She switched on the radio and music blared from the
speakers. Glancing over her shoulder, she caught Daniel's eye and quickly tuned to a station that played clas-
sical music. "How's that?"

"Fine," he said. "It's not that I don't like music, you

understand. It's just that I like to hear my own thoughts occasionally.''

Which was exactly what she *didn't* want, though he wasn't to know that. But she turned the volume a little lower.

Natalie ran into the room, face shining and hair already brushed. ''I'm ready. I even made my bed. Can we go now?''

''Not so fast, Possum. We need to eat first.'' Daniel smiled and caught Karina's eye, as if to share his enjoyment of his daughter's excitement.

Karina smiled back, her heart contracting with bittersweet pleasure. ''How about scrambled eggs?'' she suggested, knowing they were Natalie's favorite.

So they breakfasted on scrambled eggs and toast in the sunny, homey kitchen where not even Daniel could entirely eliminate the clutter. Karina and Daniel ate in the comfortable silence that came from knowing each other well enough not to always have to talk while Natalie chattered excitedly about the coming day.

When they were done, Natalie ran back upstairs to brush her teeth. Karina carried the dishes to the sink and started to rinse out the cups.

''Leave that,'' Daniel said, glancing at his watch. ''We can clean up later.''

Karina did a double take, splashing water across the counter. ''Don't look now but you just used the *L* word.''

''Beg your pardon?''

''*Later,*'' she explained with a laugh. ''My bad habits must be rubbing off on you.''

He chuckled. ''And here I was congratulating myself that I'd passed on my fetish for neatness. Look at you, doing the dishes.''

Karina groaned and dried her hands on a towel. "Caught in the act of cleaning. My reputation will be ruined."

Daniel gazed down at her, laughter in his eyes. "I promise I won't tell a soul."

"Thanks." She paused. "And, Daniel?"

"Yes?"

"I also want to say thanks in advance for today. I have the feeling you've gone to a lot of trouble."

He shrugged. "This is your day. I want to make it as special as possible."

"Why?" She felt her cheeks flush and instantly regretted asking. It sounded as if she were fishing for some sort of declaration of affection.

Daniel leaned an elbow on the door frame. "You took Nattie and me in when you didn't want to, and I'm grateful. Helping you through today is a way of showing my appreciation."

"Oh." Friendly but basically impersonal. That's what she wanted. Wasn't it?

"Too bad Joanne couldn't come with us today," she said, turning away.

"Did she tell you why?"

Karina glanced back at him, surprised by the faint sharpness in his tone. "She has to take her mother to the dentist. Mrs. Simpson doesn't drive."

"Oh. That's all right, then." With another glance at his watch, he straightened away from the frame. "We'd better get going."

"Okay." She cast him a last, puzzled glance, then ran upstairs to finish getting ready. When she came back down a few minutes later, Daniel and Natalie were waiting for her on the front steps. She grabbed her jacket off its hook in the foyer, slung her purse over her shoulder and slipped into a pair of flat shoes.

"Shall we take Sammy?" she asked, coming out and locking the door. "It'd be a bit of a squash, but we could put the top down."

"I'll drive," Daniel said, ushering her down the path to his newly washed white pickup. "You don't know where we're going."

"You could give me directions."

"And spoil the fun? A birthday adventure is supposed to be like life itself—you never know what's going to happen next."

"You do," she argued as she climbed into the cab of the truck behind Natalie and buckled herself into place on the burgundy vinyl bench seat.

Daniel went around to the other side and got in. "On my birthday, you can call the shots. Fair enough?"

Karina didn't answer. The thought of spending birthdays together was far too appealing for a relationship that was supposed to be temporary.

DANIEL DROVE NORTH out of the city, and soon they were climbing the winding road through dense forest to the Malahat mountain pass. As they neared the summit, the trees thinned to granite outcroppings topped with spindly firs and Karina caught glimpses of blue water far below. Under the steady hum of the truck engine, Natalie's enthusiastic chatter gradually faded, and soon she was fast asleep.

Karina glanced down at the small blond head leaning against her shoulder with a weight so slight she hardly felt it. "How did it go at the school the other day?" she said to Daniel. "Was Natalie okay?"

Daniel shifted down to second as they came to a steep

section of the road. "She took it in her stride like she does everything. I don't know why I worry so much."

"Just wait till she starts going out with boys."

Daniel scowled and gripped the wheel with both hands. "She wouldn't dare."

Karina laughed. "I can just see you, demanding to know their intentions."

"I wouldn't have to ask. I *know* what a teenage boy's intentions are."

"Oh?" she teased. "And what might those be?"

He glanced over at her, his gaze traveling from her tank top down her snug-fitting jeans to her bare ankles. "Roughly the same as any healthy adult male's."

Karina turned to look out the window to hide her blush. Yet she couldn't disguise from herself the way her body tingled where his eyes had lingered. She focused on the scenery flashing by and emptied her mind of futile yearnings.

After a long moment of silence, Daniel startled her out of her thoughts. "All right, out with it."

"Pardon?" She shifted in her seat, propping up Natalie's head when it started to slip down her arm.

"I can always tell when something's brewing in that convoluted brain of yours," he said. "But I can't always tell what it is."

"I suppose I should be grateful for small mercies." Buying time, Karina reached forward to examine the carved wooden tiki hanging from the rearview mirror and realized it was the source of the faintly spicy aroma that permeated the cab. "What a wonderful scent."

"Sandalwood," he replied. "It makes a change from eucalyptus. So...?"

"It's Natalie," she said, seizing on a topic that had

in fact been bothering her. "Do you know about Mrs. Beeton?"

Daniel frowned. "What about her?"

"Does it worry you that Natalie spends so much time with an imaginary friend?"

"Of course it does."

"I didn't realize till the other night who Mrs. Beeton was," Karina went on. "I'd always thought she was one of Natalie's dolls. Strange, isn't it? We think it's all right for a child to talk to dolls or stuffed toys but not a being created from their imagination. Why is that?"

"Maybe because it makes us realize there's something lacking in their lives that we can't provide." He glanced across at her, openly concerned. "The hell of it is, there's nothing I can do about it other than give Natalie as much love and attention as I can. And as many opportunities to play with other kids as possible."

"You're a wonderful father, there's no question of that."

Daniel just nodded but she could tell by the way his tanned cheeks reddened slightly he was pleased she thought so.

"Even so," he said, "there are times when I don't know if I'm doing the right thing or not."

"I imagine most parents feel that way." She held a hand out the open window and let the cool, moist wind buffet her fingers. "Not that I'm an expert or anything."

They crested the summit, and Daniel slowed to allow the car in front to pull off into a view point. He glanced at her, his expression softening. "You know how to act with kids. You're natural and you like them. They pick up on that."

Karina glowed, unable to speak.

He flashed her a quirky smile and accelerated. "Don't

you dare say anything nice to me in return or we'll have to call an official meeting of the mutual admiration society."

She laughed, then checked on Natalie. The child was still sleeping soundly, her breath coming soft and regular through her partly open mouth.

"It seems to me she misses her mother more than any friends," Karina said, lowering her voice anyway.

Daniel let out a heavy breath. "I know. But I can't give Francine back to her and I'm damned if I'm going to marry just to provide my daughter with a mother."

"What was Francine like?" she asked, quickly adding, "if it doesn't bother you to talk about her, that is."

They had started down the long descent through thickening stands of evergreens. Daniel took a moment to shift gears before answering. "What do you want to know?"

"I suppose Natalie got her blond hair from her?" The question was merely a conversation opener, for Karina had seen the small, framed photograph of Francine on Natalie's bedside table.

"Yes," he said. "And her blue eyes. She's got my mouth, though, I think."

Karina's gaze traced the wayward, curving lines of his expressive mouth and the tiny creases in the corners that hinted at the humor lying below the surface. "Yes, she does."

"Francine was beautiful in a Nordic sort of way," Daniel told her. "Into sports of all kinds. That's how she and Brian met, at a tennis match."

A faint crease appeared between his eyebrows. Was he thinking about Brian and the golf tournament? For the first time she realized just how difficult their situation might be for him.

"What did she do for a living?"

"She was a political reporter for the *Melbourne Age*. She was very good, if somewhat obsessive. When she wanted something, nothing stood in her way."

"Like a fiancé?"

He glanced sharply at her. "Maybe."

"You must miss her very much."

He didn't reply.

Karina stared straight ahead. "Sorry," she muttered. "That was a stupid question."

Daniel remained silent for a long time. The road flattened, and the forest thinned to pastureland as they entered the farming delta of the Cowichan River. Karina fished in her purse for her sunglasses and put them on.

"I'm sorry she died," he said at last. "I miss her for Natalie's sake."

Was that all? Behind her dark glasses, Karina's eyebrows lifted. He'd implied it hadn't been a good marriage, but hadn't he sacrificed his relationship with his brother for the woman? She shouldn't press him, but for some reason she had to know. "Only for Natalie?"

Daniel's fingers gripped the steering wheel until his knuckles whitened. "I didn't love her. For a while I thought I did. God knows, I *tried* to love her. But once the initial infatuation wore off there was nothing there. Nothing at all."

Objections to what must have been years of loveless marriage swirled through Karina's head. "You didn't have to *stay* married."

His mouth twisted bitterly. "It sounds stupid in retrospect, but at the time I felt I had to stick it out if only to give some meaning to what I'd done to Brian. By the time I realized how totally unsuited Francine and I were, she was pregnant. I couldn't leave her then."

"No, of course not."

"After Natalie was born things got better for a while, but that didn't last. I asked for a divorce and custody of Natalie, who was almost three."

"What did Francine say?"

Daniel scowled. "She was actually considering it. I couldn't believe she'd be willing to let Natalie go. I'd have stayed married rather than lose my child."

His anger faded suddenly, leaving him pale beneath his tan. "As it turned out, she didn't live long enough to choose."

He fell silent, mouth stretched tight. He may not have loved Francine, Karina thought, but he'd cared about her.

"Oh, Daniel, I'm so sorry." Karina reached across the sleeping child and put her hand on his shoulder. "At least Natalie still has you."

Daniel frowned, looking unconvinced.

"What I mean is," she explained, "Natalie is lucky to have a father who shows his love in a dozen different ways every day. A father who..." her voice fell to a whisper "...who lets her grieve."

Daniel glanced up sharply. He geared down as they approached the town of Duncan. "What do you mean? Didn't your father allow you to mourn your mother? I know there was a problem, but..."

She gazed out the window at rows of fast-food outlets and car lots. *Please, don't let him ask about her father*, she prayed.

"It helps to talk about it."

She waited, expecting more and dreading it.

Just then Natalie lifted her head, blinked her eyes open and stretched tall in her seat to look out the front window. "Are we there yet?"

Daniel patted her knee. "Nearly, sweetheart. Just a little longer."

He stopped at a red light and consulted a sheet of notepaper covered with handwritten directions. The light changed and he made a left, driving across town and out the other side. Another turning took them down a narrow country road past well-kept farms with black-and-white cattle grazing in lush, green pastures.

Twenty minutes later, they turned into a gravel drive and pulled up in front of a portable office. In the field beyond, a trio of hot air balloons sprouted like multicolored mushrooms.

They signed a waiver in the office, then followed the pilot, a short, grizzled man named Frank, across the field to where a bright yellow balloon tugged at its tether, as if it, too, wanted to be up and away on this fine summer morning.

Natalie skipped ahead, beside herself with delight. Karina felt like skipping, too, but forced herself to walk sedately at Daniel's side. She glanced up at his animated face and was struck by a feeling of intense liking for this man.

He'd arranged this day for her at a time when his own personal life was tainted with unhappiness. Yet he looked anything but unhappy now. Just seeing his eager grin sent an extra thrill of excitement through her.

Smiling down at her, Daniel laced his fingers through hers. His touch combined the unknown and the longed-for, giving her excitement a physical edge. She tensed, ready to pull away. Then she saw the uncomplicated gladness in his eyes and squeezed his hand instead.

She gave a little shrug. "Today isn't like other days."

He nodded and she knew he understood.

"Your daughter's a lively little scamp," Frank said

over his shoulder to Karina. "Hope we can keep her inside the basket."

Karina glanced uncertainly at Daniel. He just smiled and shrugged. She opened her mouth to explain that Natalie wasn't her daughter, but it was already too late. They'd reached the balloon and Frank was setting the wooden steps in place so they could climb aboard. With an odd mixture of pride and guilty pleasure she took Natalie's hand to help her up the stairs.

Then she forgot everything else in the excitement of takeoff. Frank cranked up the gas jets, inflating the balloon until it strained at the ropes binding it to the earth. One by one he released the lines. Smooth as an elevator, the balloon lifted skyward and the earth dropped away.

Karina's stomach leaped skyward, too, with a thrilling sensation of lightness and butterflies. She laughed with sheer delight. "It feels like we're really flying."

Once aloft, Frank turned off the gas jets, and the sudden quiet was deafening. They floated in eerie silence over farms and lakes and silver, winking rivers that wound through field and wood. To the north and west, mountains rose from the valley floor, cloaked in dark green.

Karina gazed over the side, enraptured. The fresh air swirled around her head, loosening tendrils of hair from her braid. "This is so beautiful! Natalie, look!"

She turned to beckon the girl. But Natalie had overcome her usual initial shyness and engaged the bemused pilot in a game. Karina laughed as the child clicked her heels together and pleaded with the Great Oz to take her back to Kansas.

Daniel shook his head and leaned his elbows on the edge of the wicker basket beside Karina. "Poor man," he murmured. "He doesn't know what he's in for."

"I think he's enjoying himself," Karina said, watching the pair.

"Look," Daniel said, and raised his arm over her shoulder to point to a clearing in the middle of some woods. Karina gazed in the direction he was indicating and saw a doe grazing peacefully, a fawn close by her side.

"She looks so tiny. How high are we?" Karina pressed a hand to the sudden flutter in her stomach that had more to do with the warmth of Daniel's barc arm brushing her cheek than the altitude.

"Frank said we'd get to about five hundred feet." Daniel withdrew his arm and gazed at her, so close his hazel eyes resolved into forest green flecks embedded in amber. "Your mother would have been proud of you today."

At the reminder of her mother, an ache rose in her heart. She glanced at Daniel, who'd resumed his survey of the scene below. His high, straight nose and slanting jaw were sharply delineated against the deep blue of the sky. A thick lock of chestnut hair strayed over his forehead.

The ache in her heart intensified. But for the grace of God...

"Yes, she would have been proud," Karina agreed quietly. "She never had time to overcome her fear of flying." She was silent for a moment. "I guess we all have something we just can't face. Something we have to simply forget."

"You can't forget your mother," he said softly. "You told me so yourself. All the music in the world, all the laughter and people and parties won't make you forget."

Karina didn't reply. He was right. But she was frozen

in the past, unable to grieve, unable to go forward. "You don't know what it's like."

Daniel put one hand over hers where it rested on the edge of the basket, and with the other brushed away a wisp of dark hair that had blown across her cheek. "Tell me about your mother. I have a feeling I would have liked her very much."

Karina smiled. "Everybody liked Mama. She was fun and funny. She was always laughing. And she loved to sing. The house was always filled with music."

"Sounds like someone else I know," Daniel murmured.

Gripped with remembrance, Karina hardly heard him. "She grew tomatoes and garlic and...oh, all sorts of herbs. She'd make mountains of pasta and invite half the neighborhood for dinner. She was always busy—sewing, painting, she could do anything."

"Did she work?"

Karina nodded. "She was a nurse before she had my brother and me. She didn't go back to work afterward because she wanted to stay home with us." Karina chuckled. "She called me her *bambina*. I used to hate it when she used the term in front of my friends."

Her smile faded. What she wouldn't give to hear Mama's dear voice murmur *bambina* to her just one more time.

Daniel's thumb stroked soft circles over the back of her hand. "What else?"

Karina shrugged. "She wanted to have lots of children, but for some reason she never had any more after me." She paused. "Sometimes I think she should never have had any at all."

Daniel shook his head. "She sounds like a wonderful

mother. Better to have a short time with someone like that than no time at all."

"But don't you see?" Karina protested, turning to face him. "If I hadn't been born, Mama wouldn't have suffered at having to leave me. I wouldn't have suffered when she died."

"Nor would you have laughed and sang and done all the other things that have given you such happy memories."

She fell silent. Did the good really outweigh the bad? This birthday forced her to confront her greatest fears, her deepest sorrows, and yet... Wasn't she also having a wonderful time with Daniel and Natalie, doing something new and exciting?

"There's a difference between sorrow and fear," Daniel explained. "One makes you stronger and gives you greater understanding. The other limits your ability to grow."

Karina gazed into the fathomless blue sky. The way he put it seemed so clear, but when she tried to apply the concept to herself, her mind stumbled. Grief and fear of loving had been linked in her heart for so long the chains seemed indestructible.

Behind her, Frank cleared his throat, breaking the silence. "You folks want some brunch?" he asked, nodding to a large picnic basket wedged in a corner.

"Goody!" Natalie cried at once. "I'm starving."

"Me, too," Karina said, glad of the diversion. With Natalie's help, she delved into the basket and pulled out a plastic container. "Cold barbecued salmon," she announced, lifting the lid. "Whew! I was afraid for a minute the 'new and different' would include roasted grasshoppers."

"They're at the bottom of the basket," Daniel replied straight-faced. "Right next to the fried ants."

She made a face and tossed a plastic wineglass at his head. "Catch."

With a swift movement, Daniel reached high, his fingers closing around the stem just before the glass went over the side. He looked at her and just shook his head.

"Sorry." She suppressed a giggle. "I'm used to eating on the fly, but this is ridiculous."

Daniel uncorked a bottle of champagne and filled their glasses. The bubbles spilled over the top and ran down Karina's fingers. Laughing, she quickly sipped at the froth, glancing at Daniel over her raised glass.

Maybe it was the altitude, or the sparkling wine, or maybe it was the look in Daniel's eyes... Suddenly Karina felt light-headed and quivery, as if she were on top of the world. What she felt for Daniel was far more than liking, she realized on a shock wave of exhilaration.

*She was in love with him.*

Her moment of pure happiness lasted all of two seconds.

Then, an old hand at blanking out unwanted thoughts, Karina began to whistle under her breath. She turned back to the picnic basket and feverishly unpacked the rest of the containers and plates and cutlery.

*Later.* She'd worry about her feelings for Daniel later. Today she was going to enjoy herself if it killed her.

# CHAPTER THIRTEEN

DANIEL GLANCED OVER at Karina as he cruised down the tree-lined street toward her house. She looked tired but contented, which was exactly how he felt. He'd had her all to himself, more or less, for one perfect day. As he watched her, she glanced up at him and her mouth curved in an oddly shy smile.

He smiled back and resisted the urge to reach over and stroke her cheek.

Natalie had fallen asleep again, this time with her head lying across Karina's lap. But as he pulled in to the curb and cut the engine, she sat up, rubbing her eyes.

"I wonder what Joanne's doing here," Karina said, nodding at the familiar blue Volvo parked ahead of them.

"Probably came to give you a birthday present," Daniel suggested.

"Maybe Julie's here, too," Natalie said excitedly, and scrambled across Karina.

"I doubt it," Daniel said, but she was already out the door. Then he remembered Joanne would have things to take inside, and tossed his keys after his daughter. "Here. You can get Joanne to open the front door."

He was wondering how he could distract Karina for a few minutes when he felt her hand on his arm.

"Daniel?"

"Yes?" God, but she looked beautiful, her cheeks flushed, her eyes dark and sparkling.

She cleared her throat and turned slightly pinker. "I know of another birthday custom. I didn't invent it but it's a good one."

His gaze drifted down to her mouth. "What is it?"

"The birthday kiss."

To Daniel, it seemed the entire day had been leading to this moment. One by one, Karina's barriers had fallen. All the small moments of contact lovers took for granted had been allowed him today—his hand on her shoulder as he pointed out the sights, his lips at her ear as he teased her over the roar of the balloon, his thigh brushing hers as they contemplated the world from five hundred feet in the air.

With each glance, each touch, his awareness of her had grown until it was like a second skin surrounding him, making him ultrasensitive to every nuance of expression, every smile of delight, every laughing light in her eyes.

As he gazed at her now, the cab of the truck seemed to shrink around them, enclosing a space that belonged to them alone. He leaned toward her, his heart thundering.

Just before he kissed her, the thought of Brian flashed through his mind. A moment of guilt, an instant of unconcern, a fleeting sense of bridges being burned. Then Daniel pressed his lips against Karina's and thought was no longer an option.

Her mouth was warm and deliciously soft, tasting of champagne and strawberry shortcake. He heard her moan softly and twined his fingers in her hair, drawing her closer. Beneath his palm, her cheek felt like warm satin. His elbow brushed her breast, and the sudden swelling in his groin made him urgently aware of how much he wanted her.

Her own urgency as she wound her arms around his neck surprised as much as it pleased him. He had no illusions she would surrender unconditionally, but at least she was acknowledging her desire. With all the pent-up longing of the past weeks raging inside him, he parted her lips with his tongue.

"Daniel," she gasped, blissful seconds later. "I'm sorry. I shouldn't have. We mustn't."

"I know," he murmured. And kissed her again.

Dimly he heard a dog barking in the distance, the tinkle of an ice-cream truck and the sound of children's voices in the street. All he felt was Karina's hand slipping inside the collar of his shirt to lightly caress his shoulder.

Gradually, one child's voice separated itself from the rest. It was calling to them through the open window on the passenger side of the truck. "Daddy! Karina!"

His mind glazed with confusion, Daniel slowly disengaged himself from Karina. His daughter was beside the car, trying to tell them something.

"What is it, Natalie?" he said, leaning across Karina. "What's wrong?"

"Karina's brother is on the phone from Toronto. He wants to say happy birthday." Natalie glanced with bright, curious eyes from him to Karina. "Were you guys *kissing?*"

Daniel groaned.

Karina touched his lips lightly with her fingertips and smiled. "I'd better go talk to Tom," she said, and climbed out of the truck.

Daniel watched her run up the steps, then glanced back at Natalie. Covering his lap with one arm, he rubbed the other hand across the back of his neck and patiently began to explain.

Karina smiled to herself as she went through the door. She'd give anything to know what Daniel was telling the girl, but she wasn't about to stick around and find out.

She met Joanne coming down the hall, making weather talk with her brother on the cordless phone. Sultry and warm in Toronto from the sounds of it. Here, too, she thought, lifting her blouse away from her chest.

"Good time?" Joanne mouthed as she handed over the phone.

Smiling, Karina nodded. "Hi, Tom!" she said into the receiver.

Joanne lifted one eyebrow. "Your lipstick's smudged," she whispered into Karina's ear before drifting back to the kitchen.

Karina dabbed at her mouth in the hall mirror as Tom wished her happy birthday. Goodness, she looked wild—hair everywhere and blouse rumpled. Joanne was wrong, though. Her lipstick wasn't smudged, it was kissed right off.

She chatted to Tom, telling him about her day and asking after his wife and kids, pleased to hear they'd be coming west for Christmas this year. As she said goodbye and hung up, her mind leaped ahead. Maybe she could convince her father to join them.

Natalie skipped through the door and past her, down the hall toward the kitchen. Daniel lingered in the foyer, casting a glance into the darkened living room.

"Everything okay with Natalie?" she asked. She followed the direction of his gaze. "I wonder why the curtains are drawn at this time of day." She started into the living room.

"We probably just forgot to open them this morning.'' He took her by the elbow and steered her back into the hall. ''I explained to Natalie about birthday kisses. She wants one, too.''

''I'd be delighted.'' She moved a step ahead of him and half turned out of his reach. All this talk of kisses while his warm hand cupped her bare elbow was too distracting. ''I'd like to take you both out for dinner by way of thanks.''

He shook his head and smiled his slow grin. ''You already thanked me.''

Her gaze ricocheted away from his. ''O-kay.'' One more second of that devastating smile and she'd be prostrate with gratitude.

''The next item on your agenda is a long, hot bubble bath,'' he said, guiding her toward the staircase. ''Don't worry about dinner. Everything's being taken care of.''

Karina nodded and fled up the stairs.

She was too keyed up to lie in a bath, so she opted for a shower instead. As she lathered scented shower gel over her body, she thought how grateful she was to Daniel for turning her birthday from a requiem into a celebration. Her fears had been, if not buried, at least put into perspective. Telling him about Mama hadn't been nearly as hard as she'd expected.

In fact, it had felt good to talk about Mama.

Happily humming along to the radio in the medicine cabinet, she stepped out of the shower, splashing drops of water on the floor.

One thing was certain, she realized more soberly as she reached for a towel—she couldn't kiss him again. She was playing with fire, as careless of the consequences as a child. But she wasn't a child. In spite of her implicit promise this morning to suspend barriers, in spite of the birthday kiss, she had to draw back. It was only fair to Daniel—and Natalie.

She brushed her teeth, blow-dried her hair into glossy, dark waves and reached for her robe in its usual spot on the back of the bathroom door. *Darn*. Too late, she remembered throwing it into the laundry the night before.

Wrapped in a royal blue towel, she peeked cautiously out the door. Silly to worry. It was only two steps to her bedroom. No doubt Daniel was downstairs with Joanne, plotting the next instalment of her birthday surprise.

She'd taken only one of the two steps when Daniel's door opened and he stepped out of his room onto the landing. He stopped short, looking as surprised as she felt. A few weeks ago she would have simply breezed past. Now her pulse roared into overdrive and she stood rooted to the spot, clutching the towel.

His gaze strayed to her bare shoulders and points south before he brought it abruptly back to her face. "Done in the bathroom?" he said at last.

"I...yes. It's all yours." Heat crept up her chest into her neck and face. This time Daniel's gaze went to the flushed tops of her breasts where they swelled above the towel, and stayed there.

He took a deep breath and plowed a hand through his hair. "Get dressed," he said. "I'll just have a quick shave and meet you downstairs."

"What should I wear?"

"Anything. You look good in anything." His gaze lingered on the towel.

Karina managed a light laugh. "I should know better than to ask a man for his opinion on clothes. Are we going out somewhere? Fancy? Casual?"

"Dressy," he said firmly. "Wear something dressy." Then he turned on his heel and beat a hasty retreat.

Dressy. Karina went to her room and flicked through her wardrobe. *Aha.* She reached to the back and brought forth a hanger barely weighted down by the slim slip of black fabric draped over it. Perfect.

DANIEL WAS CHECKING last-minute arrangements with Joanne when Karina sauntered into the kitchen. He glanced at her and his mouth dried up in midsentence. Below his freshly shaven jaw the pulse in his neck began to beat faster.

"*What?*" Karina glanced down at the thin-strapped dress that clung to every curve of her body. "Not dressy enough?"

"It's fine." He cleared his throat. "You look fine."

"What he means," Joanne said, bustling from fridge to stove with something on a baking tray, "is you look sensational."

"Too right!" Natalie chimed in. "You look super!"

Daniel continued to stare at Karina, trying to pinpoint exactly when she'd started having this paralyzing effect on him.

Karina peered around him at Joanne. "Looks like we're eating in. What can I do to help?"

"Nothing," Daniel said quickly. He glanced at his watch, then at Joanne. "I think it's time."

Karina glanced from him to Joanne. "Time for what?"

"Time for...a drink," Daniel said. "Some champagne?"

"Maybe a mineral water to start. I'm parched."

Karina started to reach for the fridge handle, but Daniel whisked the bottle out and quickly shut the door before she could help herself. He and Joanne had worked so hard he didn't want the surprise blown at the last minute.

"What's going on?" Karina asked, laughing. "You two are acting very suspiciously." She turned to Natalie. "What's in the fridge they don't want me to see?"

Behind Karina's back, Daniel held a finger to his lips and cast a warning glance at his daughter.

"Nothing," Natalie said, her round blue eyes the picture of childhood innocence.

Daniel released his breath. "We just want you to relax on your birthday," he said, and handed Karina the glass of fizzing water. "Take a seat in the living room. The food won't be long."

"All right." She glanced once more at each of them and started back down the hall.

Daniel waited until she was almost to the door. Then, motioning to Joanne and Natalie to follow, he led the way on tiptoe into the dining room. They took their place behind a lacquered Japanese screen and waited.

Karina stepped into the living room through the other door and flicked on the light.

Smiling faces popped up from behind the couch, the chairs, and poured out of the dining room toward Karina with a chorus of, "Surprise! Surprise!"

Karina jumped. Her water spilled. She burst into laughter, her hand on her heart. "Kevin...Betty...and the baby, too! Hi, Doug, Carol—" She didn't get another word out. Everyone was trying to hug her at once.

Daniel stood at the edge of the crowd and watched, taking pleasure in Karina's delight. Then her gaze scanned the room and came to rest on him and Joanne. She narrowed her eyes at Joanne and mouthed the word "You!"

Beside him, Joanne shook her head.

Karina's gaze shifted to Daniel. He just grinned. Karina's answering smile took his breath away. Had she always smiled at him like that?

He started to move toward her, but as Karina attempted to meet him she was cut off by another friend wishing her happy birthday. Never mind, he thought, they had all night.

Daniel sipped his drink. Karina was laughing and talking at the center of a small crowd of her friends. Her body swayed lithely as she illustrated her golf swing, only to double over with laughter at her own amateurish efforts.

He couldn't get over the way she looked in that black clingy dress with the midthigh hemline. He'd suggested dressy and she'd come up with knock-down-drag-out sexy. Hell, when he thought about it, she always looked sexy, even in those oversize shirts she wore when working on her papier-mâché.

Joanne tugged on his sleeve. "Can you give me a hand getting the rest of the food to the table?"

"Sure." He followed her back to the kitchen and went to the fridge. "That was a close call earlier." He started handing plates out to Joanne.

"No kidding. Everyone went overboard bringing food, and the cake takes up almost a whole shelf on its own."

"Mississippi mud cake," he said, sneaking a dab of chocolate icing. "She'll think she's died and gone to heaven." Joanne glanced sharply at him and he winced. "Sorry, bad choice of words."

"Was she all right today?" Joanne placed the last plate on the counter. She reached for a packet of blue tortilla chips and emptied it into a bowl.

Daniel nodded and began loading hors d'oeuvres onto

a platter. "We were so busy she didn't have time to think about being sad. She told me about her mother. Sounds like she was quite a lady."

"She told you about her mother?" Joanne's hands stilled, her eyebrows rising.

"Nothing heavy," he replied. "Just how she liked to sing and cook pasta for the neighborhood."

"Still, that's a breakthrough. She never talks about her mother. Not even with me." Joanne crumpled the empty chip bag and tossed it into the trash. With a wink and a smile, she added, "I'd say that's pretty significant."

Daniel nodded calmly, but inside pride and pleasure coursed through his veins. Karina had trusted him with memories she'd never shared with anyone else. With a jaunty step he followed Joanne to the dining room, three heavily laden plates on one arm and two more on the other.

Engulfed by party guests drawn by the sight of food, Daniel set the platters on the already overburdened table. Maybe there was a chance for him and Karina. He'd never have thought she'd be the type he'd want to marry, but now he couldn't imagine marrying anyone else.

Her mother had died young, he reminded himself. As much as he knew the odds of it happening to Karina were slim, it was still a possibility. Francine's death had been hard enough, and he hadn't even been in love with her. Karina's death would be too awful to contemplate. Natalie loved her, too, and so did—

Damn it all, who invited Brian?

His brother stood next to Karina at the table, speaking into her ear. She laughed and met his gaze. Daniel did a slow burn.

He'd left the guest list up to Joanne, never dreaming

she'd invite Brian. In hindsight, he could see how it might have seemed reasonable—Karina had played golf with Brian, and they were going to the tournament together. For the first time in his life, Daniel wished he'd taken up golf. If he'd been the jock in the family, this never would have happened.

Brian picked up a prawn, dipped it in cocktail sauce and fed it to Karina with his fingers. The bile that churned in Daniel's gut rose in his throat.

Then Brian spotted him. "Danny boy!"

"Hello, Brian." Daniel noted his brother's flushed cheeks and loud voice. Brian had had a few drinks already.

"I've got a bone to pick with you," Brian scolded, draping his arm over Karina's shoulder. "Karina missed a golf lesson to go ballooning with you."

"It's her birthday, Bri," Daniel said, forcing a smile. "There's more to life than golf."

Why wasn't she moving away from Brian's arm? Daniel looked directly at her, but her gaze was innocent and smiling. Either she had no objection to Brian's attention or she didn't think it worth making a fuss about.

"Sacrilege!" Brian rejoined with mock horror. He smiled at Karina and squeezed her shoulder. "Golf is like life, eh, Karina? You have to play to win. I'm not sure Danny understands that."

Karina smiled. "You'd be surprised what Daniel understands." She winked at Daniel and slipped out from beneath Brian's arm.

Daniel followed her with his eyes as she was caught up in another group of people. He walked over to Brian and forced himself to act civilized. "It's nice to see her in such good spirits."

"She's fantastic!" Brian said, shaking his head. "Everything a man could want in a woman.'' He clapped Daniel on the back. ''You made up for past sins when you introduced me to Karina, Danny boy.''

''Karina introduced herself, if you recall,'' Daniel said between his teeth. ''Are you serious about her?''

Brian nodded, still gazing at Karina. Then he glanced at Daniel, his blue eyes intense. ''Wouldn't you be?''

''We're not talking about me.''

''Good Lord, Danny, quit glowering at me. In a minute you'll be asking me my intentions. Lighten up. The lady is a fox and I'm the hunter.''

''She's not into marriage.''

''Oh, I think if she had the right offer, she'd be into anything,'' Brian replied with a nudge and a wink.

Daniel gripped his glass almost to breaking point. Surely any jury would consider Brian's comment justification for fratricide. ''You haven't got a clue what she's really like.''

Brian laid a hand on Daniel's sleeve, his expression sobering. ''I was only joking, Danny. She's a wonderful person and I don't mean the slightest disrespect. Any man would be damned lucky to land her.'' With a smile, he smoothed back his hair and straightened his tie. ''And tonight, I feel lucky.''

''What makes you think she's interested in you?'' Daniel sipped at his wine, half dreading the answer.

''Who knows what women think, Danny boy? But I'll tell you one thing, she kisses like a goddess.''

The wine turned to vinegar in Daniel's mouth. ''Things have progressed that far between you, have they?'' He forced himself to speak casually, but he felt as if his fingernails were being ripped out one by one.

Brian smiled modestly. ''I guess I shouldn't be kissing

and telling but, hey, you're my only brother. Who else can I confide in?''

''Maybe she's got someone else in her life.'' *Like me.* But he knew a moment of doubt. Should he warn Brian he wasn't the only one Karina was kissing? Was he doomed to face divided loyalties every time he fell in love?

Brian looked at him thoughtfully. ''She says not.''

## CHAPTER FOURTEEN

DANIEL GLANCED AT his watch. It was long past midnight and the party was still going strong. *Karina* was still going strong. He'd put Natalie to bed hours ago, right after the birthday cake. He wished he could escape the noise and crowd himself, but he'd promised Karina he'd see her through her birthday.

He'd hardly had a chance to speak to her all night. Every time he'd tried, someone else had joined the conversation or taken her away to dance. Still, he was glad she was having a good time. It meant she wasn't brooding over her mother. Or herself.

Then she looked at him across the room. Her eyes seemed to hold a special warmth just for him. He smiled at her, willing her to break away from her friends and come to him. To his pleasure, she excused herself and did just that.

"Are you enjoying yourself, Daniel?" She touched him lightly on the chest. "I didn't think you liked parties."

Beneath his shirt, his skin burned where her fingertips rested. "Dinner parties are more my thing. Most of the time," he added, thinking of the last one he'd attended.

She laughed. "I'm glad to see you're on better terms with Brian."

"We're...working things out." He paused, wondering

exactly how she felt about his brother. "Brian really likes you, Karina."

Her mouth slanted upward. "Good. I like him, too."

Salt in a wound couldn't have burned more fiercely. Daniel forced a smile. "He's always been popular with the ladies."

Karina tilted her head to one side and studied him. "Funny, that's what he said about you."

"He's dreaming. Or rewriting history again. Brian was always the most popular guy in the most popular group in high school. At university, too, or so I understand."

"And you? Surely *you're* not going to tell me you couldn't get a date?"

"I wouldn't say that," he replied, wondering at the inflection in her voice. "I usually had a girlfriend, but only one at a time. Crowds of any sort have never been my thing."

"They don't seem to bother your brother." Her gaze settled on Brian as he held forth in the center of a little gathering. From the expressions of humorous anticipation on the faces of his audience, he was telling a joke.

"He has a way with people." Dammit, why did they have to spend these moments together talking about his brother? Everything she said seemed to confirm that Brian was more her style.

But he had things in common with her, as well, Daniel thought. As much as she liked to party, she also loved her home, children, creative pursuits. The odds weren't stacked overwhelmingly in Brian's favor.

He glanced sideways at Karina. She was still moving to the music. "Care to dance?"

She flashed him a brilliant smile. "I thought you'd never ask."

They danced through three tracks before a slow song came on and he could finally take her in his arms. When Karina leaned into him and released a sigh that pressed the warm, sweet weight of her breasts against his chest, he knew he could have danced all night just for this moment.

"How are you doing?" he murmured into the damp, jasmine-scented tendrils of hair that curled around her temple.

The arm she'd twined around his neck tightened in a hug. "Wonderful, thanks to you." She lifted her head, her eyes lit with a smile. "You've worn me out today, Daniel Bowen. Not many men can say that."

"Worn out, my eye," he replied, entranced by the feel of her heart beating against his breast. "That engine of yours will purr for hours yet."

The room was darkened, lit only by a table lamp and the winking fairy lights. A few other couples were on the floor, but Daniel was aware only of Karina, her scent, her warmth, her softness as he held her in his arms. Pressed together, they moved in sensual rhythm to the slow, bluesy music.

Then he felt a hand on his shoulder.

"May I cut in?"

Daniel dragged his gaze from Karina's to see Brian standing behind him. Instinctively he tightened his hold on her. "Sorry, mate, this dance is mine."

"The next one, then." This time Brian's words were directed at Karina. She gave Daniel a questioning glance.

He wanted to say, "No, you're mine. Not just for this dance or the next one, but forever." But Karina was no more his possession than she was Brian's. "Whatever you want."

Karina hesitated, then nodded at Brian.

Brian melted into the crowd. Daniel pulled Karina back into his embrace and pressed his cheek against her temple. But the warm awareness that had built between them was shattered. At the end of the dance he released her and watched painfully as she went from his arms to his brother's.

AT LAST the party was over. The house was quiet and the landing dark when Daniel climbed the stairs. Karina had gone up half an hour ago. He'd heard the shower running and killed time clearing dishes until the bathroom was free.

There was no light under her door when he went into the bathroom to brush his teeth. She must have been worn out after all, he thought as he stepped into the shower a minute later. Too tired to do anything but sleep.

He finished his shower quickly. Wrapped in a towel, he slipped out of the bathroom and started across the landing.

He paused. A yellow glow that hadn't been there before shone from beneath Karina's door.

He listened. Not a sound penetrated the silence. What could she be doing? He pressed his ear to her door. Nothing.

He knocked. He heard a faint gasp, then a deeper silence, as though she were holding her breath.

"Karina?"

"What is it?" Her voice was low and strained.

"Are you all right?"

No answer.

"Karina, I'm coming in." He waited a moment to give her a chance to put on a robe if necessary. Then, with only a brief thought for his own unsuitable attire, he opened the door.

She was huddled on the bed, wrapped in a colorful silk shawl. Her eyes were huge and dark, her face pale and drawn in the light of the ceramic oil lamp on the bedside table. As he entered, she turned the framed photo she was holding facedown.

Wordlessly he crossed the room and sat on the bed beside her. Any sexual thoughts he'd entertained about entering Karina's private chamber vanished when he saw the heartache in her eyes.

Without hesitation he put his arms around her and pressed her head to his shoulder. She lay passively yet tense, as though afraid of falling apart. Daniel stroked her back but found no response. How could he break through the brambled walls of grief that had grown around her over the years?

"Talk to me, Karina," he said softly. "Tell me what troubles you the most."

She was silent for a long time. Finally she said, "I can't cry for my mother. I've never been able to cry for her. The pain builds inside me till I'm ready to explode but no tears come."

"You've never cried?" He could hardly believe someone as passionate about life as Karina would be able to stop the grief.

She shook her head and he felt the dry heat of her cheek on his bare chest.

"The day she…" Her voice faltered. "The day Mama died, my father told me we had to be brave, that Mama wouldn't want us to weep for her."

Daniel stifled an oath and searched for some understanding of the man who'd been so insensitive to his daughter's pain. "He must have been hurting very badly himself. He probably didn't know how to deal with his own grief, much less yours."

Karina drew away from him a little, her face cast down. "It was a long time ago. It doesn't matter anymore."

Daniel stroked back a strand of ebony hair and tucked it behind her ear so he could see her face better. His other arm gently tightened around her shoulders in case she had any thoughts of ending the conversation.

"It *does* matter," he said. "If you're still hurting, it matters very much. I'm sure if your father knew, he'd be appalled at what you're going through because of him."

"Oh, Daniel, it was so awful," she said with a shudder, her voice cracked and pained. "If only we could have talked about her, maybe we could have helped each other. Instead, he locked himself away in his grief and left me alone to deal with mine."

Daniel thought of Natalie's sorrow and confusion after Francine's death, and of the tears he would first encourage, then dry, night after night. "Children need help to deal with grief."

"I guess Dad didn't know that. He destroyed every family photo that included her. He gave away all her belongings. He wouldn't talk about her. He wouldn't even let me say her name. I had nothing left of her. It was as though my mother never existed." Karina broke off, hiccuping.

"What about your brother? Couldn't you talk to him?"

"Tom was almost as bad as my father. He went all stoical and silent, although I knew he was just as miserable as I was. He was sixteen. Said he wasn't a little boy to be blubbering for his mommy."

Daniel held her tightly, rocking her as he would have Natalie. "It's okay, love." He stroked her hair, pressing soft kisses against her temple. "It's okay to cry. You *need* to cry to heal." He pulled her even closer, as though he could insulate her from pain with his own body.

The warmth and caring in his voice penetrated deep into Karina's swollen, aching heart. She felt the tears clogging her throat, burning her eyes.

"Let it go, Karina," Daniel murmured. "Let it go."

She could hold on no longer. A painful, racking sob tore through her chest and her control broke at last. Great burning tears rolled down her scalded cheeks. The oil lamp flared and hissed. She sobbed, gasped for breath and felt Daniel's arms tighten around her. She pressed her face against his chest, soaking his skin with almost two decades' worth of tears.

Anguish washed over her, building and breaking like waves on a rocky reef as she wept in his arms. Her own arms struggled out from between them and went around his waist to hold him as tightly as he held her. Daniel stroked her hair and back, whispering meaningless phrases that bespoke comfort and safety and, above all, the assurance that she wasn't alone. That someone cared for her. Someone who loved her unconditionally.

She cried and cried until she didn't have a single tear left to shed. As her sobbing slowly ebbed, the tightness in her chest eased. She heaved a last great sigh and went still against his chest, breathing softly. She never wanted to move again.

For a very long time she lay nestled against Daniel, absorbing his warmth, taking comfort from his strong arms and gentle hands. Today he'd taken her out of herself with his adventures and his companionship. Tonight he'd forced her deep into her pain and pulled her through to the other side, whole and intact. She felt bonded to him in a way she never had to anyone else.

Finally a cramp in her leg forced her to move. She pulled away a little, smiling sheepishly at Daniel as she twisted her ankle this way and that.

His eyes searched her tearstained face. "Are you okay?"

She nodded, knowing he wasn't talking about her leg.

Daniel reached for a tissue from the box beside her bed and dabbed at her eyes. "At least you've got the portrait in the living room," he said. "How did that survive your father's purges?"

"It belonged to my aunt Maria, Mama's sister. She gave it to me much later. It was taken when Mama was eighteen, before she was married."

Daniel reached for another tissue and handed it to her. "Blow."

Dutifully, Karina blew her nose and threw the wadded tissue in the wastebasket. "I've also got their wedding photo," she said, reaching over to the table to show him.

She watched him study the photo of her mother and father. Their youthful faces were alive with love and happiness, blissfully unaware of what was to come.

"I snuck it out of my parents' room when Mama was still in the hospital," she told him. "I had no idea my father was going to destroy the rest of them. I just wanted something to have beside my bed at night. For seven years I hid it in my dresser and only took it out when I was alone."

Daniel replaced the photo on the table and tilted her head up until she met his gaze. "My poor darlin'."

Her bruised and battered heart swelled with the warmth in his eyes and voice. His thumb trailed down her wet cheeks, wiping away the last traces of moisture.

Slowly his lips descended to hers, touched, withdrew and touched again with the utmost gentleness. Drawing her close once more, he pressed his chin against her forehead.

Karina sighed softly. He was too good a person to lead on. She should move apart from him, now, before anything happened. Even as the thought entered her mind, he slipped his hands beneath the shawl, gently massaging the tension from her shoulders. His hands moved down her back, the callused tips of his fingers circling each vertebra. Karina breathed a sigh of deep relaxation. Nothing else could possibly feel so good.

But no sooner had she relaxed than tension returned in a tingling awareness of his touch. His hands framed her sides now, and his wrists brushed the edges of her breasts as his fingers kneaded her back muscles. With each nudge of her breasts, waves of exquisitely subtle desire pulsed through her, and she gripped his waist tighter.

She lifted her face, felt the roughness of his unshaven chin on her forehead and smelled the clean, woodsy scent of his skin. Then somehow her gaze was all tangled up in his and she couldn't seem to breathe.

He dipped his head, their noses bumped and warmth rose from her skin and mingled with his. She wanted to laugh, she wanted to cry. Beneath her lips, she felt one side of his face stretch in a smile.

"Karina." He spoke her name as though it were a phrase of music. "Let me love you."

It took all her strength, but she forced herself to pull back. "Daniel, I'm sorry, we can't do this."

"Are you worried about protection?" he murmured. "I've got condoms somewhere. Hang on." He started to get up.

"No, it's not that. There are some in my bedside table."

He tilted her head, forcing her to gaze directly into his eyes. "Then what?"

Oh, how she wanted him. Needed him. "They're not one-hundred-percent foolproof. I...I don't want to take a chance on getting pregnant."

He stroked her cheek with the back of one finger. "Nothing's one-hundred percent, darlin', except abstinence. I'd rather wait awhile, too, before having children. But maybe you don't realize how I feel about you."

"Oh, Daniel..." His gentle warmth brought back the aching need in her heart. It wasn't just her body that craved him but her soul, as well. Surely just this once she could allow herself the love she longed for. And longed to give to Daniel.

Leaning away from him, she opened the drawer of her bedside table and searched around until she found a condom. She turned the plastic packet over in her hand, inspecting it. "I hope these things don't have use-by dates."

Daniel chuckled softly. "I don't think so."

She hesitated a moment, then placed the packet in his palm.

Closing his fingers around it, Daniel looked into her eyes. "Are you sure?"

With a tremulous smile, she nodded.

"If you were to get pregnant, I'd be there for you," he said, still serious. "I'd welcome a baby. Our baby."

His words sparked a longing so deep she could hardly bear it. Pressing a finger to his lips, she whispered, "Just love me tonight, Daniel. That's all I ask."

His eyes shut briefly. Then he bent his head and his

lips met hers. Born neither of yearning nor passion, the kiss was a pact of love, warm and giving, wholehearted yet sensual.

She trembled, hardly daring to breathe as he drew back to kiss the tip of her nose before slipping the shawl from her shoulders. From beneath lowered lashes, she saw his gaze drop to her breasts and heard his almost inaudible sigh.

Then his eyes lifted to hers once more. He slipped one thin strap of her nightdress over her shoulder. Then the other. The slippery material slid down, catching on the fullness of her breasts. Her breath shortened, her heart pounded against her chest.

Lowering his head, he pressed his lips to her breast. Her skin burned at every tiny kiss laid on each soft mound. Trailing behind his lips came his fingertips, sending out shimmers of sensation like the ripples of moonlight on water. His touch lingered on the tiny scar on her right breast, and he raised his head in mute enquiry.

"It's nothing," she murmured. Trembling, she arched her neck. Her nightie slid farther down, exposing the dark brown tip of her nipple.

Cupping her breast in his hand, Daniel guided it to his mouth. She heard him groan deep in his throat as his lips closed over the hardening peak. Tremors of desire shot straight to the tingling warmth between her legs, inflaming her.

*I love you. I love you. I love you.* Over and over, the words formed in her brain. Words she didn't dare speak aloud.

She ran her hands over Daniel's chest, wanting to know every ripple of muscle, every rib, every inch of tanned, supple skin. When she encountered damp terry towel, she pushed at it impatiently.

He stood, pulling her up with him. Satin slithered across her heated skin as her nightgown slipped all the way to her waist and clung precariously to her hips. Daniel's towel fell away, leaving him naked. In the candlelight, his lean body glowed, shadowed by ridges of muscle and bone.

Then he pulled her close, and she gasped softly as her breasts touched his bare chest. He pressed his hips into hers, letting her feel the strength of his desire. And all the while his mouth clung and tasted, his hands moved and touched as though he would never get enough.

She could feel his erection hard against her belly and wriggled closer, wrapping one leg around his to press herself against his thigh.

His breathing was ragged now, his eyes glazed with need. With a groan he pushed up her nightdress and cupped her buttocks. Overbalancing, they fell on the bed, tangled in each other's limbs.

She shifted, her legs parting around his. Mindless with need, she bit her lip at the effort of controlling the primal urge to rock her hips upward and take him inside herself. "Daniel," she murmured. "Now. Please!"

His eyes fixed on hers, he ripped open the condom packet and, with a trembling hand, sheathed himself. A strangled groan emerged from his throat as he surged into her, filling her with a sweet, hard heat. She thrust upward, pulling him deep inside.

Daniel blanketed her in fiery love, his face animated by desire, his eyes penetrating her soul. His body moved with hers in a fit so perfect they might have been dovetailed by a master craftsman.

Deep in the moment she didn't think about tomorrow.

Filled with the love she'd longed for she didn't fear losing it. Daniel took her spinning through the distant reaches of time and space, the pain in her heart left far behind, a universe away.

Calling out his name, she arched upward. Explosions of neon-splashed ecstasy fused her body and soul in formless pleasure. Daniel plunged into her again and again, until at last his body shook with a final convulsive shudder.

"Karina," he whispered, and lowered his spent body onto hers.

When conscious thought returned, she was still wrapped in Daniel's embrace, his body a welcome weight on hers. She breathed in the musky scent of their lovemaking, savoring the intimacy of limb on limb, skin on skin.

With his face buried in her hair, she stroked her fingernails lightly down his back and up his sides. The skin over his ribs shivered at her touch and he wriggled his hips, setting off an aftershock that rippled through her body.

"Mmm, Daniel... Ohh!"

Daniel peered up at her, hair falling over his eyes as he smiled cheekily. He moved his hips again. Her eyes started to close as another pulse of lingering bliss washed over her. Just before her lids fluttered shut she saw his expression change to adoration and wonder.

At last she lay still, replete and exhausted, her limbs heavy. Daniel eased his weight off her and rolled them over onto their sides, still inside her. Her eyes half-closed, Karina smiled dreamily, savoring recent memory.

Daniel traced the outline of her lips with the tip of his

finger. "You look like the cat who swallowed the canary," he said, and laughed softly.

Her smile widened. "When you guarantee a girl a good time on her birthday, you really come through."

Daniel grinned and leaned forward to touch her lips with his. "Satisfaction or your money back. Don't forget to tell all your friends."

"Not a chance. I want you all to myself."

"Darlin', I'm yours."

Caught up in the banter, she'd spoken without thinking. He'd spoken lightly, matching her tone. Then she saw something flicker deep in his clear, hazel eyes.

"I want you all to myself, too," he said. This time he wasn't joking.

"I, uh…" She didn't know what to say. She was fine when everything was lighthearted, but how did she deal with this? One expectation led to another.

Her damp skin cooling rapidly, Karina wriggled under the covers, bringing the duvet up to her nose. "No problem," she said, taking refuge in further teasing. "Just knock aside the dozens of men beating a path to my door."

Daniel crooked one finger around the edge of the quilt and pulled it down far enough to plant a kiss on her lips. "Including Brian?"

Karina just laughed. Then her laughter faded as she realized she had to put this night in perspective, for both their sakes. "Seriously, Daniel, today was really special and I want to thank you, but—"

"I was that good, was I?"

The teasing light was back in his eyes, and for that she was grateful. "I meant about taking my mind off things."

"Nothing like sex to take your mind off your troubles.'' His expression sobering, he brushed a strand of damp hair off her face. ''Does this mean you've come to terms with your grief over your mother?''

The image of Mama, smiling and serene, came into her mind. Karina knew with a startled certainty the crippling sorrow had, if not disappeared, at least greatly diminished.

''I'll probably never get over it completely, but having you with me, being able to cry...yes, it helped. You wouldn't believe how much.''

''I'm glad. Maybe marriage won't seem such an awful fate to you anymore.''

She went still in his arms. ''Marriage?''

He smiled. ''I know you've heard of it.''

She rolled out of his arms, put her legs over the side of the bed and reached for her shawl. How could she not have seen he wouldn't be content with one night of lovemaking, or even a brief affair? Wrapping herself in her shawl, she rose, putting distance between them while she searched her mind for plausible reasons to put an end to this conversation. Any reason would do—except the real one.

She laughed, hoping it sounded casual. ''I'm not ready for marriage. If I get my promotion, as I expect I will, I'll be traveling a lot, spending more time at the office.'' Somehow that didn't sound as appealing as it once had. ''How could I take care of a family?''

He propped himself up on one elbow. ''Karina, I work at home. Natalie is going to school soon. It's not an issue.''

Karina began to pace. He hadn't come right out and asked her to marry him, but there was no mistaking his intent. ''As a wife, I'm not a good bet, Daniel. You've seen what kind of housekeeper I am—''

"Karina, if you don't love me, just say so."

His quiet words tore at her heart. She stopped pacing and faced him. "You want a family. Natalie wants a baby brother or sister. I want you both to have all the things you want."

"I want *you*, Karina."

He sounded so certain, she knew a moment of doubt. What if she was wrong to deny them a future together? Then she closed her mind to the thought.

"Aren't we getting ahead of ourselves with all this talk about babies and marriage?" she pleaded. "Let's just enjoy this night together and worry about tomorrow when it comes."

He was silent for a long moment, his expression sober. Then, slowly, he nodded. She crossed to the bed and let the shawl fall away from her breasts.

His gaze remained on her face. "I want more than tonight with you, Karina."

Instead of answering, she reached into the drawer and dangled another condom in front of him, letting her smile speak for her.

He sighed. Then a humorous light appeared in his eyes and he reached for her. "But for now, I'll take what I can get."

She grinned and straddled his thighs. "Spoken like a true pragmatist."

His hands slid down her back, urging her higher. "Being a romantic isn't doing me much good at the moment. But tomorrow—"

Karina laid a finger across his mouth. "Shh." She moved her hips against his and felt him swell beneath her. "Do you like that?"

Daniel's eyes closed. "You're absolutely ruthless."

She brushed the silky fringe of the shawl across his

chest, watching his nipples rise and harden in its wake. Then she stretched her arms forward over his head, enclosing the two of them in a glowing silken tent.

She bent her head and kissed him, her mouth warm and giving. She didn't want to think about tomorrow. Or the tomorrow after that. She just wanted to let him know without words that she loved him with her whole being, this minute and forever. Even if they couldn't have forever.

"Daniel," she whispered against his lips just to hear the sound of his name. She began to move against him more insistently, enticing him into slow, seductive lovemaking.

Much later, through a pleasure-hazed exhaustion, she was dimly aware of Daniel drawing the duvet over them. Just before she sank into sleep she felt him press a kiss, soft, warm and infinitely tender, on her temple.

THE CREAK OF the floorboards on the landing woke Karina sometime in the darkness before dawn. She opened her eyes a crack to see a small figure with tousled blond hair and dinosaur pajamas stumble into the room and crawl into bed on her side.

"Daddy, are you in here?"

Natalie's eyes were half shut, and it was clear she was more asleep than awake. Karina grunted softly as small hands and elbows dug into her stomach.

"*Mommy?*" Natalie's sleepy voice took on a bewildered note. "Mommy, is that you?"

The hope and rising expectation in the little girl's query tore at Karina's heart. On the other side of the bed, Daniel flicked on the table lamp. Squinting against the light, Natalie awakened fully and recognized Karina.

Her startled expression was swiftly followed by one of crushing disappointment.

"What are you doing out of bed, Nattie?" Daniel said, rising on one elbow.

"Shhh, Daniel," Karina said quickly. Natalie looked ready to burst into tears.

"I had a sad dream," Natalie said, her voice quavering. "I dreamed Mommy was back. And then I thought…" She broke off, gazing uncertainly at Karina. "But it wasn't—" Two big tears broke free and rolled down her cheeks.

Daniel started to get up. Karina stopped him with a hand on his chest. "I'll take her back to bed." She rose and wrapped herself in her shawl. Placing an arm around Natalie's slender shoulders, she led her out of the room.

Karina tucked Natalie back into bed and pulled the coverlet up under her chin. She stroked wisps of hair back from the girl's forehead. "You miss your mommy, don't you, sweetheart?"

Natalie nodded, swallowing. "It's worser when I dream. I forget she's not here, but when I wake up…she…she's always gone." Her thin voice trailed off as more tears snaked down her cheeks. "I'm sorry," she said with a sniff.

"Don't be sorry, darling. And don't ever be afraid to cry. Someday it won't hurt quite as much and you'll be able to think about your mother without crying. You see—"

She paused, unsure whether to burden the child with her own grief. Then she thought of how alone she'd felt before Daniel had been there for her. Understanding and caring could never be a burden, she decided.

Taking Natalie's hand in hers, she soothed, "You see, Nattie, my mother died, too, when I was young. Not as young as you, but pretty young. It's very hard to live without your mommy. I...I still hurt inside."

Natalie's tears slowed and she gazed solemnly at Karina. "You do?"

Karina nodded. "I think part of me will always hurt when I think of her, but I also remember the good things. Things that make me smile."

"Like what?"

"Oh, like when she used to let me play dress-up with her old clothes. And every year I helped her pick tomatoes and make a special sauce with them. But I think my happiest memory is of her singing to me."

"Mommy used to sing to me, too," Natalie confided with a tremulous smile. "She knew lots of funny songs that made me laugh. Like you."

"There you go. Hold on to those beautiful memories, darling. And don't forget you've got a daddy who loves you very much and...and you've got Mrs. Beeton to take care of you." It was a poor second and Karina knew it, but she also knew the child needed to take comfort where she could.

Natalie's eyes widened. "Mrs. Beeton's gone."

"Gone?"

Natalie nodded. "She had to go help another little girl who needs her."

"Don't you need her anymore?" Was Daniel aware of this new development? she wondered. He'd be so pleased.

"No, 'cause I've got you now." She snuggled under the covers.

Speechless, Karina contemplated the enormity of her responsibility. She had neither the heart to deny, nor the courage to confirm, Natalie's casual but confident assertion.

The girl's long lashes fluttered sleepily. "K'rina?"

"Yes?" she said faintly.

"Would you sing me a song?"

Karina swallowed. "Of course." She drew a deep breath and softly, she began to sing, "'Hush little baby, don't say a word....'"

She could barely get the words out past the lump in her throat. Her heart was so painfully swollen with love and grief for this poor motherless child she was afraid she'd break down before the song was over.

Natalie fell asleep within seconds but Karina sang on, the tears rolling down her cheeks as she mourned the mother she'd loved and lost.

Daniel was asleep when Karina crept back to bed in the grey light of early morning. His face was smooth and at peace. A tiny smile curled the corners of his beautiful mouth. She lay for a long time just watching him and loving him....

And knowing she could never marry him.

The responsibility was too great and the potential for tragedy too awful. Seeing Natalie's trusting face in the lamplight had brought home how theoretical her fears had been until now. The child was a live human being, not some hypothetical baby. Natalie was already fragile and vulnerable from losing her mother. How would she ever recover if she lost another?

# CHAPTER FIFTEEN

KARINA TOSSED AND TURNED for hours until finally giving up all hope of sleep. She slipped out from beneath the covers and dressed quickly and quietly, casting a last longing glance at Daniel. If only they could make love just one more time, she thought, her heart quietly breaking. But it would be wrong.

She went downstairs and moved mechanically around the kitchen, flipping on the radio, making coffee. While the coffee brewed, she went down to the basement, and a few minutes later, climbed the stairs dragging a roll of chicken wire behind her. When her inner self was in turmoil, nothing was as soothing as the feel of paste or as distracting as creating a new papier-mâché creature.

With little conscious thought she molded the wire into a stout body with four spindly legs. What she would create this morning she wasn't certain, but she knew it wouldn't be beautiful or elegant. Sure enough, before long she'd fashioned a short, thick neck with a long, upturned snout.

Karina stood back, eyeing the mass of chicken wire critically. Yes, she thought grimly, a warthog was exactly what she felt like. A warthog who'd had no sleep and had precious little happiness to look forward to.

She sipped at a cup of coffee and with one hand pinched the top of the head into small, pointy ears. Thoughts of Daniel crept into her mind as she worked but she cast them aside, focusing all her attention on the beast in front of her.

She couldn't help glancing at Felix the Clock every now and then, wondering when Daniel would wake up and what he'd think when he saw she wasn't beside him.

That was how she knew it was exactly 8:37 when the telephone rang. Absently wiping a hand down her shirt, she picked up the receiver with two fingers and clicked it on. "Hello?"

"Good morning," said a pleasant female voice. "Is this Mrs. Bowen?"

Karina hesitated, startled by the unexpected temptation to lay claim to that title. "Er, no. May I ask who's calling?"

"My name is Diana Wallace. Is Mr. Bowen in?"

"He's not available right now. Can I take a message?"

"Certainly. I'm from House Rentals Plus. Mr. Bowen asked us to locate a house for him. I'm pleased to say we have one that will suit his needs perfectly. It's just two blocks from the primary school he mentioned and it has a huge garage."

"Sounds perfect," Karina replied dully.

"It's available from the first of September," Diana Wallace went on. "But there's a good possibility the present tenants might vacate earlier."

"I...I'll let him know," Karina said, and copied down the address. "Thanks for calling."

She clicked the phone off but made no move to hang it up. *Daniel would be leaving.* She shivered, cold all over.

It's for the best, she told herself, rubbing her arms to bring some warmth back into them. He would have had to leave anyway. At least now she'd know he and Natalie had a home to go to.

Daniel entered the kitchen to see Karina standing by the window, the telephone hanging from her hand as she stared into nothingness. In the middle of the floor was the biggest, ugliest-looking pig he'd ever seen. Petunia had been positively dainty by comparison.

Sneaking up behind her, he snaked an arm around her waist and planted a kiss on the back of her neck, bared by the ponytail that hung halfway down her back.

"Mornin', darlin'. You're up early."

To his surprise, she backed away from his embrace without meeting his gaze. "Everything okay?" he asked. He was eager to touch her, to kiss her, to drag her back upstairs to her bed. Or his. He wasn't fussy.

"Fine." She slanted him the briefest of glances before slipping the phone back into its slot on the wall. Silently she tipped some powder from a bag into the basin on the table, added water and began to mix up a fresh batch of paste.

Daniel frowned, perturbed by her withdrawal. "Was Nattie upset about finding us in bed together?"

Karina shook her head. "She was too troubled by her dream to notice. I think she thought you were helping me with a nightmare."

He gave a short laugh. "I'm a bit of an expert on nightmares."

"I can imagine." The paste prepared, Karina began to cut strips of cloth from a piece of dark plaid spread flat on the table.

"A little subdued for your taste, isn't it?" He fingered the cotton fabric, his gaze never leaving her averted face.

"It suits my mood."

Why should her mood be so dark after the night

they'd spent together? He placed a hand on her cheek and gently brought her face around to his. "My kisses are renowned for their mood-lifting qualities," he said, smiling.

She ducked away again before he could claim her lips. Her fixed smile disappeared as she gazed over his shoulder. Worry, sorrow, fear—and something else that he couldn't decipher—shifted across her face.

Daniel crossed his arms over his chest, tired of the cat-and-mouse game. "Okay, Karina, what's wrong?"

She shrugged. "There's a message for you from Diana Wallace at House Rentals Plus. She's got a house for you."

He pushed a hand through his hair. "I'd almost given up on them."

Karina dipped a piece of fabric into the paste and laid it over the warthog's back. "She said the house is perfect for you and that you can move in at the beginning of the month."

He moved toward the phone. "I'll ring her back and tell her I don't need it anymore."

Karina stepped in front of him, blocking the way to the telephone. For the first time since he'd entered the kitchen, she looked him directly in the eye.

"I think you should take it."

The skin on the back of his neck prickled. "I don't want it."

Karina rested a hand on the chicken-wire frame, her fingers closing around the open mesh. "It's close to Natalie's school."

"I can drive her."

"It's got a big garage for your exclusive use."

"I'm all set up here."

"*I want you to go.*"

He stared at her in disbelief. "Why?"

"I just do. Don't ask me any more."

She meant it. Through his mind-numbing pain, he saw that Karina was on the verge of tears. He wanted to reach for her but didn't. She was suffering, but he was suffering, too. The time for comforting was past. It was time for some answers.

"I—" Her voice cracked and she cleared her throat. "I'll give you a good reference."

Daniel's head snapped up. "Reference! Forget the reference. Forget the damn house! Just tell me what's going on. Why are you acting this way?"

She turned back to the basin and picked out another strip of fabric, squeezing off the excess paste with trembling fingers. "I just don't see how we can go on living in the same house when...when..."

Coming up behind her, he gripped her shoulders. She shuddered at his touch. Her reaction gave him a sick feeling in his stomach but he couldn't bring himself to let her go.

"Karina, I love you. I want to marry you."

Her head went back, eyes closed. Tears squeezed beneath her lids. "I can't marry you, Daniel. I'm sorry."

"Dammit, Karina, do you love me or not?"

"Love has nothing to do with it."

"The hell it doesn't." His fingers dug into her shoulders as he turned her to face him. "What's the real reason you won't marry me? Is it Brian?"

"Brian?" she repeated. "What does Brian have to do with you and me?"

He shrugged, an attempt at nonchalance he didn't feel. "You and he are...close."

"Daniel, for once and for all, I feel nothing for your brother beyond friendship."

''You kissed him.''

She wrenched herself away. "For your information, *he* kissed me. There's absolutely no reason for you to be jealous of him."

"Then why are you turning me down?" His hand crashed onto the table, shaking the basin of paste. "I'm not some young fool you can make love to, then cast off like last year's fashion. Tell me the truth!"

Natalie skipped into the kitchen, oblivious of the tension. "Can I help?" she said, spying the new papier-mâché animal. "Can I, please?"

Karina turned away to lean against the kitchen counter but not before Daniel saw more tears spring to her eyes. He grabbed his daughter's arm as she went by and turned her back toward the hall.

"Have you made your bed this morning?" he asked, knowing she rarely did such a thing without prompting. "No? Then off you go upstairs. When you've done that *and* have your hair brushed, you can see if Karina needs help."

Grumbling, Natalie ran up the stairs. Daniel stalked back to find Karina still leaning over the counter, her forehead resting against the cupboard. He jammed his hands in his back pockets to avoid touching her and made an effort to sound reasonable.

"Why won't you marry me? You've begun to grieve for your mother. That's a sign of healing—"

"It's not that simple, Daniel," she interrupted, a sob in her voice. "I've got a family history of breast cancer."

"I know. And I'll do everything I can to give you whatever emotional or material support you need. But I don't see that as a reason not to marry. Karina, *look at me*."

She turned, her fear and frustration plain on her face. "Don't you see, if I were to—" she swallowed hard "—*die* and leave you and Natalie and...maybe another little one, I could never forgive myself."

"Where is it written you're going to die? You're too smart to let anything like a lump get by you."

"But it almost did!" she cried. "Last spring I found one in my right breast. That's why I changed my mind about renting."

*The scar on her breast.* His heart seemed to stop beating. "Oh God, Karina. You mean..."

Eyes wide, she reached out a hand. "No, it's all right. It was benign. But it could just as easily have been malignant."

Relief turned his knees to water and he leaned against the counter. "Okay. But even if it had been malignant, that still doesn't mean you'd have succumbed to an early grave."

Karina went to the coffee jug and fumbled the lid open. From clear across the room he could see her hands shake as she poured herself a cup. "You don't know what you're talking about."

"Then tell me."

The pain in her tear-filled eyes when she looked at him almost made him wish he hadn't asked.

"My grandmother died of breast cancer in her thirties. As did my great-aunt and God knows how many others on my mother's side. It's in my genes."

"That still doesn't mean you're doomed. Treatment has advanced since your mother's day."

She threw up her hands. "Oh, don't be so damned *rational*. Think of Natalie if you can't understand for yourself. I know I could never take her mother's place, nor would I want to, but if we were to marry, she'd get attached to me."

"She's already attached."

Karina's eyes pressed shut. "I know. I love her, Daniel. I love her so much I don't want to cause her a single moment of pain. How do you think she'd feel losing another mother? How many Mrs. Beetons do you think she can conjure up?"

Daniel's fists clenched inside his pockets and he turned away. This time he didn't have any answers. He gazed at the molded chicken wire, so frustrated he wanted to kick it. "What is this thing anyway?"

"A warthog."

He stared at it with loathing. They could have been making love right now, or planning their future. Instead she'd deserted his bed—okay, *her* bed—to make a damn warthog.

He tried another tack. "Your mother must have known the odds of getting breast cancer were pretty high, yet she still had you."

Karina set her cup down on the counter so hard the murky brown liquid spilled over the side. "That's what makes her actions so irresponsible. She knew it was in her family, but she had me anyway. And then she *left* me."

"Is that the trouble? You haven't forgiven your mother for dying?"

"Don't be ridiculous. She didn't *want* to die. How could I blame her?"

She dropped her face in her hands, shoulders heaving as she fought for control. When she looked up, her eyes seemed to plead for understanding. "I would *never* knowingly inflict that kind of suffering on a child. Daniel, do you understand? *I will never have children.*"

*She really meant it.* Daniel read the agonizing truth in her eyes and the strength of her determination in every line of her slim, rigid body. He'd never known the joy that children brought until Natalie had come along. But like a blind man suddenly gifted with sight, once he'd found out what he'd been missing, the prospect of some-day having more children had become as expected and as necessary as the rising sun.

His heart breaking, he said, "I want a family, Karina. With you. Think of it, our babies..."

"Don't!" she cried, her voice raw with pain. "I'd give anything if I could be part of it. But I can't."

He grasped her by the arms, desperate to make her see reason. "Yes, you can, if you only want to. You've told me the worst. I'm willing to take a chance."

*"Well, I'm not."* Her eyes blazed up at him. "I couldn't inflict that suffering on you, either. Not after seeing what my father went through."

"Karina," he pleaded. "Talk to your doctor. Assess the probabilities, discuss the options...."

"I *have* talked to my doctor. Endlessly. If it were simply a rational decision I'd say yes right now. But it's not, and I can't." Tears streamed down her face. "I never wanted to hurt you, Daniel. I...I hope you find what you're looking for. I hope Natalie will be happy. I hope..."

Daniel pulled her into his arms, and this time she didn't resist. With all his heart and soul he wished he could erase her anguish. And his. It hurt knowing his love, deep and strong as it was, still wasn't enough to overcome her fears. But she'd made her decision long before she'd even met him. The sooner he accepted the fact her path would never converge with his, the better. For all of them, he thought, remembering Natalie.

"I'd better pack my bags," he said, drawing back.

She clutched his arms, gazing up at him in alarm. "Where will you go? The house isn't available for two more weeks."

"I'll find some place to stay, don't worry."

"Daniel, I'm so sorry." Fresh tears started from her eyes.

"Shh, love." He dropped his head and his lips met hers with all the love and tenderness he could place in one brief kiss. He tasted the salt of her tears and the bittersweet nectar of love gone awry. He could hardly bear to look into her eyes as he lifted his mouth from hers.

"Goodbye, Karina, my love." His fingers trailed down her wet cheek and lingered a moment at the edge of her lips. "Goodbye."

"FOR CRYING OUT LOUD, Karina, do you know what time it is?" Joanne hung on to the doorjamb with one hand and clutched her head with the other. Her purple dressing gown hung open over a Snoopy nightshirt.

"I thought you were always up early with the kids." Karina edged past Joanne into the house. From the living room came the sound of Yogi Bear's voice entreating Boo Boo to steal a picnic basket.

"*They* let me sleep in on Sunday mornings, unlike some people I know."

"Sorry. Can I make some coffee?"

Joanne sighed. "Sure, why not. Just let me wash the sleep out of my eyes so I can see you while we're talking."

Karina went through to the kitchen and put on the kettle. The fridge bristled with colorful children's drawings, and small handprints in plaster decorated the walls.

A family kitchen. Marbles underfoot, crayons on the counter, sticky patches on the backs of the chairs. Nothing had ever seemed so desirable. Or so impossibly remote.

Joanne reappeared a few minutes later wearing a faded tracksuit, her hair brushed and damp around the temples. She went to the sink, filled a glass of water and popped a couple of painkillers.

"You really danced up a storm at the party last night, Jo. Feeling frisky, were you?" Karina turned away from the counter, a cup of instant coffee in each hand.

"Feeling good," Joanne said with a sudden smile. "I didn't get a chance to tell you. Peter got a promotion! From now on he'll manage projects from the office instead of doing the fieldwork. He'll still have to go away sometimes, but for much shorter periods."

"That's wonderful," Karina said, brightening at her friend's good fortune. She handed Joanne a cup. "You must be so happy."

"You bet. We've been waiting for this for so long. Next time I go to a party, I'll be dancing with my husband."

Karina removed a toy truck from a stool and sat down at the breakfast bar. "I don't know how you two have survived as a couple with all the time you've spent apart."

Joanne shrugged. "It's been hard at times, but...we love each other. You can get through a lot of tough stuff that way." She hoisted herself onto another stool and looked expectantly at Karina. "So, what's up?"

Karina reached for the cream and sugar. She'd come here because she wanted to be with someone rather than mope alone. And because she couldn't bear to be around

Daniel after all they'd said to each other. Now she realized she badly needed to talk.

"I...I had a fight with Daniel."

Joanne's eyebrows shot up as she reached for her coffee. "What? Are you kidding me?"

"I wish I were."

"When I left last night you two were wrapped tighter than wisteria around a trellis. What happened? Was it Brian?"

Karina frowned. "What is this obsession with Brian? He had nothing to do with our disagreement. It started long after the party was over."

Joanne sipped at the black steaming liquid and squinted over the cup at her. "So, you and Daniel stayed up after the party was over. That sounds cozy. What's that old saying, 'Make love not war'?"

Karina fiddled with the lid to the sugar bowl, spinning it around until Joanne slapped her hand away.

"Honestly, you're as bad as the kids." Sudden comprehension lit her face. "You slept with him, didn't you?"

Karina heaved a resigned sigh. "Yes."

"Fantastic!" Bug-eyed, Joanne ogled her. "Was it?"

"Yes." Karina was annoyed to feel herself flush. "For God's sake, Joanne, quit looking at me like I swallowed a baby bird or something."

"But it's so exciting," Joanne gushed, undeterred. "This is a first since Joel, isn't it? That's what, two years?"

Karina nodded, but there was really no comparison. What she'd had with Joel went nowhere near as deep as her relationship with Daniel.

"So how did you go from loving to fighting?" Joanne asked. "Usually it happens the other way around."

Karina hooked her feet around a rung of the stool and leaned an elbow on the counter. "It all started when he asked me to marry him."

"Holy cromoly, Karina. What did you say?"

Karina frowned. "*No,* of course."

"Oh, of course." Joanne rolled her eyes. "The greatest man you've ever met in your entire life asks you to marry him and you just naturally say no."

"Greatest man I've ever met?"

"Well, isn't he?"

Karina shrugged. "Okay, so what if he is? That's not the point. I made a promise to myself never to get married."

Joanne leaned forward, incredulous. "So break it. No one else would hold you to such a silly promise. Think about it, Karina. He's creative, he's intelligent, he's got a sense of humor, he's sensitive without being a wuss, he's good in the kitchen, he's good with kids, he's good with his hands, he's good in bed, *and*—" she finished on a triumphant gasp "—he loves you. What more do you want?"

There was nothing left to ask for, Karina thought, except infinite patience. And even that might not be enough.

"It doesn't matter what I want, Jo. I can't seem to come to grips with this fear I have of dying young and leaving the ones I love behind. I know my feelings aren't entirely rational but..." She paused, searching for words. With a sigh, she gave up. "It's hard to explain."

"Try," Joanne prodded.

Karina clutched her head with both hands and struggled to overcome her confusion. "Well, for instance, last night Natalie had a nightmare and came into my room looking for Daniel. She was half asleep and for a moment she thought I was her mother.''

Tears filled Karina's eyes at the memory. "Jo, you should have seen the look on her face when she realized *again* that her mother wasn't ever coming back. It brought home to me how much responsibility goes with having children.''

"Responsibility? Well, of course,'' Joanne said, frowning slightly. "But the most important thing is to simply love them.''

"You have to be alive to love them,'' Karina argued, rubbing her thumb around the rim of her cup. "If you can't guarantee you'll be around to see them grow up, then you shouldn't have them.''

"Karina! I can't believe anybody so smart can be so dumb. No one can guarantee their children that. All anyone can do is care for them as best they can.''

Karina burst into tears. "That's exactly what I'm trying to do!'' When she'd told Joanne all that had passed between her and Daniel, she wiped a hand across her eyes. "I've turned into such a baby, Jo. I don't cry. I never cry. Suddenly I'm crying every half hour.''

Joanne got off her stool and pulled her into a hug. "Everything will turn out all right in the end, you'll see.''

"I don't see how it can.'' She snuffled into the piece of paper towel Joanne had handed her in lieu of a tissue.

"It will. And don't worry about crying. No one can be strong all the time. It's not healthy.''

Karina nodded, thinking about her father and how his outer strength hid an inability to adapt and accept. Maybe it was time to stop protecting him with her complicity. It wasn't too late for them to reestablish a relationship. She'd grown up some. Maybe *she* could help *him* now.

"Give yourself time," Joanne said. "You've been fretting over this for so many years you can't expect to rid yourself of all your worries in a single night."

"Daniel seems to think I should be able to."

Joanne squeezed her hand. "You caught him at a bad time. Don't forget, you'd just turned down his marriage proposal."

"I can't expect him to wait for me indefinitely." With a sigh, she got to her feet. "I'd better go. Thanks, Joanne," she said, hugging her friend. "I'll see you later."

Joanne followed her to the front door. "What are you going to do now?"

Karina turned on the step. A breeze caught a length of her hair, blowing it across her face. "I'm not sure," she said, brushing the hair out of her eyes. "I guess the first thing I need to do is get home before Daniel leaves. I didn't even say goodbye to Natalie."

"You two will work it out," Joanne assured her.

Karina couldn't answer that. Whatever lay between her and Daniel was complicated by what she felt for Natalie—a fierce, protective desire that nothing she did should ever hurt the child.

Talking things over with Joanne had made her feel better, but nothing was resolved in her mind. She didn't feel any closer to being able to say yes to Daniel than she had before.

She started down the steps, then turned back to Joanne. "I'm really glad for you. About Peter's job, I mean."

"Thanks. Me, too. Take care." Joanne waved once more and closed the door.

Karina steered Sammy toward home. By the time she pulled up in front of her house, she was eager to see Daniel. One thing had changed, she realized as she ran up the steps. She desperately wanted to try to work things out. Maybe with his help, she could overcome her fears.

# CHAPTER SIXTEEN

THE FRONT DOOR was locked. Frowning, Karina rattled the knob. She was sure she hadn't locked it when she'd fled to Joanne's. She scrabbled in her purse for the key and quickly opened the door.

All was quiet. To her frazzled nerves, the silence seemed to scream out loud. Daniel never could remember to leave the radio on when he went out so there'd be music to greet her on her return.

She pushed the door shut harder than necessary just to break the stifling hush. With hurried steps she went from room to room, searching in vain for some trace of Daniel and Natalie. Surely they couldn't have packed up and left already?

She ran up the stairs, calling his name. The tinny sound of the transistor in the bathroom seemed to mock her as she hurried across the landing.

Without knocking, she flung open Daniel's door. Her anxious gaze whisked from corner to corner. Her heart sank. The room was empty of all his belongings.

It was only when she retreated to her own room that she found the note pinned to her pillow.

DANIEL LAY ON the hotel bed and gazed glumly at the bland, characterless walls with their color-coordinated pieces of pseudoart. A week in this cold, impersonal hotel had been more than enough to show him how lackluster his life was without Karina. He never thought he'd see the day when he'd miss her weird and wonderful creature collection.

He glanced at Natalie, asleep in the other bed, clutching her doll to her chest like a lifeline, and tried to count his blessings. The current tenants of the house he'd rented had moved out early. He'd picked up the key this afternoon, and tomorrow he and Nattie could move in. The house was just as perfect as described. Except for the fact that Karina wouldn't be there.

For the thousandth time, he pondered the note he'd left and wondered if it was too impersonal. Maybe if he'd been more forceful. Maybe if he'd pleaded. Maybe if he hadn't been so worried about Natalie, he would have said the right words to convince Karina to take a chance on him, on them, on life itself.

He'd hoped she would ignore his note and come looking for him. But she hadn't even called. God, how he missed her. Her laughter, the tapping of her high heels, her endless commotion, and yes, even her ever-present music.

Wearily Daniel rolled off the bed to turn down the neutral brown bedspread and slide beneath the cold, starched sheets. On top of everything else, he'd forgotten to give Karina her birthday present.

KARINA STARED forlornly at her TV dinner. Her appetite had disappeared with Daniel, along with everything else worthwhile in life.

The house echoed with emptiness. In vain she listened for the sound of Daniel's rich, accented voice as he calmly countered her outrageous comments with maddening logic. Or Natalie's happy laughter as she played her endless games of make-believe.

Gone was the smell of good cooking, the fragrance of the eucalypt sawdust that clung to Daniel's clothes and the scent of childhood in Nattie's newly washed hair.

All gone.

Pushing the tray aside, she got up and wandered onto the deck. Looking at the garage made her think of all the tools and wood still sitting out there. He'd have to come back for them, but he'd probably do it while she was at work. He didn't want to see her again, he'd said as much in his note.

She'd read the note so many times it was little more than a rag, yet she knew it by heart. "Dear Karina," he'd written, "Natalie and I will be gone by the time you get back. I don't fully understand your feelings, but I respect your wishes. I won't try to see you again. If you change your mind about us, call me. Otherwise I think it's best we have no further contact. Thank you for everything. Natalie sends her love. Daniel."

Straightforward, unemotional and definitely final. Well, what had she expected? A torrid declaration of undying love and a desperate plea for one more chance? He wasn't the type to beg, and she wouldn't respect him if he did. Yet her heart ached for the smallest sign of the warmth and affection she'd come to associate with him.

On a separate piece of paper he'd written the name and address of their hotel. Several times she'd picked up the telephone only to slam it back into its cradle. He obviously didn't have enough faith in a future together to keep trying. Or maybe he simply didn't love her enough. In which case, why prolong the agony?

Leaning over the balcony, Karina noted apathetically that the tomatoes were ripe and badly needed to be picked. Behind the fence she spotted a wriggling black shape between the cracks in the boards. Piper saw her, too, and let out an encouraging yip.

"Okay, Piper," she called. "I'm coming."

She picked up a long-handled woven basket from the deck, donned her gardening gloves and clumped down the steps to the backyard. Life went on.

A short time later she knelt back on her heels and wiped a sun-warmed arm over her damp brow. Piper danced around her, kicking up bits of dirt and snuffling at her heels.

"Piper, you cheeky mutt! Bring back that tomato right now."

He paid no attention at all. Laughing around the tomato gripped in his slobbery mouth, the dog ran off, ears and tail flying like flags.

Karina ignored him and turned her attention back to the tomatoes. They were all that tomatoes should be—ripe, red and firm. She breathed in the tangy scent the plants gave off as she moved among them. Inevitably her thoughts turned to her mother.

She plucked a large, red globe and smiled at the memory of Mama surrounded by mountains of tomatoes, chopping the ripe fruit, stirring the big pot of pasta sauce. The air would be redolent with garlic and herbs, the counter lined with glass sealing jars. She'd taught Karina the secret family recipe, explaining how it had been handed down from her mother and her grandmother before that.

Who would *she* pass things on to? Karina wondered with a painful quickening of her heart. At least she was there to remember her mother. Who would remember *her* when she was gone?

The thought nagged at her as she climbed the stairs with her load of tomatoes and set the basket on the counter. Going to the shelf beside the fridge, she pulled out an old and tattered volume from her sparse collection of cookbooks.

The book bulged with loose pages, recipe cards and half-torn pockets filled with newspaper clippings of long-forgotten summer favorites. There were yellowed scraps of paper in cramped Italian script, so faded she could hardly read them. She'd have to go through it all someday and sort things out.

She flipped to the section that contained her mother's recipes, handwritten in Mama's elegant slanting script. Her mother had given her the book just before she died. Who would she leave it to when she was gone? Her brother? Joanne?

With *La Traviata* playing in the background, Karina went to work preparing the jars and measuring the herbs that went into the sauce. It wasn't any fun this time, she thought dismally. It was supposed to be a family ritual, not a solitary ordeal.

She ladled the steaming red sauce into the sealing jars, screwed on the lids and put them in the pressure cooker to boil. She'd been counting on Natalie to keep her company, she realized, and wondered if she would even bother growing tomatoes next year.

Felix's white-gloved hands pointed to midnight when she finally took the last jar from the pressure cooker. They were lined up two deep on the counter, gleaming dark red in the low light of the range hood. Karina sank onto a chair, staring blankly at them, the dying strains of Violetta's final aria drifting through her head.

She sat on in the semidarkness, her head resting on her hand, and drifted off....

A door slammed in the breeze from the open window. She awoke with a start. Her elbow flew out, knocking the recipe book off the table. It crashed to the floor in a scattered heap of pages and papers. Karina bent to gather the bits and pieces together.

What in the world—?

She reached for one of the overflowing pockets. What was a photo doing in with the recipes?

She pulled it out and crossed to the counter, where the light was better. The photo had been taken here in the kitchen one sunlit day—years ago, judging by those old green curtains. A row of sauce-filled sealer jars lined the counter, just as they did now. And a woman who looked exactly like her smiled down at a young girl with long, curling dark hair.

*Mama.* And she was the girl.

Tears filled her eyes. Aunt Maria must have taken the photo. Yes, she'd come out from Toronto that summer.

Karina breathed in on a sigh, and the scent of tomatoes and herbs filled her nostrils. They permeated the kitchen, just as they had then, and the smell brought that day forward with crystal clarity. There'd been a bowl of roses on the table. And a canary singing. Funny, she'd forgotten about Tweety Pie.

Karina peered closer at the photo. Yes, and there were the dangly beaded earrings she'd given her mother for her birthday that year.

A shiver ran over her shoulders and skittered along her arms, making her go cold all over. Mama's thirty-second birthday. Six months after this photo was taken she was dead.

It was hard to believe that someone so vibrant and alive could have died so young, she thought, lightly touching the photo. Behind Mama's smiling face, tragedy lurked.

In the dark, silent kitchen, memories quietly flowed

back into Karina's mind. Memories she thought she'd buried forever.

Mama, sending her to the basement for more sealing jars. The light was dim down there and she didn't like the spiders that hung in the corners. The jars were dusty but she gathered as many as she could carry. Then she was standing on the top step, trying to reach around the armful of jars for the knob....

And she heard something she wasn't meant to.

Mama, her beautiful voice troubled, telling Maria about a lump in her right breast. Aunt Maria begging her to see a doctor, take some tests. Mama's voice fearful but evasive, promising nothing, reminding Maria of the suffering their mother had gone through. And all for nothing in the end....

But wait, the visits to the doctor, the biopsy...all that hadn't started until *October* of that year. She remembered because Mama hadn't been able to finish her costume for a Halloween party; she'd been too upset by her first appointment with the specialist.

Karina doubled over, struck by a squeezing pain behind her breastbone. Her hand closed around the photo, crumpling it. *Mama knew.* Not just that she was predisposed to cancer, but that she *had* it. And she hadn't gone for treatment until it was too late.

Karina tried to breathe, tried to whistle, but her throat was dry. *Mama might have lived.* Why hadn't she gone to see a doctor in time? If not for herself, then for her family. How could she have let them down?

Anger forced air into Karina's lungs, but she no longer had the urge to block out her thoughts. They were too powerful and too insistent not to vent. Hardly knowing what she was doing, she jumped up, grasped the wooden spoon and smashed it down on the counter.

"Mama!" she shouted. "How could you have done that to us!"

Her angry cry rang through the dark and silent house. All those years, all that pain and grief. Wasted. No wonder she'd never been able to cry. She was too furious with her mother for dying.

Karina had allowed herself nothing. *Nothing.* All because of Mama. No husband, no children, no future.

*No Daniel.*

Once again she raised the spoon. And with a slashing blow, broadsided the row of sealing jars.

*Damn you, Mama! Damn you to hell!*

Glass shattered against glass. Heavy jars slid over the counter to smash on the floor. Red splashed the blue-and-white linoleum and spattered the cream-colored wall.

She hit out again. And again. Every blow was a blow against her mother. For all the moments in her life, large and small, when she'd needed Mama to be there—her first date, graduation night.... And for all the times Karina had called out for her in the night and she hadn't come.

"*Ma-a-mma!*" she called out now into the emptiness.

All the jars lay smashed on the floor, tomato sauce bleeding between shards of glass, dripping from the walls. Karina dropped the wooden spoon from her cramped hand. Gasping, she sank to her knees. Her hair fell around her face as she bowed her head and wept. Pain racked her body and she rocked back and forth on her heels, hugging herself.

Mama hadn't had to die. She *should not* have died.

*She* was going to die like her mother.

Karina stopped rocking, still clutching her sides.

*No.* She was not her mother, no matter how much

alike they were. She was her own person. One who could learn from her mother's mistakes. Mama's death need not have happened. But that thought, which a moment ago had caused her anger and despair, now filled her with hope for the future. If the future brought cancer, she would face it. Defeat it. *She would not die.*

Rising to her feet, she made a new promise to herself—a promise to survive. A fierce, exultant joy swept through her. She would marry Daniel, be a mother to Natalie and, God willing, bear Daniel's children.

Her mother had looked so proud of her in the photo. Well, she would give her something to be proud about.

*The photo.* What had she done with it?

Frantically she glanced around the room and spied the photo on the floor where she'd thrown it, one corner steeped in tomato sauce. She snatched it up, sponged the sauce away with a towel and hugged the unexpected treasure to her chest.

Poor Mama. Maybe she'd been angry, too.

Karina sat again, her eyes closing as images of her mother filled her mind. Here in the kitchen where so many memories of Mama dwelled, she felt her mother's presence all around her. A wave of love washed over her, refreshing her parched heart with the living memory of a mother's love, flooding her soul with joy and serenity.

Soon another pulse of love wove in with the first, like a second melody. It was her love for Daniel. More vibrant, more compelling, but just as pure and strong and filled with the promise of a future.

Karina let the waves of love and joy ripple and flow through her like a symphony. Her heart healed and swelled to contain the expanding love she held inside, for Mama, for Daniel, for Natalie.

*Thank you, Mama.*

Tears of forgiveness and gratitude streamed down her face. Mama might not have had time to teach her all the ways of a woman, but she'd given her the greatest gift a mother could give a child—life itself.

Mama had had a passion for living and a talent for loving. Surely the greatest tribute Karina could pay her would be to pass those qualities on to her own children. To give of herself to those she held dearest.

Karina pushed herself out of her chair. She had to talk to Daniel. Squinting at the number of his hotel she'd tacked to the corkboard, she picked up the phone and began to punch in the numbers. Then she glanced at Felix.

*Shoot.* It was 2:00 a.m.

Slowly she replaced the receiver. She might not be a mother yet, but at least she knew better than to wake a child in the middle of the night.

Never mind. Tomorrow would soon be here.

"NOT SO MUCH JAM on your crumpet, Nattie," Daniel chided. "And sit up straight."

Though it was barely 7:00 a.m., they were already in the hotel coffee shop having breakfast.

"Gee, Daddy," Natalie complained, "why are you so grumpy today?"

"I'm not grump—" He broke off, catching sight of his reflection in the window. His face was set in a disagreeable frown, and he was hunched over his plate like an old bear.

Well, who wouldn't be grumpy? Today the woman he loved was going away for the weekend with his brother.

He forced a strained smile onto his face. "Sorry, Possum, I haven't been sleeping very well lately. I guess I am a bit grumpy.''

"You're *very* grumpy," she declared. Then, in a small voice, she added, "I haven't been sleeping well, either."

Daniel grunted sympathetically and buttered a slice of toast for which he had no appetite. "Did you have another nightmare last night?"

Natalie nodded sadly. "I miss Karina. And Mrs. Beeton won't come back."

"Don't worry, Nattie," he said, trying to put some animation into his voice. "I called Grandma last night and she said she'll come and visit us soon."

"Oh."

Daniel reached across and felt her forehead. Natalie should have been over the moon at the prospect of a visit from her grandmother. Maybe she was coming down with something. And he thought he recognized the symptoms—Karina withdrawal.

"We're going to move into our new house today," he said, making another attempt to cheer her up.

"I don't want to move to a new house," Natalie wailed. "I never even got to say goodbye to Karina. She was going to show me how to crochet an elephant."

This struck Daniel as bizarre, even for Karina. "An elephant? Wouldn't that take an awful lot of wool?"

"Not a *real* elephant." Natalie's mouth crooked up in a tiny smile. "A *toy* elephant."

"Oh, I see," he said with a chuckle. He reached for his coffee and sipped pensively, his smile fading.

"Why did we have to leave, Daddy?"

They'd been over this at least a dozen times in the past week. Nothing he said, no reason he could give, satisfied the little girl. Or himself, for that matter. If only Karina hadn't been so stubborn.

"I told you, sweetheart, Karina wanted us to go."

Natalie looked crestfallen. "Doesn't she like us anymore?"

"Of course she does," Daniel said, mentally kicking himself for his thoughtless words. "She loves us. She definitely loves you, and I'm practically positive she loves me."

"Did you ask her nicely if we could stay?"

"I asked her to marry me."

Natalie's face brightened. "Goody!"

Good God, now why had he gone and said that? "Don't get excited, Nattie. She said no. That's why we're at this hotel instead of Karina's house."

"But, Daddy," Natalie persisted, trying to puzzle things out. "If she loves us, why won't she marry us?"

Daniel picked up his toast, searching his mind for an answer that would make sense to the child. And to him.

"It's complicated. You see, sweetheart, her mother died when she was young." He wasn't sure he should be talking about this to Natalie, but he knew she needed answers just as much as he did.

"I know. She told me."

"She did?" He was surprised at that.

Natalie nodded. "After I had the nightmare. She told me someday it wouldn't hurt so much to think about Mommy. She told me to think about the good things instead. But you know what, Daddy?"

"What?"

"It already doesn't hurt quite so much. Not after Karina told me about *her* mommy." Natalie smiled bravely and tears swam in her eyes. "I wish we still lived with her."

With all his heart, Daniel wished the same thing. He took a bite of his toast and chewed mechanically.

"Daddy?" Natalie fixed worried eyes upon him.

"Yes?"

"Karina won't get sick and die, will she?"

The toast turned to cardboard in his mouth. "Did she say that?"

"No. But I loved Mommy and she died. I just thought..." Her small voice trailed away as she gazed at him, fearful yet trusting.

"Sweetheart, Mommy didn't die because you loved her."

"I know, but..."

Daniel rubbed the back of his neck with one hand. He couldn't tell her about Karina's fears; the child would be terrified. Besides, even though he understood why Karina felt the way she did, he refused to accept the possibility she might be right.

"Nobody knows exactly how long they have, Possum," he said, taking his daughter's hand and squeezing it. "But *I* believe Karina will live to be a very old, very nutty lady who makes papier-mâché unicorns from her rocking chair."

Natalie giggled. "I could help her reach the high parts."

Daniel smiled at the thought, then sobered. "Problem is, Nattie, we won't be around. For reasons of her own, she doesn't want to have babies. But she knows I want more children. She also knows you want a baby brother or sister and she doesn't want us to be disappointed."

Natalie sniffed, and pushed her crumpet around her plate. "I'd rather have Karina than a baby brother."

Daniel froze with his toast halfway to his mouth. "What did you say?"

"I said I'd rather have Karina than a baby brother."

His hand dropped to the table. How could he have

been so stupid? The way out of their misery was blindingly simple. Yes, he wanted more children. And not having them would leave a huge gap in his life. But that was nothing compared to the black hole that threatened his universe when he contemplated a future without Karina.

"Do you really mean that?" he demanded.

Natalie nodded, on the verge of tears again.

Daniel tossed the piece of uneaten toast on his plate. Karina might be as stubborn as a mule, but he was the biggest jackass that ever lived. He didn't deserve to have her if he wasn't willing to take her as she was. With or without children. If he truly loved her, he should be with her now, helping her continue the fight against whatever fears she had yet to confront.

She would still be worried about Natalie, but somehow he would have to convince her she needed their love as much as they needed hers. That the gain would outweigh the risk.

He started to get up, then stopped. Before he could ask for Karina's future, he had to resolve the past with Brian. She might not have feelings for his brother, but Brian had implied more than once that *he* had feelings for *her*. Daniel was fed up with trying to atone for Francine, but keeping secrets was what had damaged his relationship with Brian in the first place. He wasn't going to add to the hostilities by repeating that mistake. For good or ill, it was time to come clean about his love for Karina.

"Come on, Nattie," Daniel said, pushing his chair back. "We've got to go, right now."

"Back to Karina's house?" the girl asked eagerly, her crumpet forgotten on her plate.

"No. To Uncle Brian's." He pulled some bills from his wallet and tucked them under a saucer. "Let's go."

"Don't forget," he said to Natalie a short time later as they rode the elevator to Brian's floor, "what I have to say to Uncle Brian is serious and private. I want you to stay in the living room and—"

"I know, watch TV while you talk in the kitchen." Her face took on a mischievous expression. "Don't worry, I won't hear a thing. I'll turn the TV up really loud."

Daniel rolled his eyes and cuffed her lightly on the shoulder. Control of the TV's volume was a continuing battle of wits with Natalie and he'd just lost a round.

But that was the least of his worries.

"So, DANNY BOY, what's up?" Brian lounged against the gleaming white kitchen counter, coffee mug in hand, and glanced pointedly at his watch. "I have to pick up Karina in an hour."

Daniel fought down the surge of irritation his brother invariably provoked in him. "It's Karina I want to talk to you about."

Brian's eyes narrowed over the rim of his mug. "What about her?"

Daniel leaned over the central cooking island and planted his hands on either side of the pristine chopping block. "I'm in love with her. And I believe she loves me."

"In love, you say. Big step, Danny boy." Brian thoughtfully smoothed the crease line of his front-pleated pants.

Ignoring Brian's mocking tone, Daniel continued, "I wanted to tell you how I felt about her in person, rather than have you find out the hard way."

Brian glanced at him sharply. "Like last time, you mean, when you sent a telegram from Australia saying you'd married my fiancée?"

Daniel shoved a hand through his hair and felt the sudden dampness around his temples. "I tried to tell you about Francine and me but you wouldn't listen."

"I might have believed it was serious if *she'd* said something. Right until the end, she never once let on she was leaving me." His voice threatened to break on the last two words.

"She meant to, I know," Daniel replied, trying to make amends for what never should have happened. "But everything was so chaotic those last few days before we left."

The skin around Brian's mouth tightened. "Thank you, brother. That informative little twist of the knife opened up the wound nicely. To be rejected is bad enough, but to be forgotten, as well..."

Daniel wiped his hand, damp with perspiration, on his jeans. "The point is," he persisted, "Karina and I have things we need to work out. I'd rather you didn't go away with her this weekend."

Brian, about to take a sip of coffee, set his mug back on the counter and laughed. "You think Karina would give up her golf tournament even if I agreed to do as you ask? Think again, Danny boy."

Daniel pressed two fingers to the bridge of his nose and closed his eyes. "Look, Brian," he said, glancing up. "You're my brother. I want to be friends with you. But I also want Karina."

Brian's laughter faded, to be replaced by the familiar derisive hostility. "And you think you should be able to have anything you want."

"No. Yes. In this case, yes." Daniel straightened and glanced away.

Brian tossed the dregs of his coffee down the sink. "Are you telling me you and Karina are getting married?"

If only he *could* say that. Daniel stalked across the white-tiled floor and halted in front of the breakfast table with its view of the ocean.

"I want to marry her, yes." The bald statement didn't begin to convey the extent of his love for her. Or his need to protect her and to make her the mother of his child. But Brian wouldn't be interested in all that.

"I take it she said no?" Amusement tinged his brother's voice.

Daniel nodded sharply, his gaze fixed on a bobbing scrap of white sail rounding the breakwater. "So far."

Brian chortled. "She obviously prefers me, Danny boy. Why don't you bow out now and save yourself some heartbreak?"

Daniel spun around. "Because I *love*—" He broke off, shocked at the triumphant gleam in Brian's eyes. Triumphant not because he thought he'd won, but because Daniel was suffering.

"I thought you were in love with her, too," Daniel said slowly, starting toward his brother. "But you don't care about her at all, do you?"

Brian shrugged. "Did I ever mention the word *love?*"

Daniel halted, boxing Brian in against the counter. "You orchestrated your whole involvement just to get revenge on me." Sick with anger, he jabbed his fingers at his brother's chest. "Didn't you?"

Brian raised an arm as if to defend himself—or was it to strike out at him? "What if I did? I'm going with her this weekend whether you like it or not. You're going to know how it feels to lose the woman you love to your brother. By Sunday night I'll have Karina falling into my arms." A nasty glint came into Brian's eye. *"And you know I can do it."*

Daniel went cold. Karina had too much sense to be carried away by Brian's surface charm. But she was in a confused and vulnerable state, and it wouldn't be the first time his brother had dazzled a woman into wanting him.

"Karina's not stupid," he said, his voice rough. "And she's not naive. You can't *make* her love you."

"Care to make a bet on that?" Brian demanded. "Maybe she refused you because she's holding out for something better."

Daniel clenched and unclenched his fists. "Her reasons for not wanting to marry have nothing to do with you or me. If you hurt her, I swear I'll kill you. It's time you thought of someone besides yourself for a change."

"Like you were thinking of others when you ran off with Francine?" Brian pushed forward, forcing Daniel to back up past the cooking island. "You're no paragon of virtue yourself, Danny boy."

Daniel's fist crashed down on the cutting board. *"Don't call me Danny boy!* And stop throwing Francine in my face! I'm through feeling guilty over her. *If she'd really loved you, she would have stayed with you."*

Brian stopped as though struck, his sharp intake of breath audible. "How the hell can you say that? Francine and I were made for each other."

"Then why were you always flirting with other women?"

"Other women came on to me."

"You didn't have to encourage them. How do you think that made Francine feel?"

"No one else mattered to me. *She knew that.*" Brian turned away, his face contorted in pain. "I *loved* Francine."

Daniel stared at Brian's hunched shoulders, his gut twisting with doubt. For once his brother's voice held an undeniable ring of sincerity. Daniel felt himself go hot, then cold, all over. Why had he always imagined Brian incapable of deep feeling? To excuse his own actions? To make himself look superior in his own eyes?

Brian straightened and turned back, wiping a shaking hand down his face. "If I'd known what was going on, do you think I'd have let her go without a fight? You two ran off so fast I didn't have a chance to win her back. And, *you*, Danny, saw an opportunity to do me over and took it." Brian gazed at him with hatred in his cold blue eyes. "I'll bet you loved every minute of it."

"No!" Daniel said. "Of course I didn't."

A thin lock of blond hair fell across Brian's brow as he jutted his head forward. "Face it, you've been trying to one-up me since junior high."

"Don't be a jerk."

Yet somehow he couldn't quite look Brian in the eye. Jamming his hands in the hip pockets of his jeans, he backed off a step. "Since when did you feel threatened by your little brother? You were always the favorite. At school, at home—"

"Are you kidding?" Brian said. "Mom and Dad were hardest on me. I always had to break new ground. You just cruised along afterward, taking it all for granted."

"But it was *you* Dad spent time with. Coaching your team, taking you to ball games..." The old hurt rose in him, sharp and fresh as yesterday. Words he'd never spoken aloud, feelings he hadn't known were trapped inside, burst out of him. "It was *you* he saw as his *real* son."

Brian threw up his hands. "You always had your nose in a book! Or you were off in the woods building a tree fort or something."

"So I wasn't a chip off the old baseball bat. I would have liked some recognition of who *I* was."

"Get real, Danny! Mom and Dad were always telling people how many A's you got on your report card, how you mowed Granny's lawn without being asked, even how thick your goddamn hair was, for crissake!"

Daniel jerked his head in disgust. "Listen to us. We sound like children."

Despite himself, images of their younger days flashed through his mind. Brian, the Number One Son, following in Dad's footsteps on the basketball team, the football team, every damn ball team there was. Brian, the Greek god, offering to get Daniel a prettier date for the prom.

Daniel squeezed his eyes shut, trying to get a clearer picture on the past. He'd never actually wanted to *be* Brian. He'd just hated his brother acting as if he were some sort of crown prince.

Then Francine had come along, convincing him he was so much more interesting, so much more attractive than Brian. He'd been too young to sort out lust from love, vindicated pride from true commitment.

"All right!" he shouted. "I *was* glad she chose me over you. I *enjoyed* beating you at your own game. I was young and stupid. If you want to punch me in the nose for what happened a decade ago, go ahead."

He braced himself for a blow. But instead of bunching up to strike, Brian's shoulders sagged. A cold, sad smile washed over his face.

"You were always so damned noble. All I wanted was to tarnish your gilt a little."

"*My* gilt?" Daniel's hand dropped to his side. "*You* were the golden boy."

"Maybe that's how you saw it. Things looked different standing in my shoes. You were the smart one, the good one. You never seemed to worry whether people liked you or not, but they always did."

Maybe it was a trick of light, or the release of long-pent-up emotions, but suddenly everything was turned around. Daniel had the dizzying sensation of looking at himself through his brother's eyes and seeing all the old hurts and resentments, real and imagined. It made no difference who really was the favorite, or if there'd been a favorite at all. Perception was all that mattered.

Then the moment passed and he was gazing directly into Brian's tortured eyes. He glimpsed the tangled skein of ancient wounds. *God.* They could snarl themselves forever in the past....

Or they could get over it.

He took a deep breath. "Brian, I...I'm sorry." He almost choked on the words and realized it was because, for the first time, he truly meant them. "I'm sorry you suffered over Francine. I'm sorry that for so many years I missed out on having a brother. I'm sorry I hurt you."

Brian's expression turned coldly impassive. "Sorry won't change the past."

"That's true," Daniel said, searching for a way out of their impasse. "But we have to forgive each other or we can forget about the future, as well. We've got to learn to relate to each other as adults, not kids."

"We don't have a future. You decided that when you took off with Francine."

Daniel almost thumped the counter again in frustration. They were going around in circles. "I was in no state of mind to rationally decide anything then. I acted on hormones and impulse. But I'm not the same person I was ten years ago."

"Are you saying you'd do things differently now?" Brian asked with a return to mockery. "Show a little brotherly love? That's convenient."

"For God's sake—" Daniel broke off as the faint sound of Natalie laughing at something on TV filtered through the door. "Look, Brian," he said, "there's a little girl out there who's lost her mother and could do with some family. Whether you like it or not, you and I are family."

Brian turned his back on him, but not before Daniel saw the flash of bitterness in his eyes. "So I should forgive you because of the kid?"

Daniel gripped his arm and spun him around. "Not just any kid, Brian. Your niece. Francine's daughter. You don't have to forgive me, but don't shut us out. For Natalie's sake if not for mine."

Brian squeezed his eyes shut, and stress lines appeared around his mouth. "It's too late. There's too much bad blood between us." He turned away, waving a hand at Daniel. "I'm tired of this. Go on, get out of here."

"Not until I'm finished. I can't stop you from going away for the weekend with Karina, but for God's sake, don't use her to pay me back. She's a good woman, and she doesn't deserve to be screwed around because of something I did a long time ago."

Brian's head shot up. "Francine was a good woman, too!"

"Yes, she was." Daniel took a deep breath and gazed steadily at his brother. "And for what it's worth, I think you would have made her happier."

Something of the old Brian flashed into his brother's
eyes then. Not the crown prince or the jaded Rolls-Royce
salesman, but the young boy Daniel had caught tadpoles
with, the boy he'd raced to the Christmas tree on frosty
mornings. The big brother he'd always looked up to but
never seemed to catch up with. Daniel's throat tightened
and he looked away.

When he glanced back, the spark of boyhood had
faded from Brian's eyes. Turning away, Brian crossed
to the counter to pour himself another cup of coffee.
Daniel watched in agonized silence, hearing the coffeepot clatter on the edge of the cup, seeing Brian's
white-knuckled grip on the countertop.

"Brian? Are you okay?"

"I said, get out of here."

Daniel's shoulders sagged and his eyes closed. It was
no use. Nothing he'd said had gotten through to Brian.
What he thought he'd seen in his brother's eyes had been
an illusion created by his own need.

Drained and weary, he turned to go, his footsteps ech-
oing quietly on the marble tiles. His hand was on the
doorknob when Brian cleared his throat.

"Daniel."

He paused without turning. "What is it?"

"My golf clubs are in the hall closet."

Daniel went still, not daring to believe what he was
hearing. "Your golf clubs?"

"You heard me. Break any and you'll pay."

As an olive branch it was pretty thin, but Daniel was
prepared to grasp at twigs. "I...I'll take good care of
them." He turned. Brian was stirring his coffee, avoiding his gaze. "Maybe after I bring them back we could
catch a ball game sometime."

There was a long silence while the coffeepot bubbled

in the background. Finally Brian said, "Don't push it, Dan."

Daniel forced himself not to mind, to be grateful for what progress they'd made. "All right, Brian. Thanks—"

Brian cut him off with an impatient wave of his hand. "Why are you still hanging around? Karina's waiting."

Daniel nodded. "Okay. I'm going."

He opened the door to the living room, paused and glanced over his shoulder. "But I'll be back."

# CHAPTER SEVENTEEN

GOLDEN SUNLIGHT sifted through the chinks in Karina's blind, waking her. She opened her eyes with a smile. Overnight her happiness and peace had grown into a sense of joyful purpose.

Nothing had changed, yet everything was different. Marriage was no longer a thing to be feared and avoided, but a natural progression of her love for Daniel. Her heart sang at the thought of watching Natalie grow up, of someday holding her and Daniel's baby in her arms.

Daniel. She could call him now. Throwing back the covers, she swung her legs over the side of the bed and glanced at the clock. Nine-thirty! How could she have slept in, today of all days?

Dressing quickly, she ran downstairs to the telephone and dialed the number of Daniel's hotel. But when she asked for him, the desk clerk informed her Daniel Bowen had paid his bill and left early that morning.

"He can't have checked out already!" Panic crept into her voice. "He's not moving into his new house for another week."

"Sorry, ma'am, I wouldn't know anything about that."

"Did he say where he was going? Did he leave a forwarding address?" She sensed hesitation on the other end of the line. Not caring how desperate she sounded, she added, "Please, it's really important."

"I probably shouldn't say anything...."

"What? Tell me."

"Mr. Bowen made a couple of phone calls from the desk just before he left. I didn't hear everything because I was busy with another customer, and of course I wasn't eavesdropping...."

"Of course not." Karina paced the kitchen floor. *Get on with it, man.*

"He mentioned the name Brian."

"Brian. Of course. Thank you very much. 'Bye."

"Wait, there's more. I think he was also talking to someone at the airport, inquiring about tickets to Australia."

*Australia.* "Thank you," she said, and hung up. Karina sank onto a chair, still clutching the receiver. Surely Daniel wouldn't go back to Melbourne without telling her.

Her mind in neutral, she dialed Brian's number. The telephone rang. And rang. On the fourth ring, his answering machine came on.

"Damn," she muttered and hung up before the beep. He was probably on his way to pick her up for the golf tournament. She had to hurry and find Daniel before he arrived.

She called Betty and Kevin, but they'd had no word from him. She tried the hotel again but he hadn't returned, hadn't checked for messages. With little hope of success, she tried to get a telephone listing for him at his new address. No luck there, either.

At least when Brian got here she could ask him if he knew where Daniel was. Her bags were packed and standing by the front door, the golf clubs she'd borrowed propped against them. But unless she sorted things out with Daniel, she wasn't going to any tournament. What had once seemed like the key to a new life now loomed before her as an obstacle to happiness.

Frustrated, she went outside and sat on the top step to watch for Brian's Jaguar to slink around the corner. Then, too restless to sit still, she jumped up and paced the footpath, snapping dead heads off the dahlias. What if she'd driven Daniel away for good? The thought was too horrible to contemplate.

Without him, what was left for her but to climb the corporate ladder? Not so long ago, that had been her top priority. Without a family to help care for, there would be no limit to the heights she could attain. And with success would come the material trappings—a bigger house, overseas trips, clothes, parties....

The thought of another party suddenly seemed inexpressibly tedious. As did the empty house that would await her at the end of each and every night.

*Fool.* She tossed a shriveled flower aside and strode back up the path to the house. A fool and a coward, that's what she was. She had the address of Daniel's new house. Maybe he was there right now. She'd drive over and camp out front until he showed up.

Karina ran up the steps onto the porch. Forget the golf tournament. Forget the job. Don't think about the look on Brian's face when he showed up and she wasn't there. There wasn't a second to waste.

Next year she'd go to the tournament. But she'd go as CEO of her own company. Yes, that was it. She'd quit procrastinating and install that computer in her basement next week. To hell with Ross and his cronies. To hell with the art department. With Daniel and Natalie around, she'd never be lonely. And if she could poach Kevin from SignCity, she'd be laughing.

Karina grabbed her purse and car keys off the hall

table. She heard the sound of a vehicle and spun around to glance out the door. Brian?

Her heart missed a beat. Not Brian, but *Daniel.*

She came slowly out of the house and down the steps, half afraid she was just imagining that his white pickup was pulling in at the curb across the street.

Then she saw his tall figure emerge from the driver's side and Natalie run around the truck to stand next to him.

*Daniel was back.*

Now they were crossing the road, Daniel holding his arm in front of Natalie to stop her from running blindly across the street.

Karina ran down the path to meet them. Natalie broke away from Daniel the moment her toes touched the sidewalk. Crouching low, Karina scooped the girl into her arms and hugged her to her chest. Tears coursed down her cheeks, through the creases of her smile.

"I thought I'd never see you again!" Natalie cried.

"I thought I'd never see you!"

"I didn't want to go away, but Daddy said you wanted to live here all by yourself. It's not true, is it?" Natalie pulled back and her tear-filled eyes blazed at Karina.

"No, sweetheart." She wiped the wet streaks away from the child's flushed cheeks with trembling fingers. "It isn't true anymore. I want to be with the two of you."

"Truly?"

At the sound of Daniel's voice, Karina looked up. His eyes, shadowed and grave, searched her face. He was asking for more than confirmation of her words, she thought with a leap of her heart. He was asking for her future. *Their* future.

"Truly."

He took a step toward her and she gently disentangled herself from Natalie. "Oh, Daniel," she said, and went into his arms. He was warm and solid and felt so right. The time for tears was over. From now on there would be nothing but kisses and sighs and loving—

His hands moved to her shoulders, and before she could taste the love on his lips, a gap had grown between them. She swallowed a moan of regret and looked questioningly into his eyes.

"I forgot to give you your birthday present the other night," he said.

She stared at him, startled back into uncertainty. Had she got it all wrong? Had he come back just to give her a birthday present? A sick feeling grew in her stomach as Daniel handed her a wrapped parcel.

"I made it myself," he said.

Karina swallowed hard. "Thank you." She stripped away the tissue paper and stared at the carved ebony box in her hands. "It's beautiful," she murmured. "Just what I needed."

Except it wasn't. What she needed was Daniel and wedding bells and happy-ever-after. And babies. Lots of babies.

She ran her fingers over the polished wood. Despite the numbing cold enveloping her heart, she couldn't help but admire the intricate pattern of paisley swirls and spiraling horns.

"Good grief," she said with a choking laugh. "Is that a *pig?*"

Daniel smiled, but it was Natalie who answered, "Yes. And look, there's a unicorn and your flying ladies. Open it up," she chattered excitedly. "There's a secret compartment and inside is a—"

"Shh, Nattie," Daniel admonished, tugging on the child's braid. "Let her find it herself."

The top of the box lifted easily, but it took Karina a few moments to work out how to open the secret compartment. Her fingers poked and pushed without success until finally she twisted a partition and a thin layer of wood slid back to uncover a small chamber buried in the heart of the box.

Inside, nestled in royal blue velvet, lay a ring.

A ring made out of yellow construction paper. With a red crayoned ruby in the center.

She laughed, and there was a sob of joy in her laughter. "There's an inscription," she said, astonished and delighted but not fully comprehending. Removing the ring, she turned it in her fingers and read, "'I.O.U. one engagement ring'."

She glanced at Daniel, her eyes blurring with tears. "Then you still want me?"

"Forever." His curving mouth was set in a solemn line and his eyes were full of love.

"Oh, Daniel—"

"Wait. Before you answer, there's something else I want to say. If…" he took a breath and cleared his throat "…if you really don't want children, well, that's hard, but I'd rather have you that way than not at all. And so would Natalie."

Karina's heart swelled to bursting at the depth of his sacrifice. He was giving her a second chance, a gift of happiness more precious than all the jewels in the world.

"Marry me, Karina."

She nodded vigorously, her throat too constricted to speak. "Yes," she gasped at last. "Yes. Yes! *Yes!*"

"See, Daddy?" Natalie said, looking up at her father. "I told you she'd say yes."

Daniel gently prised Karina's fingers loose from the jewelry box. "I promise you can have it back in a minute. But I'll need your hand for this next bit."

She laughed, her fingers trembling as she relinquished the box. "I was just scared of dropping it."

Daniel slipped the ring on her finger. It caught on her knuckle and almost tore. By the time it was in place on the third finger of her left hand, her heart was pounding.

She turned her wrist to catch the light in the shiny red crayon, savoring the bliss of wearing Daniel's ring. "I've never seen anything so beautiful," she said, and meant it.

He grinned. "If I'd known you were this easy to please, I'd have asked you to marry me a long time ago."

Though his words were teasing, the look in his eyes left her in no doubt of the depth of his love and the strength of his commitment. And when he pulled her into his arms and touched his lips to hers, she responded with all the joy in her heart.

It was every kiss they'd ever exchanged and more. Longing and love, passion and promise, fulfillment at last.

Finally Karina broke away, her fingers lifted to her mouth. "Brian," she said breathlessly. "The golf tournament."

"Don't worry about it." Daniel pulled her close again and began planting tiny kisses behind her ear.

"Daddy, Karina, let's go." Natalie skipped up and down, tugging on her father's sleeve.

"Okay, okay." He loosened his embrace and glanced down at Karina. "Coming?"

She nodded happily, not knowing where they were going and not caring. Daniel picked up her bags and started in the direction of the truck. She glanced at her watch and felt a pang of guilt. "Brian's due any minute. I'd better wait and tell him—"

"You can tell him whatever you like when we get back from Parksville."

"Parksville?" she said as they crossed the street. "That's where the tournament's being held."

"You didn't really think I was going to let you go with my brother, did you?" Daniel opened the door for her and Natalie, a smile playing around the corners of his mouth.

"Frankly, yes," Karina said. "But I'll pick that bone with you later." She got in beside Natalie and waited while Daniel hoisted her bags into the back of the pickup.

"Does this mean you're not going back to Australia?" she asked as he slid behind the wheel.

His head jerked sideways, a bemused expression on his face. "Whatever gave you that idea?"

"The clerk at your hotel said you were inquiring about flights to Australia."

"Not *to* Australia. *From.* Natalie's grandmother is coming over for a visit and I was arranging a ticket for her."

"Oh." Her relief was inexpressible. She paused for a moment, trying to take it all in. "And is Natalie coming with us to the tournament?"

"No. We're dropping her off at Betty and Kevin's for the weekend."

"They've got a pony," Natalie exclaimed happily, bouncing on the seat.

Karina gave the girl a quick smile before turning her attention back to Daniel. "And have you patched things up with Brian?"

Daniel shrugged. "He lent me his golf clubs. It's a start."

"And you did ask me to marry you?" Best to be absolutely sure.

He laughed out loud. "Yes! Natalie insists on being a fairy princess flower girl. Is that okay?"

"Nattie can be anything she likes," Karina replied with a big smile at the little girl sitting between them. Then she had a worrying thought. "How will you get into the tournament?"

"I reckon D. Bowen could easily be mistaken for B. Bowen. Besides, you're registered as a player. If anyone asks, which I doubt, you can simply say you've got a new partner. For life."

Karina laughed. Then she narrowed her eyes at him. "But can you play golf?"

He started the engine. "I'll fake it."

"I don't think you can fake something like golf."

"Then I'll caddy for you. It'll impress the board of directors no end."

"I don't care about that anymore." At his surprised look, she added, "But it won't hurt to have a few high-level connections when I start my freelance graphics business."

"Good on you." Pride shone in his eyes.

"Oh, and Daniel," she said shyly, "I've changed my mind. I do want babies."

He didn't say a word. Just gazed at her with eyes brimming with love while his mouth slowly stretched into that beloved smile. And time stood still for the space of a heartbeat.

"Hey, what are we waiting for?" Natalie said with all the patience of a six-year-old.

Daniel laughed and ruffled her hair. "We've done waiting, Possum. It's time to get on with life."

He put the truck into gear and stretched an arm along the back of the seat as he reversed out of the parking spot.

There was something truly delicious about his fingers caressing the back of her neck, Karina thought dreamily as they pulled away from the curb. And something both thrilling and comforting to know that very soon they would live together as husband and wife, until death did them part...a very long time from now.

"Wait!" she cried, suddenly. "Go back."

Daniel hit the brakes and the truck screeched to a halt. He glanced at her, eyebrows raised.

"Go back to the house," she repeated. "Please."

"What is it?" Daniel said as he backed down the street. "You haven't changed your mind again, have you?"

She laughed. "Nothing like that. There's something I forgot to do."

He threw the truck into neutral and waited with the motor running while she ran back into the house. The rhythmic beat of a rap tune grew louder and louder as she hurried down the hall to the kitchen.

With a lopsided smile, she reached across the table and switched off the radio.

Silence.

She listened a moment. Not bad. She could get used to it. Maybe in time she'd even get used to her own thoughts.

Daniel gave her a questioning glance as she climbed back into the truck. Karina just smiled and leaned over

Natalie's head to plant a kiss lightly on his lips. She would always love music, but now she didn't need to hide behind it.

Not when she had so much to live for.

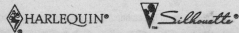 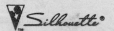

**Coming in August 1997!**

## THE BETTY NEELS RUBY COLLECTION

### COLLECTOR'S EDITION

This August start assembling the
Betty Neels Ruby Collection. Six of the
most requested and best-loved titles have
been especially chosen for this collection.
From August 1997 until January 1998,
one title per month will be available to avid
fans. Spot the collection by the lush ruby red
cover with the gold Collector's Edition banner
and your favorite author's name—Betty Neels!

Available in August at your favorite retail outlet.

**HARLEQUIN®**

Look us up on-line at: http://www.romance.net          BNRUBY

**Make a Valentine's date
for the premiere of**

◆ HARLEQUIN® **Movies**

**starting February 14, 1998 with**

# Debbie Macomber's
# This Matter of
# Marriage

on **the movie channel** tmc

Just tune in to **The Movie Channel** the **second Saturday night** of every month at 9:00 p.m. EST to join us, and be swept away by the sheer thrill of romance brought to life. Watch for details of upcoming movies—in books, in your television viewing guide and in stores.

If you are not currently a subscriber to The Movie Channel, simply call your local cable or satellite provider for more details. Call today, and don't miss out on the romance!

**the movie channel** tmc
*100% pure movies.*
*100% pure fun.*

◆ HARLEQUIN®
*Makes any time special.™*

# DEBBIE MACOMBER

*invites you to the*

**HEART OF TEXAS**

Join Debbie Macomber as she brings you the lives
and loves of the folks in the ranching community
of Promise, Texas.

If you loved Midnight Sons—don't miss
Heart of Texas! A brand-new six-book series
from Debbie Macomber.

Available in February 1998
at your favorite retail store.

## Heart of Texas by Debbie Macomber

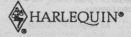

**HARLEQUIN®**

HPHRT1

# Don't miss these Harlequin favorites by some of our top-selling authors!

| | | | |
|---|---|---|---|
| HT#25733 | THE GETAWAY BRIDE | $3.50 U.S. | ☐ |
| | by Gina Wilkins | $3.99 CAN. | ☐ |
| HP#11849 | A KISS TO REMEMBER | $3.50 U.S. | ☐ |
| | by Miranda Lee | $3.99 CAN. | ☐ |
| HR#03431 | BRINGING UP BABIES | $3.25 U.S. | ☐ |
| | by Emma Goldrick | $3.75 CAN. | ☐ |
| HS#70723 | SIDE EFFECTS | $3.99 U.S. | ☐ |
| | by Bobby Hutchinson | $4.50 CAN. | ☐ |
| HI#22377 | CISCO'S WOMAN | $3.75 U.S. | ☐ |
| | by Aimée Thurlo | $4.25 CAN. | ☐ |
| HAR#16666 | ELISE & THE HOTSHOT LAWYER | $3.75 U.S. | ☐ |
| | by Emily Dalton | $4.25 CAN. | ☐ |
| HH#28949 | RAVEN'S VOW | $4.99 U.S. | ☐ |
| | by Gayle Wilson | $5.99 CAN. | ☐ |

(limited quantities available on certain titles)

| | | |
|---|---|---|
| **AMOUNT** | $ | _____ |
| **POSTAGE & HANDLING** | $ | _____ |
| ($1.00 for one book, 50¢ for each additional) | | |
| **APPLICABLE TAXES*** | $ | _____ |
| **TOTAL PAYABLE** | $ | _____ |

(check or money order—please do not send cash)

To order, complete this form and send it, along with a check or money order for the total above, payable to Harlequin Books, to: **In the U.S.:** 3010 Walden Avenue, P.O. Box 9047, Buffalo, NY 14269-9047; **In Canada:** P.O. Box 613, Fort Erie, Ontario, L2A 5X3.

Name: _____

Address: _____ City: _____

State/Prov.: _____ Zip/Postal Code: _____

Account Number (if applicable): _____

*New York residents remit applicable sales taxes.
 Canadian residents remit applicable GST and provincial taxes.

Look us up on-line at: http://www.romance.net

075-CSAS

HBLJM98